PLAY TO WIN

JA'NESE DIXON

PUBLISHING

ALSO BY JA'NESE DIXON

Rockstar Secrets

Play to Win

Black Diamond

Platinum Love

Yuki's Luck

Resort to Love

You Owe Me

PLAY TO WIN.
Copyright © 2020 by Ja'Nese Dixon.

All rights reserved.

This is a work of fiction. All of the characters, organization and events portrayed in this story are either products of the author's imagination or are used fictitiously.

No part of this book may be reproduced in any form or by any electronic or mechanical means, including information storage and retrieval systems, without written permission from the author, except for the use of brief quotations in a book review.

Warning: The unauthorized reproduction or distribution of this copyrighted work is illegal. Criminal copyright infringement, including infringement without monetary gain, is investigated by the FBI and is punishable by up to 5 years in prison and a fine of $250,000.

ISBN-13: 978-1-950405-24-4 (paperback)

Printed in the United States of America.

Photo by Lindee Robinson Photography.

Model: Jonathan Holloway.

Design by Danja Tales.

TABLE OF CONTENTS

Rules are meant to be broken, and when it comes to love, this ex-quarterback and single mother are playing to win.

Kamal Montgomery owned the football field, and now he's one-fifth of Southern Soul, a family-owned soul food restaurant. Nothing and no one is off-limits until Jayda enters his restaurant in need of a second chance.

Jayda Dallas returns to Houston with her baby on her hip and her ex in the dust. He refuses to pay child support for their third-year-old daughter, and rather than take his sorry ass back, she's getting a J-O-B.

Jayda stands back, watching women fall at Kamal's feet. His smile is more deadly than his arrogance. But seeing him with her daughter has her wondering if she should take a chance.

Every rejection will only make Kamal's victory sweeter. He plans to lick, taste, and devour her like the delicacy she is until the world, her ex, and Jayda knows his name is tattooed on every inch of her curvy body.

Kamal's never played a game by halves, and Jayda's got a thing or two to show this deviously handsome player. But when an unknown enemy wages war on their budding relationship will their new love survive.

PLAY TO WIN

GOLDEN RAYS CUT through the curtains below eye level, casting a faint shadow over my beauty room. Time is passing faster than I can record today. Rocking forward, I flick the blinds a little wider, turning my head to the side, dodging the direct glare of the last hint of the day. I need the light to finish my last video for the week.

The national cosmetic brand paid me five grand to shoot this makeup look for my YouTube channel. The red light signals the camera is recording, and I pick up the fluffy contour brush.

I stare at the camera. "Drugstore makeup can deliver a comparable look to high end makeup if you use the right technique. Watch as I use this foundation as my bronzer." The brush glides over my naturally high cheekbones. The rich brown powder blends with the rose gold highlight.

"Mimicking an 'e' shape will bring the eyes to the center of your beautiful face." I say to my viewers with my eyes on the mirror. Like a trained makeup artist, I dust across my forehead, paying close attention to my temporal bones. My viewers love educational videos and tutorials, throwing in quick tips for help. "And don't forget the little area between the bridge of your nose and your brow bone."

I work quickly because I need to edit this video tonight after Reese goes to sleep. I have this video and four others lined up to publish on my channel while I'm in Houston taking meetings with potential brands with my boyfriend Brett.

In less than five minutes I'm applying my signature natural lip, racing the sun. I reach for my finishing spray.

"Mommy." The door to my beauty room pushes open, not wide enough for me to see in the monitor.

That's my girl. I smile, angling my head to the side, blocking the view from the camera.

"Honey, can Mommy get ten minutes?" Reese peeks around the corner and I hold up both hands, wiggling my fingers, and she nods. "Here, sit with me, they love when you're in my thumbnails." I pat the bench.

She skips through the door with a delightful smile on her face. I can tell she's adding a little extra effort to make her hair fall over her shoulders based on the click-clacking sound of the wooden beads on the end of her braids.

She jumps to an abrupt stop, giggling as the beads slap around. I scoop Reese up and sit her beside me.

"Can I have lip gloss?" She wiggles, getting comfortable while inspecting the makeup and brushes spread out in front of us.

I cut an eye at her. My baby is a genius. I know I'm biased, but she only has to see and hear a thing once to input it into her overactive imagination. It's a task to stay a few steps ahead of her quick wit. She pairs times and sequences with the ease of an older child. At least, I think so, since I had next to no experience with children until I had her. So, we're both learning as we go.

"Yes, but quickly, honey." I kiss the top of her head and rub off the pink residue. Reese yanks open her special drawer in my vanity and digs out her tube of gloss. I smile, watching as she applies it with focus and a steady hand. My nod of approval has my baby beaming as she returns to her drawer for a coloring book. She works on the end of my vanity and I return to finishing my look.

Reese understands makeup is for mommies only. But she also knows I keep special items in the top drawer to keep her occupied while I work. Her favorite item is no doubt her tube of strawberry gloss.

I used to tell her makeup was for big girls only, then we started referring to her as a big girl for going to the potty on her own. My little genius asked within days if she could wear lipstick. I had to think quick, and that's when "we" created Mommy Rules. The first being, lip gloss is for big girls, and makeup is still for mommies.

As a full-time YouTuber, people used to drag me in my comments for letting my daughter wear "makeup." But I block them without a second thought. I draw the line concerning Reese. No if, ands, or buts about it.

What they'll never understand is the power that comes

with embracing your beauty. It's not the lipstick or the gloss, but the whisper of confidence that comes with knowing you're the shit, and can't nobody tell you different, even when I find it hard to embrace.

My mother never told me I was beautiful. All I heard was my skin was too dark, my lips were too big, my hips were too wide. I was too much in her eyes. But I can't recall her ever calling me beautiful.

I took to beauty products, hoping to change my appearance with the magic of makeup. Then I worked up the courage to sit in front of the camera.

I started teaching my viewers how to use makeup instead of going under the knife. Pouty lips without fillers. Snatched noses without rhinoplasty. Chiseled cheekbones without surgical sculpting.

It took one video going viral to change my life. More views garnered more attention. More attention brought on more admirers. And I found myself with fans that embrace my ethnic features because I learned to love my wide nose, my full lips, and my striking facial structure.

But in this house, and with Reese, I tell her she's beautiful, inside and out, every single day. Because no one ever told me, except for men interested in my body.

I stop, looking in the mirror. Time to take a few pictures. I face the camera.

"Gems, this is the final look. This is a great base to glam up, or for a beginner playing in makeup. Make the eye more pronounced for a night out with your man or use a bolder lip for drinks with your girls. We're out." I glance down at Reese, who's closing her book, and back to the lens to give my signature sign-off. "And remember Gem, makeup doesn't make you beautiful. You're gorgeous because God made you that way." I wink and give a flirty goodbye wave with my fingers. "Toodles."

"Let me see." Reese stands on the bench with her glossy smile. Her golden skin mirrors her father but her eyes, nose, lips, are all me. "Gorgeous!"

"Thank you, Reesie Piecie. Now let's take this thumbnail." I switch the camera off video to take our picture and pass her the remote. "Ready?"

She nods, hiding the thumb size remote in her little hand. Reese will never doubt her beauty or her worth, and she'll never need a no-good man to tell her she's absolutely perfect.

"Need me to count."

"No, ma'am." Reese stares into the lens like a professional.

"Well, all right then, honey. Let's give them some face."

The camera chimes with the capture of each picture. Reese hits them back to back, giving us time to make slight moves. But we never take our eyes off the camera.

"Silly pose!" Reese squeals. I expand my cheeks like a human blowfish and cross my eyes. "Mommy..." She laughs with a squished face capturing the final picture.

Our laughter echoes through the house. I'm thrilled because we beat the sun. Now that's how to end a night of work. And suddenly the sweetest form of happiness settles over me. To think I never wanted children, but life gave me what I needed, Reese Dallas Hardin—my four-year-old clone.

"How about pizza for dinner?" I close the blinds and turn the camera off.

"And chicken?" Reese drops the remote into my side drawer.

"Yes, I'll order wings too. But you need to take your bath first. Deal?"

"Deal."

"Then chop chop, honey." Reese jumps down and I follow her down the hall with a full face of makeup like I have somewhere to go. But this is my life. Recording videos as an influencer and taking care of my number one priority, Reese. "Get your pjs and I'll start your water."

"Strawberry bubbles, please."

"You got it."

Reese disappears into her bedroom across the hall. It's only seven. I wonder if Brett will make in home in time for dinner. I sit on the edge of the tub pouring in the liquid bubble bath. The sweet fruit fragrance fills the bathroom, and I smile, emptying the basket of her favorite toys into the sudsy water.

"Don't forget your shower cap." I call out, pulling out my cellphone and opening the Message app.

My fingers fly over the screen. *We're ordering pizza and wings. Want your usual?*

I suck in a quick breath, holding my phone. The muscles in my fingers tense from my tight grip. My chest burns from the lack of oxygen, so I exhale until my shoulders buckle. The weight of trying to make our little unit a family is making itself known.

Deep down I know Brett's answer, but that doesn't stop me from hoping that this time I'm wrong. That he'll pick us over his entourage, his boys, and the owner of the pink panties.

"Mommy."

I jump, startled by her standing in the doorway with her nightshirt gathered to her chest. "Yes, baby."

"I need help." I help her out of her clothes and into the tub.

"I'll be right back." I slip out and grab my makeup wipes.

Multitasking is the name of the game in this house. I work around Reese's and Brett's schedules. I'll wash off this makeup and get back to editing the footage after she's in the bed. Before I reach the bathroom, I order the food after checking my messages for Brett's response once more. And true to his nature, there's nothing.

Somehow, we've found ourselves in an awkward "friend zone." It seems no matter how hard I try, or how hard I plead, we're stuck. We live in the same house, share the same bed, yet we live separate lives.

Brett parties all night and sleeps most of the day. I sleep through the night to wake early to care for our child. The moment she's off to school I work to build my relationship with cosmetic and lifestyle brands. Which went nowhere until Brett connected me with his team. His name wiggled me past the gatekeepers.

Thanks to their efforts I work around the clock. They got me on the public relations list for every major brand. I can barely review all the products I receive, even with recording from sunup to sundown. Hence this trip. His help shifted me from buying products with my money to receiving paid product placements and potentially brand deals. Brett gave me exactly what I wanted but the skeptic in me wonders why, and whether the pink lace panties have anything to do with it.

I turn out the light in Reese's room and hurry down the hall to get my wipes. When I stop at the sink, I chuckle at her splish-splashing in the tub before dropping my phone on the counter and facing my reflection.

For a quick tutorial it turned out well. I lean closer, inspecting my face. Dark brown skin and makeup can be friends or enemies. One brand may cause my rich hue to appear ashy, while another may cause my skin to radiate an inner glow. Overall, I'm pleased. I just hope the footage reflects the flawlessness finish of this soft matte glam look while I'm editing tonight.

Reese strikes up a conversation as I scrub away the layers—powder, foundation, blush, primer—that beautifully cover my imperfections. She flicks water around the bathroom, submerged in her rendition of her playtime fiascos. I don't trip over the small stuff. I'll clean it up after she's in the bed. Instead, I laugh and ask questions, allowing her animated story time to mask the imperfections of my life.

"Tomorrow you're going to Grannie Minnie's. How's that sound? Like fun?"

"Good."

"Yes, ma'am."

I lean over the sink to rinse my face, and I glance up at my bare face. "There you are," I whisper. The doorbell rings and I quickly dry my hands. "That's the food. Finish up, sweetie, so you can eat while it's hot."

I run out the bathroom and down the stairs. Living in a mansion never crossed my mind. My plan was to date for fun and snag a man who could take care of me. The older me laughs at the naivete of my younger self. It was on and popping until the pregnancy test came back positive. And in a flash, I thought my life had ended.

The team sidelined Brett due to an injury, and the pregnancy came at the right time. He had something to focus on other than himself, overlooking the extra pounds I put on and the change in our relationship. I went from a woman he showed off every chance he had, to the mother of his only child.

Ugh. I hate having my identity distilled to my reproductive organs. Almost more than I hate being his girlfriend for almost five years, or that he and Reese share the same last name. But on the flip side, I can't see forever with Brett.

Not like this. Not since the scales fell from my eyes twenty-three days ago—the moment I found a pair of lace panties in his Bentley. Panties, that don't belong to me. Panties that I would have missed if it wasn't for the circumstances surrounding our trip.

My car was due for a regular service appointment and my list of chores to prepare for staying a week in Houston had me coming and going in circles. So, I needed to drive his car. I stopped by the bank and went fishing in his armrest for a pen, and there I found them. Hot pink lace, folded, tucked away, damn near neon against the charcoal black interior.

I should be pissed. Right?

Throwing shit.

Cussing his ass out.

Reminding him I gave birth to his child. Flaunting every stretch mark, my less than perky breasts, and my fuller hips. Reminding him of how he begged me to have Reese, to move into his house, and to make our situation-ship a family.

How can a slither of lace untangle the fabric of the life I'm desperately trying to hold together? I stop by the table in the front hallway and grab some cash for the tip from the drawer.

I guess... I stall for a moment, attempting to make sense of the unreasonable. But I guess I'm not pissed, because I'm not shocked. The panties, oddly, confirmed what I already knew. Brett and I haven't had sex in months. It's been so long I refuse to put a date to it, and if he's not getting it from me, he's getting it from someone.

I know.

I was that girl.

The girl who didn't care about a man's responsibilities at home as long as he kept me clothed in designer labels and rocking the most expensive handbags. But somewhere between giving birth to our daughter and finding those cheap-ass-lace-hot-pink panties, I realize I've changed.

Apparently, it took me four years to grow the fuck up and now the overwhelming question is… What do I plan to do about it?

I plaster a smile on my face and open the wooden door. The delivery guy and I make small talk as he stacks scorching hot boxes in my arms. I bid him goodbye and hustle to the kitchen, placing them on the island.

Because the old Jayda Dallas would have told his ass to kick rocks. But the new Jayda knows it's not about me anymore. This is my baby's life too. So, instead of wilding the fuck out, like I wanted to do… like I want to… I swallowed my frustration with this relationship, my discontentment with my lack of autonomy, and I had a come to Jesus moment.

I prayed.

Prayed hard. So hard the sky parted and rained. I figure the Man upstairs had a good laugh at my expense.

Me, who had no regard for others. Me, who strongly considered whether to keep my child. Me, who has absolutely nothing to offer the world except my pretty face and makeup skills.

I spread the boxes out like a makeshift buffet, placing the roll of paper towels at one end and the pitcher of juice on the other. Then I pull down two plates, one for her and one for me.

Funny thing is, I didn't know when the shift began.

Those panties make it hard to pretend I'm happy. That our relationship is the same. But what other choice do I have?

I cook and clean like normal. I record videos and smile for the camera. However, deep in my soul, I wonder if this is payback for the hell I've caused. I went from an independent woman to a woman with a child, living in his house, driving his cars. So, I brushed it under the carpet.

Then a few weeks ago, Milton, the new brand manager, invited us to Houston to meet with a few luxury boutiques. I jumped at the chance to fly back to Texas. Houston isn't home, but my best friend, Catrina, lives there. My hope, I guess, best case is Brett and I can rekindle our relationship. Worst case, Catrina and I can down a bottle of wine and help me get my shit together.

"Mommy."

"Coming and don't stand in the tub, I'm on my way." I take the stairs two at a time, stopping by the hall closet for a towel. I push the door open, and my heart drops. The sight of my child stops me dead in my tracks.

"Reese, how did you get bubbles in your hair?" I fight to hold back my laughter. We spent hours braiding her hair.

"I'm a princess."

"With a bubble crown?"

"Yes, ma'am."

I squat beside the tub, cupping her face in my hands and kiss the tip of her nose. "Baby, the point of the shower cap is to not get your hair wet."

"Sorry, Mommy."

I help her up and wrap my strawberry-scented child in

the fluffy towel. I made this bed and I wouldn't change anything if it means I'd have her. So, if it means stuffing my desires to give her a chance in life, with a mother and father raising her, I'll do it. She's worth it.

Ten minutes later, we're in the kitchen talking with our mouths full, when the hum of the garage door opening silences us. And I swear my baby shrinks in her skin. The sight wraps around my heart and squeezes me so tight I can't breathe. Then a car door slams.

"Eat, baby. It's getting late." I stand and kiss her forehead, not missing her slight tremble. Her stares at the door behind me. I turn her face to mine. "Want some juice?"

She nods, and I miss the light in her eyes. The mother in me wants to give her anything and everything that will make her happy. That's why I overlook the changes I see in Brett.

The late nights. The whispering phone calls. The broken promises. The side door opens, and he's startled straight.

"I'll talk to you tomorrow," Brett mumbles, ending his phone call, stumbling a little. "Hey… my girls."

"Did you drive yourself home?" The stench of alcohol drowns out the smell of pepperoni. I stand beside Reese and she leans into me—by instinct I hold her. Brett stands taller, he towers over my five-and-a-half-foot frame, as his smokey eyes bounce between Reese and my protective arm around her shoulder.

"No, I came through the garage to keep from digging out my keys. What are you guys doing up?" He smiles down at Reese, dropping the device into his pocket.

"We're finishing up dinner. I'll make you a plate."

"Nah, I'm good, I ate with…" He stops himself.

The room falls deathly silent. I play the mediator between Brett and Reese. He regards her like an expensive possession, bragging about her and sharing her photos on social media. I know he loves her, but he's more like a friend than a father.

Which makes all my sacrifices seem futile. We stay because I want my daughter raised in a two-parent house-hold. I want Reese to have a relationship with her father. Both are things I never had, and Reese deserves that and more.

"Okay… Then join us. Are you packed for the trip?" I sit and pull Reese's plate closer to her. "Milton sent over the itinerary for the week. We have a jam-packed schedule, but it should be fun."

"I need to lie down. Goodnight." Brett walks past us.

I glare at his retreating back. I have a choice here. Follow him or let it slide. Again. Then I look down at the tears gathered in my baby's eyes. The man's using her heart like a cheap trampoline.

"Daddy's just tired." She nods beneath my chin, as if she understands. But no child should understand his asshole ways. I want to follow him, but Reese comes first. "Finish your pizza and I have a special treat for you."

She sits back and smiles. "Cookies?"

"I don't know… maybe."

I squeeze her tight and give her a shake to make her giggle and her beads clang like windchimes. I walk over to the refrigerator and grab her a juice box. Then I do what I do best, change the subject.

"Want to stop and get some new coloring books?" I take a bite of my pizza, showing my baby how to brush it off. I'll have all night to process what just happened. But for now we'll focused on the next positive thing on her list and that's spending the next with Grandma Minnie, Brett's mother. She truly makes up for where her son falls short.

"One of those big ones like last time?" She loves the huge floor-sized coloring books.

"We'll stop by the store in the morning."

We finish dinner and clean the kitchen together. I get her to bed, and she's sleep within minutes. I exhale, mentally preparing myself for the second half of my day. It's time to edit, upload, and schedule all the videos I recorded today. I drag to my feet and flick on the soft purple night-light, then I slip out, leaving her door cracked.

Reese sleeps like a rock. Once she's out, she's out. I chuckle, heading down the hall to my beauty room, and I surprised by the sound of Brett talking on the phone.

I glance at my watch—it's after midnight. He jumps a little when I yank the door open. "Would it have hurt you to sit and talk with her tonight? She missed seeing you all day."

"Don't start, Jayda. I'm exhausted."

"Not too tired to whisper on the phone." I gesture to his ever-present device.

A part of me wants to get it and see the evidence of all of his dirty deeds. But my pride won't let me do it. I promised myself the moment I turn into that woman, it's over. It's a shaky line, but it's all I got.

"Man, whatever." He rolls over in the bed, as if I'm not standing here. Then he glances back over his shoulder, "And since you're already bitchin', I'm not going to Houston."

"What? Then I'll stay home too." The words spill out, but this is a big break for me. For once, I'm carving out my own space and my own career, but it's not more important than my family.

"No, go. This trip is important. If you sign with these boutiques, more will follow."

"If it's so important, why are you staying here?"

"I'm meeting with a new potential client."

"A client?"

"Seems the word is spreading. I received an inquiry from another beauty blogger."

I can't see his face, but I hear the sarcasm in his tone. Brett was playing pro football when we met. Then he injured himself. After riding the bench, they let him go. Now, the very thing he used to laugh at is how I generate additional income.

He thought my YouTube channel was a joke until Milton approached me, and then Brett gave himself the title of my manager.

I had the followers and fans, but now I'm a brand with the verified blue checks and all.

"They'll expect to see my manager at these meetings," I remind him.

"Milton will fly out in two days. You can handle things for a few days?"

"I've handled things for years. So, you'll look after Reese? This would be a great time for you two to bond and..."

"No, my mom is looking forward to spending the week with her." He leans back against the headboard, staring at his phone.

I cross my arms. This picture is much clearer to me. His doggish ways know no boundaries. "And this will leave you plenty of time to do what you do."

"Quit tripping." He smiles, licking his lips before he completes the text message. Then he drops his phone onto the nightstand.

I stand in the dark, staring at his silhouette. All I can think about are those pink panties and the fact that I'm scheduled to remain in Houston for an entire week, and Brett will be here alone. He flips around a few times before settling, not bothering to look my way, or tell me goodnight.

Visions of panties and bras lingering over my house bombard my mind. He wouldn't... *Would he?*

Brett would. He'll have some skank in our bed before I can leave Reese at Minnie's house. And like a fool, I'm still with him. Still trying to make this dysfunctional unit a family.

I turn my head up to the ceiling, ready to plead with the Man above again. But why should He listen? I got exactly what I wanted: A man to match my swag. A man that is financially secure. A man every woman wants. A man that makes heads turn.

A man not ready to settle down, whispered through my head. And the old Jayda breaks through the haze of my uncertainty with a healthy dose of taught love.

Jayda, now might be the right time to wake the fuck up!

"Smell that?" I rolled down my window and let the aroma of my mother's fried chicken fill the rented car. If it's possible for a scent to invoke the feeling of being home, it's my mother's food.

My mouth waters, signaled by the gurgle of my stomach, and for a brief second I hate I agreed to let Trish accompany me. We're stopping on the way to Los Angeles for a gathering with mutual friends. I suggested she visit the mall or check into the hotel without me, but she insisted on joining me for brunch.

My fingers wrap around the chrome handle and a wave of excitement ripples through me. My younger brothers—Rashaad, Demetrius, and Quan—and our baby sister Miya save a table inside since it's crowded. I don't know which excites me more, seeing them or eating at Southern Soul.

I haven't visited home for more than a quick pop-in here and there since our folks remarried five years ago. And

I haven't had my mother's chicken and waffles, or shrimp and grits, or…. "Come on, let's get going."

"You're taking me here?" Her wrinkled nose and displeased gaze say she's the fancy type.

I shake my head. Why didn't I leave her in New York? That's my bad for bringing her. Emmitt, my boy since college, introduced us, and I should have known something was up when he introduced us, instead of dating her himself.

I turn back to the old building, the unpaved parking lot, and the tasty cloud lingering out back over the smoker. The line wraps across the front sidewalk and down the side, which I'd expect on a Saturday.

"Yeah, got a problem with it?"

"I guess not, but I expected…" Her eyes swept the area until her doe-like expression returns to mine. Then she hesitates, "It's fine."

I need to tell my boy Emmitt, Trish isn't my type. I like a woman that can hang in the hood, on the ski slopes, or at the governor's mansion, in the same day. My life covers it all, and any woman on my arm must adapt.

Timberlands. Stilettos. Flip-flops. I want it all, and stuck-up Trish may not make the cut.

I open the door, placing my feet on the land I know like I know the football field, like I know my own face because this place is home for me. I round the car, opening the door for Trish. We'll eat and head to do some shopping before flying out to Los Angeles.

I extend an arm to her, glancing into her eyes. This place is in the Fifth Ward in Houston. For most, it's the hood, but this is my old stomping grounds. Her heels crunch on the gravel as we approached the line. The old building seems smaller, a little more weather worn, and in need of a coat of paint.

"Yo, man, is that you, Kamal? What'd up with you?" A big man with a linebacker's build steps closer.

"Man, I can't call it. How's your family? And your folks?" Recognition settles the moment I hear Rodrick's laugh. We played ball in junior high and high school. We pound fists.

"Good. Good. Just trying to get in here and break bread with my ole lady. Can we get a picture with you? Been telling my lady I taught you everything you know on the field." His arm circles the woman beside him and pulls her forward.

"Taught me everything I know, huh? Still a bullshitter, I see." I smile, he's always had a large personality.

"Oh, then you know Rodrick well." The woman grins.

"Shut up Yvonne and take a picture with the man."

We share a laugh as the two bicker a little. I unfold Trish's hand from my arm and the two flank me.

I take Rodrick's phone and snap the picture, giving it back to him. "Don't forget to tag me."

"No doubt, man. Thanks. Wish the kids were here."

"Bring them by sometime. My number's still the same. I hop in and out of town."

"Word?" His eyebrows shoot up, as if surprised.

"I don't let this shit go to my head. We're still peoples. Now don't abuse it. But I'd love to meet your kids."

"Man, you were always my boy." He beams, stepping back in line.

"What are you up to now?"

He digs out a card and passes it over to me. "I have a private security company. We handle events, private detail, you name it I have a guy for your needs."

"I'll remember that." I slip the card in my pocket. "Look, I gotta run. Enjoy your meal and thanks for the support."

We make our way to the doors. A few more people stop me while others frown. I stop at the podium, smiling at the hostess.

"Good morning, Catrina." Her lips curl into a welcoming smile and I return it. I pull out my phone to call my brother while I scan the crowd.

"They're waiting for you over there." Catrina points to the dining room facing the street.

"Wait, this is a group date?" Trish halts, causing us both to stop.

"I told you I'm here to check on my family. You still wanted to accompany me." I hold up a finger to my brother, Rashaad, and face Trish. I glance at my watch and drop my hands in my pockets. This "date" started five hours ago. She talked the entire ride over, name dropping to show me she's part of the "in crowd" in NYC. Now, I'm ready to eat and kick it with my sibling. I glance over and seeing all of them at the table makes me eager to find a solution with Trish.

"How about I call you a ride back to the hotel?" Then I sweeten the offer. "I can make us reservations and we can hit up a few spots around town later tonight."

The sour look glued to her face since we parked disappears. "That sounds more like it."

I pull out my phone to call a car service.

"No need, I got it." She tips her head to the waiting car. "You have my number, call me when you're ready." She sashays off without a glance back.

I shake my head and chuckle. I'm not surprised. She's here to be seen and not at a hole in the wall restaurant. Southern Soul is about rolling up your sleeves and devouring Southern comfort foods. There's nothing glamorous about it, just good food in a family environment.

"Yo, Big Boy, the biscuits are getting cold," Q calls out over my shoulder.

"Don't start that Big Boy shit with me." I stroll over to the table. My brothers and sister stand to greet me. We collide in a familiar huddle, then I give each my undivided attention.

"What the superstar is too good for his nickname?" Q and I execute our signature handshake, ending with a salute. Then I gather his big ass in my arms. "Man, stop!"

The others laugh while I rough him up. Quan was the baby for years until our folks surprised us with their *oops* baby, and the only Montgomery dressed in pink, Miya. I turn and face my baby that's not a baby but a grown woman.

"Baby Miya." Her arms circle my waist and I hold her tight. "I missed you, love."

Miya glances up with a smile. "Not enough to bring your player ass home. Who was that?"

"Nobody. Trying to multitask. So, what's the emergency that required flying home?" She steps back, making room for Demetrius, the middle child always quietly observing the world. "How's the book coming along?"

"Slow, but I'm not in a rush. What about you? Are you planning to stick around for more than the weekend?" Demetrius grounds me with a firm hand on the shoulder.

The thought of staying in the city more than a weekend means I'm bound to bump into Kenneth, and I'm not there yet.

"And your niece needs more than weekly FaceTime calls." Rashaad adds, stopping behind his chair.

Their expectant faces make me feel trapped yet grounded. Each standing behind a chair awaiting my response. Man, I miss my family.

I never thought I'd settled anywhere but Houston, but our parents remarrying changed everything. The fourth largest city in the United States isn't big enough for Kenneth and I to live.

"I'll see what I can do and tell my girl I'll be by to get her for a day of the works."

"She'll be packed and ready to go. Now let's eat."

Rashaad laughs, taking the attention off me and back to food.

My chair is at the head of the table. I sit scanning the table and pride fills my chest—like a proud father. Each of my siblings are thriving and it shows. As the eldest of the five Montgomery children, I raised them like my own from the moment our mother signed the divorce papers. At thirteen I became the man of the house and I took my role seriously.

None of my siblings have seen the inside of a jail cell, although Q had a few close calls. None of them were teenage statistics. All of them are college educated and successful in their chosen fields.

"What's so important that y'all couldn't share it over the phone?" The collective shift of the energy sends a chill down my spine. "What is it? Is it Mother?" I guess since she's not here.

"You could say that." Rashaad flags down the waitress. "We're ready for our orders."

"Well, don't all speak at once."

A series of unspoken messages bounce between them until the ball drops in Rashaad's lap. He's the second oldest and the one that keeps me in the loop. My decision to live on the east coast following my retirement from the league put a wedge between us, and that's something I need to repair.

"The folks are ready to retire." Rashaad shrugs, leaning back with an arm resting against the table. The casual posture speaks volumes.

"And?" I grab a buttermilk biscuit from the basket and my stomach stirs.

"*And*… they want us to take over the restaurants." Miya bookends the announcement.

"It shouldn't surprise us. I just wasn't expecting it this soon." I glance around the room, seeing Southern Soul with fresh eyes. We were raised in this building. The school bus picked us up and dropped us off at the end of that gravel driveway.

The place once served cafeteria style, then we added waiters before I left for college. Then I had the place expanded when I landed a contract as a professional football player. We added windows to bring in more natural light and updated the restrooms and kitchen. But that was almost fifteen years ago.

"Kamal…" Q interrupts my musing. "This place isn't what it used to be."

"What do you mean? It's packed. There's isn't an empty seat in the dining room, and there's still a line outside."

"On Saturdays, but Monday through Friday it's a ghost town. Mom's not making enough to support the staff, let alone moving—"

"Moving?"

They share a grimace.

"They're ready to turn over the reins and sell the house too." Q says, the fidgety tap of his fingers captures my attention more than his words.

"Sell the house?" I turn to Rashaad. "Is it listed?"

"Not yet, but Mom's already consulted a stager and started removing our things."

"And what does *Kenneth* have to say about all of this?" I toss the biscuit back in the basket. "I'm sure this is all his idea. Probably filling her head with more of his fucking lies."

"Dad says it's her idea," Miya says.

"Yeah, right? To give up her home, her business, leave her children and grandchild behind. Sounds like more of his manipulation to me." I pinch the bridge of my nose. "It was only a matter of time. He wants to get her away from us. And then what?"

I want to stand up and walk the length of the room, but that's not possible. The last time I attempted to talk with Mother about her rekindled a relationship with our father, it was on their wedding day. She shut me down and told me it wasn't any of my business. I honored her wish to walk her down the aisle, but our relationship changed.

Now Kenneth and I respect each other's boundaries, and my mother's wishes. And our "conversations" are nothing more than common pleasantries, since he walked out on us twenty years ago.

"I think he's on the up and up," Q says.

"And you, Demetrius?" I glance over at him, sitting on the other side of Miya.

"He seems different. But I don't trust him."

"Rashaad?"

"I don't want to think the worse, but Mom's house is

worth at least two million dollars. Two point five if we list at the right time."

I whistle, not realizing the house had appreciated in value over the years. But with the renovations we did for her birthday a few years back and the new construction in her subdivision, I'm not surprised. She owns a house inside the loop. People would pay a pretty penny to get their hands on that property, even if only to level the house and build something larger.

"So, you think he's trying to get in her purse?" My heart races like the moment a play is called on the field, as I contemplate my next move.

"Man, I don't know. But she always said she'd never leave Houston. Especially with me having Lillian." Rashaad has full custody of his six-year-old daughter after his nasty divorce last year.

"Miya?" I ask.

"I think he's changed. He's not the same man he was when we were kids." Her compassionate eyes plead with each of us, but Miya's always been a daddy's girl. "I think we should give him a chance. People change."

"When people show you their true colors, you paint that shit in ink." I chuckle, but nothing about this predicament is funny. I don't trust the man. He left us once, and I don't put it past him to do again. "The moment I believe Kenneth is different is the moment y'all can commit my ass to the crazy house. Have y'all talked with Mother, alone? And why is this the first time I'm hearing about this?"

"Mom's an adult. I make it a point to stay out of her

personal affairs." Rashaad lifts a hand in the air in resignation. "I figured she'd tell you when she's ready. As for this meeting, we called you in because of our growing concern for the restaurant."

I glance around at the business in question, not pleased with being left in the dark about this matter. I open my mouth to respond and see the waitress approaching the table.

I sit back to give her room. She places the plates of food on the table while I mull over the news. Our parents were joint owners. During their divorce they agreed to split the business in half, while keeping the Southern Soul name intact.

Southern Soul Houston went to Mother, and Southern Soul Raleigh went to Kenneth. I haven't visited the Raleigh location since my early teens, and the effect of their remarriage on the business never crossed my mind. Not when the business documentation has us listed as equal owners. Therefore, any significant changes would need the majority approval of each of us. That fact gives me some relief, but our contracts mean nothing if Kenneth is playing with my mother's heart.

A plate blocks my vision for a moment. The corners of my lips turn up as the scent of my mother's signature spices tickles my nose. The oversized waffle covers the plate topped with four perfectly fried chicken wings. Miya squeezes my hand, and I know she ordered.

"You're a real one," I tell her and grab my fork.

"You know it." Miya winks, slipping the utensil from my hand, and intertwines our fingers.

I almost forgot. I sit straight up and scan their faces, waiting for me. "Demetrius, will you bless the food?"

"Father…"

All heads bow. His words float in and out of my mind. He prays over the food, our family, over the decisions we must make. We end with a boisterous "amen." I linger for a moment, looking over my siblings.

"Rome wasn't built in a day, brother," Q calls out, smothering his scrambled eggs in salsa.

I nod and pick up my fork. I guess I need to shift my schedule and head over to Mother's to get to the bottom of this change. What I know without a doubt is Kenneth won't get his hands on Southern Soul Houston.

"Eat before it gets cold. You know how you hate cold chicken." Miya passes the hot maple syrup.

"Yes, ma'am." I take her offer and cover the piping hot food with a thick coating. I'll eat now and handle this situation later. I cut into the waffles, eager for nostalgia to settle in as the sweet batter melts on my tongue.

The food lightens the mood as we shift from family business to catching up on life. Lillian in elementary school. Rashaad expanding his real estate agency. Miya considering whether to move back home for good.

"I'm glad you finally dumped that jerk."

"I'm starting to think all men are jerks." Miya picks at her food.

"Damn, throw us all under the bus with his loser ass. We told you he was a player," Q says.

"Q, you belong under that damn bus. All of y'all, except Rashaad. Lining up women like trophies. One day, you'll find you match."

"Like you found yours," he teases. Q isn't one to hold his tongue and the two of them stay at each other's throats.

"Q, keep playing with me." She thrusts a fork in his direction.

"What are you going to do now?" I ask Miya.

"Look for a job here. I want to find a place I can stretch my creativity. Maybe become a head chef."

"I have a few connections in the city," I offer.

"Not now, I plan to take some time off. Hit the gym. Focus on myself for a change."

I exchange looks with Demetrius. I caught that "hit the gym" and he did too.

"Miya, there's nothing men like more than a sexy, confident curvy woman." I have two true loves and she's one of them. Knowing some no-good man has her doubting herself makes me want to find him and express my displeasure.

"Correction. Purchased curves. Not real ones."

"Baby Miya's on a roll." Q smiles, trying to get under her skin.

I wish I could reach him. Then I look at the next best thing. "Rashaad…"

Like a mind reader, Rashaad pops the back of Q's head and our laughter fills the room.

"Don't kill the messenger," Q barks, sliding away from Rashaad.

I wipe at my tears as he rubs the back of his head. That's when I see a beauty outside the bay window.

She steps out of a silver luxury car. Her brown skin so rich it looks photoshopped. The fitted business suit contours her curvy frame, stopping midthigh.

Sexy…

She spins around to gather her luggage, when her head tips back and I assume she's laughing at the driver. Her hair floats around her oval face and I smile, as if hearing it. Then she takes the offered business card, giving the driver a sultry smile, and my breath catches.

I lean forward, unable to look away as the driver stumbles a little, spellbound. I don't blame the brother. I freeze, watching the scene unfold until the driver pulls away. Then she turns, heading this way.

"Excuse me." I drop my napkin beside my plate and head out to meet the black beauty. She's rolling Louis Vuitton luggage over gravel like it's smooth concrete.

"This ninja is always recruiting," Q says behind me, but I'm focused on the door.

I stroll through the crowd and out the door. She turns, mumbling at the luggage, lowering until she tilts her curvy backside in the air.

I see you, baby… I don't stop until I'm beside her. "Let me help you with that."

CHAPTER 3

"Look at that line." The driver stops outside the little building that looks like it once was a house. "Is it always like that?"

"Yeah, on Saturdays. I can leave you here or around the side of the building."

"Let me call my friend." I dial Catrina. "What's your favorite dish on the menu?" I ask the driver, waiting for the line to connect. The heavenly scent has me ready to change this outfit for leggings and t-shirt. Especially after flying out early this morning, I slept less than an hour before it was time to wake Reese and get her off.

"I always order the breakfast platter. It has all of their current bestsellers. So, every time you come it could change. Last time I had—"

"Let me get this." I smile at the driver in the rearview mirror. "Hey, Catrina. There's a line. Do I need to wait? Because I don't have that kind of time."

"Nah, come in. I have a table for us. My shift is almost over."

"Girl, these people might drag me for cutting in line." I laugh, gathering my purse. "She's inside," I whisper to the driver, and he hops out to get my bag from the trunk.

"I'll keep an eye out for you and meet you. Did you check in at the hotel?"

"Not yet."

"Okay. We'll eat and I'll drive you over."

"Cool. I'm heading in." I hang up and grab the handle for my bag from the driver, after submitting his payment through the app. "Thank you."

"You're welcome, gorgeous. Let me know if you need a driver while you're in town." He passes me a card.

"Thank you." I smile, and he pulls away from the curb. I navigate the gravel drive in my heels and rolling luggage until a wheel locks up. I rock the bag side to side, searching for the issue. "Where are you?"

"Let me help you with that." I look toward the deep voice and I'm met with a smile. My heart skips a little and I'm stunned.

"Uh… I think it's a rock," I say without drooling.

He picks up the sixty-pound bag without issue, moving it to the sidewalk. I open my mouth to thank him when I see all eyes on us. I nervously chuckle.

"I'll take it from here. I don't want you to lose your place in line."

"I'm already seated. I saw you struggling and thought I'd lend a hand."

"Is that so?"

"Yes, ma'am."

"Ma'am?" I laugh and he stammers a little. "I'm much too young for you to address me as ma'am, don't you think?"

"It's how my mother raised me." He flashes a trillion-dollar smile that derives straight from the steamy depths of hell because it's downright sinful. The man is a work of art.

Powerful jaw. Broad shoulders. Beneath that shirt is a chiseled body, I'm sure. I swallow around the stone in my throat as he hunkers closer and examines the wheels on my bag.

"Here's the issue."

I blink, and his face is close. Super close. I'm finding it hard to breathe and when I do, I inhale a long drag of temptation.

Can a man smell yummy? Yes.

Better than the scent of homemade Southern food lingering in the air? Absolutely.

God, yes.

"Everything all right?" A crease of concern bunches between his dark brown eyes.

"Uh…"

My lungs empty as I take a quick inventory of the man in front of me. A man rendering me speechless in the right way. This moment is going down in the books. But in my defense, I'm delusional and sleep deprived. That's what it is. I lay a hand over my galloping heart, fighting to string together a response.

I inhale and… oh hell, that damn delicious scent tickles my nose, and the sensation travels through my body, awakening a whisper of attraction. I groan.

Stop breathing, Jayda. Just stop breathing. I chastise myself the moment I lock eyes with him.

"Yeah, I…" I shake to quiet the voices in my head. "Long morning of travel."

I can't look away, and neither does he. I came to Southern Soul to meet my best friend, Catrina. I figured staying with her for the week would make up for Brett ditching me.

Damn, Texas has some fine ass men. The masterpiece before me has a beard and full eyebrows. He's groomed, but all man. His golden peanut butter complexion reminds me of Reese. And with that thought comes the thorn in my side, Brett.

"Huh, thanks. I got it. I appreciate your help." I stand and he moves with me until he's towering over me.

And he's tall. I almost groan again, but I hold it in. It's time for me to find Catrina. Unlike my boyfriend, I'm a lot of things, but I'm not a cheater. The moment I want someone more than what I have, I'm out. At least, that was before I had Reese. Now, I stay because… staying's the right thing to do.

"My pleasure. Name's Kamal Montgomery. And you are?" He extends a hand.

"Jayda Dallas." I take his hand and immediately regret it. A trail of heat flows from him to me in a timeless extension of energy, paralyzing me. "Huh, someone's waiting for me. Thanks again."

I retract my hand, but not before he flips it over. The perfect thick brow of his arches in an unspoken question. I slip my hand from the warmth of his. But the heat of his touch lingers.

I rub my hand along my skirt, trying to erase the memory as I reclaim the handle of my bag and start rolling toward the front of the line.

"Hey, Jayda!" Catrina sings, wrapping me in a sister-friend hug as we squeal like kids. When we finally step back, she takes possession of my bag. Then she stares at the man now standing beside us. "Kamal."

Kamal nods. "Enjoy your meal, Jayda." Then he disappears.

"How you pick up that fine ass man before you even get in the building good?" Catrina hisses, not taking her eyes off his fine ass, which is perfect. He sits at a table with three men and a woman, and all of their eyes are on me.

I face Catrina. "You know him."

"They're the Montgomerys. They own this place."

I discretely glance back over my shoulder and they're still looking at us. Heat floods my face and I'm embarrassed at how I'm reacting to a stranger.

"Where's our table?"

"Over there." Catrina points and walks as I try to ignore the awareness lingering in my hand. "I need to change, so people won't think I'm still on duty. I'll take your bag to the back while I'm at it. Check out the menu and I'll be back," she says in a single breath, unaware of my dazed state.

"Uh… Okay."

"Jay, you good?" She stops with a concerned look on her face.

"Yeah, just tired. I'm operating on an hour of sleep."

"We can always take the food to go." She offers and my eyes have a mind of their own, trailing back to the table across the room. Catrina glances over her shoulder and back at me. "How's my baby?"

"Reese is amazing. I can't believe she's about to turn five." I sigh.

"And the donor?"

"Brett is Brett." I lower to one of the four chairs. "Go change because my spine and my belly are having a conversation."

Catrina lets out a boisterous laugh, and every head turns in our direction, even *his*.

"Be right back."

She heads off down a narrow hall and I pick up a large trifold menu. The waiters wear jeans, white polo style shirts, and red waist aprons. Our server fills two glasses of water and tells me the daily special. I ask for a few more minutes to wait for Catrina. She smiles and leaves me to browse the menu.

The waiter said the full menu is available for brunch, which is no help at all. They have pancakes, waffles, smothered pork chops, greens, and Lord, they have banana pudding. I could order every single item and eat until I snuff out my woes. But that won't solve my problems.

I settle on taking the driver's suggestion. I fold the menu and place it in front of the free chair beside me, wiggling with excitement. Food helps me think better. Curiosity sends my gaze across the room and Kamal tips his head. I smile, thankful that my dark skin hides my embarrassment.

The sound of my phone distracts me. I answer with an enormous smile on my face. "Reesie Piecie! What are you doing?"

I lean into my hand, listening as she covers her morning. The moment Catrina returns we end the call with her sending kisses to Reese and us ordering our food.

"So, what's on your agenda while you're here?" Catrina asks, and I tell her my schedule. "I can drive you. I have the rest of the day off."

"I'd like that. We haven't hung out in a while."

"I'm surprised you came straight here. I thought I wouldn't see you until tonight or later in the week."

"Are you complaining?" I tease, making room for our food as the waiter approaches the table.

"Not at all, just surprised."

The platter is big enough for both of us to eat. I lean forward, inspecting my food. Eggs, steak, fried potatoes, biscuit, and pancakes. "How do you work around this kind of food?"

"Girl, you know food goes straight to my feet."

"What does that mean?" I unfold the linen napkin, placing it across my lap.

"I don't know, something my mom used to tell me. She called me a beanpole with feet." She laughs and I join her.

"I'm not a beanpole and my trainer would kill me if he saw me eating this. But oh well."

"Then let's do one for the Gram."

She pulls out her phone and snaps a picture with me and my oversized platter of food. And we immediately dig in. We don't talk for a while. Faint music, mumbles of conversations, and the sound of utensils on porcelain plates fill in the gaps.

Fifteen minutes in I come up for air and I sit back. "I think I just gained ten pounds."

"And it'll all go to your ass."

"Girl, hush." I push the plate forward. "Why did I wear this tight suit?"

"Trying to put us beanpoles to shame." She grabs a toothpick from the center of the table, leaning back with her keen eyes on me.

I shake my head, ready to talk. Catrina is Reese's godmother, and my best friend. She's the one person who knows about all of my skeletons, all of my passwords, and if anything happens to me, I know she'd take care of my baby. We have weathered the storms of life, and I have a funny feeling another is on the horizon.

"What's on your mind?"

"How do you know something's on my mind?" I roll my eyes.

"You only touched half of your food and you keep sighing as if your mind is running. What's up?"

"I think Brett and I have run our course." I exhale. "I can't believe I just said that."

"You did. But where is it coming from?"

"I'm tired. My life is an endless cycle of the same shit, different day."

"Okay. Where is this coming from?"

"You already asked that."

"I'll ask again until you answer. You've been tired for years. I've been tired for years. But you've been team Brett with pom-poms."

I cut my eyes her way. She's right. I was tired before I learned about my pregnancy. But I had to give my family a chance. "Reese deserves…"

"Don't put this on Reese. Please don't. We both know Reese deserves better than Brett the asshole."

"Catrina." I cut off her rant. My feelings aside, he's still Reese's father.

"Fine." She crosses her arms. Catrina is loyal and stubborn and this conversation could drag on until next week at this rate.

"I found panties in his car last week," I confess. The fact that she doesn't wince or turn away is telling of the state of my relationship.

"Did you put them with the others?"

The sting of her bite stuns me silent, and a fresh wave of embarrassment burns my cheeks. The type that weasels into the cracks and crevices of my resolve to walk away from him once and for all. The pink lace panties aren't the first pair I've found. But they are the first pair I've found in his car. Which feels like one step from being in our home.

I've found black panties tucked in his pants pockets. Red panties hidden in his suit jacket. And the others have faded into a rainbow of disillusionment. I thought having a child, building a house, meant… *forever*.

It's as if he wants me to find them. Is that it? Is Brett waiting for me to make the first move?

I stare at the tablecloth, looking for the answers in the woven fabric. When a finger settles beneath my chin and I'm staring into Catrina's eyes.

"What's the worst that can happen?" I hear no laughter behind her question. Nor the usual wit. What I see is her impatience, and I get it. If the shoe was on the other foot, I'd have my best you-don't-need-his-ass speech, along with my best *bish* please, and a few you-don't-need-his-sorry-ass high fives.

"Jayda, you're one of the strongest women I know. You raised yourself. You're building a career with blush and a fucking camera. Tell me what he has over you that makes it so hard to kick his ass to the curb and walk away?"

I asked myself the same question. Why do I stay? And I realized…

"I've never had to start over." She opens her mouth to feed me another line, but I stop her. "No, Cat, not like this. Every time I had to restart, to remake myself, I only had one person to think about—me. I could change cities with the clothes on my back. I could board a plane with a one-way ticket. But staying means my child will never know what it means to be alone on the streets. About having to find a place to sleep, keeping one eye open for manipulators, and the other open for crooks."

Catrina sits back. "Yeah, she's living in a big ass mansion. She'll go to the best schools. But what is she learning from her parents? What is she learning from her father? And what is she learning from you?" She reaches for my hand and I pull them to my lap. "You don't need a roundtrip ticket because my house is your house. You don't need a closet full of clothes when you have that fire in your gut. Brett didn't give it to you, and he can't take it away. You did it once, you can..."

"... do it again." I stare down at the princess-cut diamond ring Brett gave me for Christmas as a promise ring. He teases that it keeps the guys away, and I know it's nothing but another carat to keep me complacent.

"Let me go get your bag—can't have you late for your brand meetings." Catrina stands, and I wrap my arms around her waist. I hold her tight, thankful that she cares. "Just promise me you'll think about it."

"I will."

"Be right back." Catrina disappears down the same hallway.

What if... Ricochets in my head like an unruly ball in a pinball machine. I swallow back the questions because I don't have the answers. Because I'd have to admit that my plans to get away from him don't amount to much, and that I'm stuck with Brett.

My eyes burn with the need to cry out my frustrations, but there's no crying when you're adulting. A vision of Tom Hanks in *A League of Their Own* makes me smile. The sight of tears rendered him a yelling madman. I guess I'm the batter up.

The waiter clears the table and I nod my thanks when my eyes settle on Kamal's again. He rolls back his shoulders and lifts his head a little higher. The slight tip of his head invites me to do the same. So, I mimic his gesture. His quick wink brings a smile to my face, tampering the sting *a little*.

Catrina's question rises to the surface. What's the worst that could happen?

I pull out my phone and list my bills. Catrina offered us a place to sleep, but I'd want our own apartment. I add an apartment. I wonder how much that would run us? I tap the screen, and since I don't have the answers, I fill the note with my unanswered questions.

Now to the dollars and cents.

I have my mad money account, but it will only cover us for a few months. Then there's the account he deposits a small allowance to cover the household costs and Reese's tuition. The total isn't much either, but it means I'm not broke.

But... if I sign with one of these brands this week, I can pad my accounts a little—after I finish the approved videos. Which shouldn't be an issue. I open my calculator to give myself a goal figure.

Apartment. Car. Preschool for Reese. I punch the numbers, watching the total soar.

Food. Equipment. Clothes. The monthly figure on the screen mocks me. I hear the ungodly total laugh and the confident bravado of my audacious plan is losing its appeal with each passing second.

What about all the other months of the year? I reach for my water and take a long gulp, wishing it was something much stronger.

I can't afford this.

"Ready?"

I jump, startled, and my phone drops to the table like a hot potato. I bat my eyes, pulling myself from the overwhelming tunnel of doubt and debilitating fear, focusing on Catrina's face.

"Huh… yeah. I am." I stand and grab my phone, hiding the number from my sight with the press of the power button. "Do you know a real estate agent?"

"Sure do, there's one right over there." She points to the table on the other side of the room. "Rashaad Montgomery. He helped me find my place. I'll go get a card."

"Catrina… don't." I reach for her arm a second too late because she's gone. My ex-best friend bounces right up to the table, says only God-knows what, as they all looked back over at me. Then she walks back smiling.

I truly hate her right now.

"Here you go." She passes the card with a smirk on her face. "He said he recently signed a new complex. They're offering pre-lease specials."

"Did you have to switch your narrow tail over there?"

"Girl, Rashaad is divorced. I could be his next baby's mamma."

I laugh. "No, ma'am. We are not aspiring to be baby's mammas. We need to find ourselves some husbands."

"So, the donor is out?" That's her nickname for Brett. I hate it and she knows it. But it doesn't stop her from wiggling her eyebrows and dancing around like she's doing the potty dance from that diaper commercial.

"I'm not saying he's out, but I am saying, I'm not taking his shit no more."

"What does that mean?" She stops, planting her a hand on her hip. Her sour expression says it all.

"Not what you're thinking. I can't just throw five years away. And I can't walk away without a plan either, I have a child to think about."

"What are you going to do? And how can I help?"

I loop my arm through hers. "To start, I have a week of meetings, but maybe we can call your future baby daddy and schedule time to see a few places."

I leave Southern Soul with a whisper of hope. Catrina drops me off across town at the first brand meeting where I meet up with Milton.

For the rest of my visit, we meet with three boutiques and a custom jeweler. Each looking to contract with a brand ambassador. It all seems promising, except Milton.

I can't put my finger on it, but he seems either inexperienced, or unmotivated, or a healthy dose of both. We find a cafe to regroup and eat before heading to visit with another custom jeweler.

"I've been thinking about putting together a video reel to give them some examples of my work." I take a bite of my wrap, waiting for him to contribute to the conversation.

"You can, but I doubt it will make much of a difference." Milton flags down the waitress and orders another cocktail.

"Why not? And do you think having another drink is wise? We have two more meetings."

He chuckles, as if he's privy to a private joke.

"I'm glad you think showing up to a brand meeting sloshed is funny."

"Jayda, these are decent opportunities, but they won't pay what you're worth." He wipes his mouth, tossing the linen napkin aside. "Extra work won't change that."

"Then why are you wasting my time?" Suddenly I'm not hungry.

He glances off, as if weighing his options. Leaning against the table, his eyes are clearer than a moment ago. "Brett arranged these meetings, I'm just standing in his place."

"What does that mean?"

"You need to discuss your contract with Brett."

"What contract?"

"His contract as your manager."

"We don't have a contract."

"Are you sure about that?" Milton's slurred question

feels like a slap across my face. "I think it's time you talked with your man."

"I *never* signed a contract for management. That's what I thought we were doing." I'm confused, grasping to put this together. The sounds of the mid-day patrons around us fade in the background.

Put this together, Jayda, and you better do this shit quick. Brett hires Milton. Brett said Milton arranged brand meetings. Brett pulls out of the trip. The question is obvious.

"Why did Brett hire you?"

"To babysit."

"Babysit? Is that why this trip was extended? Was this all a hoax?"

Milton downs the rest of his drink and then slams the glass on the wood table.

"Wait… Are any of the deals real?"

Milton pins me with a look filled with sorrow as he pulls out his wallet, dropping some cash on the table. "Good luck, Jayda."

He leaves and I'm stuck in an unexplainable stupor. What just happened?

I've been in Houston for two weeks, missing my baby, and for what? Because Brett thought I needed a babysitter? But why?

Brett wanted me gone.

My excitement for this business trip evaporates, and I'm blinded by his betrayal as I dig around looking for my phone. Is Miss Minnie in on it too when she volunteered to keep Reese?

I need answers, and I don't trust Brett to get them without digging through his bullshit to find them. I laugh, but it's only to cover the crushing weight in my chest. This is the relationship I want to save. A man who would hire a fake manager to get me out of town. For what? He probably has a hoe in our bed right now.

I feel so fucking stupid. I've gone into these offices pitching myself as a brand ambassador. And Brett is home alone laughing his ass off.

I'm a fucking joke.

Tears roll down my face. I use the napkin to dry them the moment they fall, but they keep coming. So, I let them. Just this once I acknowledge the brunt of the rejection and the familiar presence of regret.

My mind flashes to all the signs I ignored, all the signs that pointed to the exit door. I should have left. I guess this is what happens when you try to hold on to a dream. *You choke the life out of it.*

"It was lavish while it lasted." I drop my head in my hands, forcing myself to breathe and think.

I want to fly back to Los Angeles and flip the fuck out.

Bleach his shit. Burn everything standing. Because I did this to us, but I won't let another man play me.

The chime of my phone makes me sit upright. I fumble with my phone, panting as if I've run a marathon and see the joy of my life on my screensaver: Reese.

She's painted up to look like a butterfly. And I smile through my haze of pity. I can't do anything that will land me in jail, and I can't do anything that will make me lose my baby.

What are you going to do, Jayda? He doesn't know, I know, rings loud and clear in my head.

I said I'd never be this woman. But he's pushed it too far this time. It's time I go on a scavenger hunt through his precious computer. But to do that, I need to get back to California.

I hit speed-dial for the only person I can trust. "Catrina, I need a ride to the airport."

CHAPTER 4

A PERFECT PRINCESS cut diamond fit her. I respect the man code—I don't entertain another man's woman. But damn.

Thoughts of Jayda resurface the moment I push open the doors and see Catrina. Her head is down, focused on a stack of menus. She twists and turns the plastic-covered menus before placing them in the slot beside the podium and glancing up at me.

"Kamal Montgomery."

"Catrina, it's been a while." I return her welcoming smile. "How are you this afternoon?"

"Good, finding ways to keep myself busy. Right this way. I set you up in the party room." She flags over a waiter, leading me through the restaurant. "You're the first one here."

"Thank you." The place is empty. I glance at my watch and it's almost one-thirty. "Is it always this quiet?"

"Yeah, on weekdays."

I nod, counting the people in the dining room. Catrina stops outside the double doors, gesturing inside. I step inside, pushing the doors until they're flush with the jam. The cream paint needs an update, and the floors could use a good polish.

"There's water, tea, and fresh coffee. Two waiters will take care of you guys. The first should arrive in about ten minutes. Can I get you something while you wait?"

"No, Catrina everything's... *Fuck*."

"Excuse me?"

"I'm sorry." There are seven place settings at the table. Kenneth's coming? I run a hand over my face. Guess it's time to face the old man. "This works. You're the manager on duty?"

"No. We run a light staff except Friday evenings and Saturdays. And if any issues arise, we're told to call Mr. Montgomery. But mostly, I'll handle what you need."

"Which Mr. Montgomery?"

"Your father."

"Really?" I face her.

I reviewed the books while traveling last week. Mother and I haven't talked because she asked that I stop by the house. The wedge between us is growing by the second, the fact that no one bothered to tell me about the financial state of the restaurant makes me feel like an outsider with my own family.

"How often does he come in?"

"Daily."

I nod. "And my mother?"

"Miss Jackie arrives early to make the baked goods. So daily and all day on Saturdays."

I hear Q's loudmouth and glance toward the sound. He and Rashaad spot me and stroll through the dining room.

"Okay. Thank you, Catrina."

"You're welcome, Kamal. I'll send in the waiter in a few minutes."

"Great." She turns to leave. "And Catrina, how long are you scheduled today?"

"Until close."

"Good to know. I'll stop by and see you after we finish here."

She stops. "Is there an issue?"

"Oh no, I want to walk through the place and see how we can spruce it up. I'd love to get your input. You know this place and I'm sure you can add a few things to my list."

"Oh, sure, no problem. I'll be right up front." Catrina walks back to her station.

"Bet."

Q and Rashaad walk side by side and for a moment Rashaad regards Catrina with a sweeping gaze from head to toe.

"Cat," he says low. The moment I hear it I give Q a, *what's up with that?* look.

Q slows to a stop in front of me. "Rashaad has officially joined you in the *never will I ever* club."

"The what club?" I laugh.

He laughs with me, sitting on the edge of the table. "It's

the never will I ever… get married. Never will I ever…" then he rubs his chin, "I guess 'Shaad's not part of the never will I ever have children since he has Lillian."

"You just sit around making shit up?" I glance at Rashaad and Catrina. "It's a wonder you get any work done."

"Am I wrong?" His challenging eyes hold an edge of humor. "Then I've made my point."

He stands up, making his way to the back table and pours a cup of coffee. He's right about marriage and children. Both are not on my radar, *ever*.

I watched my mother struggle to raise five kids while running a small business, while our father led his life as a single man. He picked us up every other Christmas and every other spring break. But the day-to-day responsibilities sat squarely on her shoulders. And if that's love. I'll good without it.

"What's that all about?" I ask Rashaad the moment Catrina's out of earshot.

"Nothing. She needs me to look into some places for her." He surveys the table. "The folks are joining us?"

"If Kenneth is, I think it's better if I catch up with you guys later. You know Kenneth and I don't see eye to eye, and it won't make for a productive meeting."

"At any moment you can start acting like an adult," Rashaad counters. "We can't get on the same page if the two of you refuse to talk."

"Here's her number." Catrina appears with a yellow

piece of paper. "I would have sent the text, but I don't have your new number."

"It's 832..." Rashaad rattles off the number.

I step back giving them some privacy, as Q leans against the door jamb watching it all go down. Catrina's eyes shine like she hit the Mega Million and judging by Rashaad's slack posture, he's clueless. Q's head drops to his chest, his shoulders shaking with laughter.

The moment Catrina leaves us alone, Q's roar fills the restaurant.

"What's wrong with him?" Rashaad elbows Q on his way to the table of refreshments.

I catch up and wave a hand in front of face, pretending to check his sight. "Shaad, man, you have to be blind if you can't see she's checking for you."

"Catrina?" He pours a cup of coffee.

Q howls, holding his stomach. "That's that old man shit."

"What's so funny?" Miya enters the room with Demetrius just over her shoulder.

"Rashaad and Catrina," I answer, accepting her hug.

"You finally gave her your number?" The glee on Miya's face sends Q into another round of laughter. "What?"

"Tell her, Shaad." Q taunts. "Please tell her."

"You're a brat," Rashaad counters. "I gave her my number. But it was to schedule a few apartment tours for her friend."

"Her friend, Jayda?" I ask, ignoring the feeling of aware-ness ignited from the mere mention of her name.

Miya snaps her mouth closed, trying to suppress her laughter. "It's a start." Then she turns her nosy eyes in my direction. "You know Jayda?"

"What am I missing?" Rashaad speaks over the commotion. We lean on the loud side when we get all together, with several conversations running at once.

"Catrina is attracted to you," Demetrius states.

"It's not even like that." He glances over at Catrina back at the podium, then she sends him a finger wave. Rashaad's face turns crimson, and it's hard for a brother to blush.

"I've seen it all. Light-skinned is blushing," Q tosses out between gasps for air.

"Just start the meeting." Rashaad brushes past me, sitting at the table.

"Yo, Q, that's enough." But it's too late because Catrina's bright smile fades.

"I'll talk to her," Miya whispers. "Q, don't be a jerk."

"A jerk?" Q sobers, sitting in a chair. "No, I'm the most honest person in this room, that's what I am." He turns to Rashaad. "She's cool but always goes out of her way to help you. Sends you business nonstop. Always buying Lillian gifts."

"That's because she's a kind person, and we're friends." Rashaad looks ghostly.

Q continues, "Buys you birthday presents every year. Keeps working here for next to nothing. Continued to work here *after* you met, married, and divorced Miranda Priestly."

We mutually agreed to keep his ex from our conversations. The wounds are still too fresh for all of us. The divorce was four years ago, but the custody battle was nasty.

"Who's Miranda?" I ask Miya, keeping my eyes glued on the exchange.

"From *Devil Wears Prada*," she whispers, walking over to stand beside Rashaad. The distant look in Rashaad's eyes tells me he missed it.

"D?" Rashaad focuses on Demetrius.

"Q lacks subtly, but he's not a liar."

"I'm not saying he's lying, but he could be wrong." Rashaad drops in a chair.

"Yeah, but not with this one." Demetrius confirms, and the room falls silent.

I feel the need to say something, but relationships aren't my thing. This is why I need to be closer to home. I'm out of the loop and this moment with Q shows Rashaad is dealing with more than he's been sharing on our regular calls.

"Let's get this meeting started since we're all here," Miya says from across the room.

"Just us?" I give Rashaad's shoulder a supportive squeeze and take my seat.

"Yeah, Mom and Dad left on a two-week cruise," Demetrius says pulling up to the table.

"I guess I don't know shit," I bark, tired of being left in the dark.

"Whose fault is that?" Q drops his arm over the back of the chair beside him, crossing his ankle over his knee. "It's their anniversary."

"Man, keep that blade you call a tongue to yourself." I brush him off, checking the calendar on my phone. "I don't see anything. What anniversary?"

"Their first anniversary? Kamal, you really need to get it together." Miya shakes her head. "So, what are we meeting about?"

I sigh. I didn't call this meeting to talk about our parents. "We need to talk about how we plan to handle Southern Soul. I reviewed the books, and she's barely covering overhead. The staff is as lean as we can make it without each of us stepping in and picking up shifts—like we used to do."

My thoughts travel off for a moment. We each know how to run this place from the kitchen to waiting tables. But I hope it won't come to that.

"The numbers are clear, and y'all each have reason to be concerned. Continuing at this rate, we'd have to close the doors. I'd like to start with what you all had in mind when you asked me to come back? And where you see Southern Soul down the road? Q?"

"Mom's worked her whole life. I'm cool with her retiring and stepping away. But I want to make sure she's straight, and you know she won't let us take care of her."

I'm with him. I nod. "Yeah, and I don't want her financially dependent on Kenneth."

They mumble their agreement before Rashaad jumps in. "I want to one day be able to pass this place on to Lillian. To give her some of the experiences we had."

Miya smiles. "That would be dope."

"What are you thinking, Kamal?" Demetrius asks and they all face me.

"I think we should try something different. Saturday is floating this place. What if we open on Sunday, too? We'd take advantage of our hottest day of the week."

"Moms ain't going for that," Q responds first.

"Sunday is family day. They've never opened on Sunday in thirty years," Demetrius reminds us, and I'm aware of this.

"But this isn't thirty years ago. They didn't have restaurants in the same parking lot and on every corner. Times are different," I point out.

"Chick Fil A does." Rashaad says.

"They're a national franchise. We're one restaurant that's struggling to keep our doors open," I remind him.

"Man, I'm for whatever will help us keep this place open. But Mom and Dad won't be on board, and until they turn over the reins, this is their business." Q states the obstacle, which is obvious—the objections of our parents.

For a brief moment, I second-guess the plan I've constructed. I knew this idea would be a tough sell, so I forge ahead. "I considered many scenarios. We're in agreement that closing the doors is not an option. So, the challenge is how will we increase the revenue?"

They pass looks between each other, and I take their silence to continue. "We could examine the overhead. But we can't cut the staff. We're already operating at the leanest we can manage. We can't increase the prices on the menu. Because Mom won't go for that either."

"We need a bridge here, guys. We're not financially secure and we agree that closing the doors isn't an option." I use my hands to bookend this issue, hoping they'll see where I'm coming from. "My proposal is to run a test. Open for one Sunday and look at the numbers."

I ignore their closed expressions. This is why they called me home. This is what I do.

"We each are successful entrepreneurs. I don't have to tell you that getting traffic through those doors is the issue and putting asses in that dining room is the solution."

I sit back. Q owns and runs one of the hottest clubs in Houston. Rashaad owns and operates one of the largest privately held real estate agencies in the state. Demetrius could not sell another book, and he'd still be a millionaire. And Miya knows the restaurant business.

"This isn't the totality of my plans but it's the cornerstone. Weekend brunch is a sweet spot for us. It's clear in the numbers. Now, if we can get those numbers to spread over Saturday and Sunday, then we'll have enough revenue to slowly turn this ship around."

A knot forms in my stomach as I wait. I'm not trying to convince laymen but business savvy entrepreneurs with a vested interested in the outcome of this venture. I thought they'd jump aboard on the strength of the existing numbers. But it seems I was wrong.

"Miya, are you with me?"

Her heavy sigh tells me her answer before she speaks. "Look. I'm all for turning this place around. But doing it behind Momma's back..." she shakes her head. "I can't support it without her approval. Sorry."

"Rashaad."

"I'm with you. However, I can't approve of the idea. Mom is the day-to-day operator of the business. Yeah, we're partners, but this is her baby, her business. Why don't we—"

I jump to my feet, not wanting to hear the last of Rashaad's statement, and face my next option. "Demetrius?"

"I'm Switzerland. Having actual numbers would help validate your idea, but you won't have a majority with my vote. So, if Q agrees, I'm in."

My hands dig into the rough fabric-covered chair, pushing it into the table. The final vote is on Q.

"Kamal, you know I'm down for reviving this place. But stepping around Mom sounds like a Kenneth move."

The weight of his words feels like a blow to the gut, and all the pent-up air in my lungs swooshes out. Comparing me to Kenneth tells me exactly where they stand.

"Fine."

I spin on my heels and leave, blocking out each of their shouts for me to return. For me to talk it out. For me to find another solution.

"Everything okay?" I slam to a stop when Catrina blocks my exit. She's looking at me, but her eyes bounce back and forth to the room. I turn back to see my siblings walking to catch up with me.

"It's better to step aside."

Thankfully, she moves. I burst out the door, glad I drove today, and within seconds I'm in the car with the city in front of me and a cloud of dust behind me.

Ringing fills the cabin of the sleek sports car. I press end until they stop calling.

"What are you going to do, Kamal?" I ask myself, driving to the airport.

I could sit back and let Mom do her thing. She could sell the place. She could keep the place. She could give it over to Kenneth with a fat red bow. But my mother is my responsibility, and we wouldn't be in this situation had I not let Kenneth's presence get in my way.

Southern Soul won't die on my watch. The four of them had months to address it—while keeping me in the dark. Yet no one had a concrete plan for addressing the decline of revenue or the decline of guests through the doors. *Then* they called me. Which means they were out of options.

A pang of disappointment throbs through my chest. There was a time when they didn't question or challenge my suggestions. But I won't sit back and watch our family business die.

Today's a new day. I'll show them that my plan's sound and the new wave for Southern Soul. But, how?

The fact that mom's traveling for two weeks gives me a tiny window to do something. But, what?

The city rolls by in a blur. The newly constructed highways after Hurricane Harvey, along with the updated buildings, give my hometown a fresh appeal.

They don't have a plan, and I do. Whether they approve of my idea or not.

Southern Soul needs more than us sitting around waiting for Mom to get with the times and decide. I will turn this place around with or without my siblings on board, and I'll use my money to do it.

I dial the restaurant.

"Southern Soul, your dining room away from home. This is Catrina, how can I help you?"

"Catrina."

"Ka—"

"Don't say my name."

"Uh, how can I help you, sir?"

"I need you to make a list of every single repair needed at the restaurant. Can you do that for me?"

"Yes, sir. Would you like that with gravy?"

"They're still there?"

"Yes, sir. That's one of our specialties."

"I need you to keep this between us."

"Why? What's going on?" Her tone drops to a twisted whisper.

I pull into the parking lot of a gas station. The car rolls to a stop and I shift into park. My mind runs through the facts, trying to devise a way to have at least two of my siblings onboard when I suggest opening on Sundays to Mother.

But can I get enough data in two weeks? And to run the Sunday opening before she returns, it will have to happen *this* weekend—in five days.

"Shit," I hiss. I grip the steering wheel tight, dropping my head back.

"Should I email Miss Jackie?"

"No. Give me a second."

Thankfully, Catrina holds the line. The soft sounds of voices fill the space between us. I'm asking for trouble with doing this without Mother's consent. However, I know she won't give my plan a chance without proof. And what if I can double the monthly revenue in two weeks?

Money talks. And if I run the test this weekend, I could probably run another one next week, depending on when they scheduled to return.

Now, with the dates nailed down, I need to get the word out.

"Do you guys send a regular newsletter?"

"No, sir." She blows air in the phone. "Look, whatever you're doing I can't lose my job."

"You won't lose your job," I reassure her. I honestly can't guarantee anything, since I have no clue how to make this happen. But I know I can't do it without her help. "Look, I need to have the place available on Sunday."

"For a private party?"

That's it! I sit upright. A wave of excitement replaces my slight apprehension. A welcome home party. Why didn't I think of that?

"Yeah." I feel the smile on my face.

I pull the car back onto the road while Catrina runs through a series of questions to make my reservation. We set the time from noon to six with the full staff. She hesitates when quoting me the figure for making that decision, but I assure her I'll cover the full tab plus a generous bonus. Catrina asks about the appetizers, buffet style or sit down, and whether I have special requests.

By the time I reach the airport for my flight, I'm booked for Sunday. Q's words hover like a ghost, eerily present yet unseen. I park, watching the crew move quickly to help me transition to the plane. My thoughts remain on my family. It's not my intent to defy my mother.

Our hands are tied.

Mother doesn't want us to fund the restaurant, and I don't want her to depend on Kenneth's support. In my mind, her financial independence rules over her desire to keep the place closed on Sunday. Finding a way to ride the wave of the weekend seems like the most logical step with the lowest risk.

My phone rings as I drop into a seat, nodding to the stewardess. The doors of the plane close and I answer the call.

"You ready to talk this thing out?" Q asks, not bothering to engage in small talk. He goes right in and most days I appreciate that quality about him. You never have to wonder where you stand with him. But I'm not feeling it.

"Not unless you've called to change your mind."

"I'll consider a change of heart when you stop running around like a hot head. Your beef is with Kenneth, not us."

"Y'all hold all the fucking details to yourselves until it's convenient to tell me. And I'm the hot head?" I slip out of my jacket, tossing it on the seat beside me.

"Take off your gloves, bro."

"I'm not fighting. We're on the same side, with the same agenda."

"Are you sure about that, Kamal?"

Part of this is business, but the other part is personal as hell. I've been the one to steer our family and at this moment I'm not behind the wheel, or even in the fucking car.

Mother's on a cruise I didn't know about. The restaurant is near financial ruin, and I'm just hearing about it. Yet, they all waited until the last minute to reach out to me, then shoot down my plan.

"Look, I need to go." I stare out the window.

"Leaving town so soon?"

"I need to take a few meetings out in Los Angeles. I'll be back by Friday."

"Travel safely and hit me up when you get back."

"No doubt, I'll call you the moment I touch down."

I disconnect the call, ready to hang with my boys, knowing I'll handle my siblings one at a time.

CHAPTER 5

I flew coach for the first time in years. All to surprise Brett. A herd of people move through the aisle to exit the plane, but I'm not in a hurry. The reality of what awaits me is unfathomable.

I bought the ticket and boarded, spitting fire, ready to tell Brett all about himself and what I'm not taking, and how I can do better than the lies and secrecy. How I'm over the deceit and this fake-ass picture we've held together.

I boarded the plane ready to upend my entire life. Now, after flying home, my fire has dwindled down to smoke. For the life of me I can't believe I'm here, not back in Los Angeles but sitting on a crowded plane trying to make sense of life.

What will I tell Reese?

God, that's the toughest question of all. To force her to leave the only home she knows. To leave behind all her things. To leave her father behind. And it doesn't feel fair. That he can disrupt our lives and *we* have to start over.

I sniffle, brushing away my tears with the sleeve of my oversized sweatshirt, glad I didn't bother putting on makeup or dressing up. I went to the final brand meetings without Milton after begging him not to tell Brett that I know the truth about my Houston trip. Which is a stretch because I don't know why Brett wanted me away.

So, I sat through that final meeting with my perfect makeup and perfect smile like a perfect puppet in Brett's plan.

I gained access to his laptop and his calendar. The only appointment he had listed was a party tonight at an address somewhere in Beverly Hills.

"Do you need help with exiting the plane?"

"No, thank you." I look up at the smiling stewardess with a box of tissues between us. I grab a few and stand to face whatever's ahead of me. But I'm legit having second thoughts.

The first rule of leaving is to have an exit strategy and a nest egg stashed in the bank. My nest egg is more like a piggy bank. An itty-bitty plastic piggy bank. And not closing on any of the contracts in Houston places me back where I started.

I drag my luggage to a bar to decide my next move. I order two dirty martinis and text Catrina. I'm one martini in when my phone rings.

"It must be a full fucking moon."

I pull the phone away from my ear and stare at the

screen. Yep, it's Catrina. "I'm sorry, I can't handle any more bad news."

"I'm sorry, boo. I wish I was there with you. But these people here are…." The phone rings in the background. "Let me grab this line. Hold on."

I take a sip of my martini. I'm back in Los Angeles early and no one knows I returned. I could pick up Reese at Minnie's house and go home as if nothing happened to buy myself some time or I can follow through with my first thought, and that's leaving Brett for good.

"Girl, you won't believe what's going on here." Catrina breaks through my thoughts and I can tell she's about to spill some tea.

"What happened?"

"*Girl*… Kamal ran out of here like his ass was on fire."

"Kamal?" I almost choke on my martini. Even amid my crazy ass week, I kept seeing his smile and that moment when he tilted his chin up. "Why?"

"I don't know. All I know is I'm staying as far away from his plans as possible."

"You act like he's trying to tear the place down." I grab a napkin to wipe my mouth dry.

"He might. One minute they were laughing and talking, and the next I heard shouting. Something about opening the place on Sunday."

"That sounds like a good plan."

"But Miss Jackie never opens on Sunday, unless it's for a private booking."

I nod, although she can't see me. I have enough problems of my own, but I'm curious about how Kamal fits into this rant. "And Kamal wants to open the place?"

"Yep."

"And the others don't?"

"Exactly."

"And what's your take on it?" I down the first one and start on the second, feeling a little more like myself.

"I don't have access to the books but somebody needs to do something." Catrina's voice drops to a whisper, and I lean in closer to hear her. "They've laid off people and the rest of us have fewer hours. We honestly can't keep going like this. Hell, I've considered looking for another job."

"When are you going to tell Rashaad about how you feel?"

"Never."

"Why?"

"It just never seems to be the right time."

"Cat, how are you supposed to survive? It's not like you're rich. You can't keep living on lower pay and fewer hours."

"I have money saved. If things get worse, I'll do something different. Until then, I'll be here."

"Waiting…"

"I guess." She sighs. "While you're dishing out advice, trying to fix my life, what about you? When are you going to tell Brett how you *really* feel?"

I finish the last of my drink. Staring at the bottom of my empty glass searching for the answer. Then I watch the traffic walking outside the bar, and I see one of those Hallmark couples floating pass. The woman smiles up at the man, holding hands, and I wonder for a moment how people get there in their relationship.

"Cat…"

"Huh…"

"Do you think love is real? I mean…" I think through the relationships that matter most, and none have stood the test of time. "I can only name two people who love me. You and Reese. Is that normal?"

"I don't know. I hope so." She sighs. "There are days when I'm certain that what I feel is the real deal, but can it be real if he doesn't feel it? I've waited and…" Her voice cracks and my heart aches for my friend. "The best I can come up with is it's not my turn."

"Your turn?"

"Yeah, we wait in line at the grocery store. We wait in line at the bank. Shit, I figure I'm waiting in line for love too."

Catrina's big throaty laugh catches me off guard, and I can't stop laughing. The people in the bar stare like I'm crazy, and maybe I am. I laugh—good and hard—until a ray of hope bursts through the dark clouds casting a shadow over my life.

"Waiting on love?" I ask.

"Yep, waiting. What about you? You're back in Los Angeles. What's next?"

"I'm sitting in a bar trying to figure it out." I dry my eyes with my sleeve. "I thought I'd march home, pack our bags, and fly back to Houston. Now that I'm here, I'm not so sure."

"I think you should leave. But it's not my decision to make. Just know, you and my goddaughter have a room here for as long as you need it. I'm here, Jay."

"And I appreciate you having my back."

"You know I'm down like four flat tires."

We laugh again. I'm no closer to an answer, but I feel more like myself. "So, what do you think will happen with Southern Soul?"

"Girl, I don't know. But I think the shit's about to hit the fan."

"Why do you say that?"

"Kamal's sticking around." Her laugh sounds like a grunt. "He and Mr. Montgomery don't see eye to eye. Ain't no drama like family drama. Hold on."

Catrina doesn't wait for my response. She gives a series of orders to someone on her end, and a part of me wants to ask more about Kamal. He branded my brain with his heated gaze that morphed to ice cold at the sight of the promise ring Brett placed on my finger like a leash. But for a hot thirty seconds, I basked in the passion in his eyes.

A shiver zips down my spine. I twist in my seat, sitting up taller.

"Chile…" I chuckle, rolling my head to the side. He's the type of man who'll make you forget your name and your morals.

Hell, I'm still thinking about him after a brief conversation and a handshake. I can't… *no*, I won't imagine how it would feel if I let anything else happen with him. I'd never move on it, not after all the pain Brett's infidelity has caused in my life. His behavior is wrecking what little we have left in our relationship.

"Jay…"

I turn my attention back to Catrina. What I need to do is figure out how to keep my man at home and leave Kamal Montgomery in Houston.

"Let me get off this phone and back to work. We have a party booked for this weekend, which means more hours. Let me know if you plan to head back this weekend, because I need to get a key made for you."

"You'll be the first to know. I'll call you tonight."

We hang up. My fear is rooted in the thought of starting over with a new city, a new life, and ultimately a new relationship. I could blame those pink panties on my predicament, but I knew what I was getting myself into with Brett.

Brett is a dog. I knew it then, and I know it now. But all men are dogs with big ass fleas. At least, I know my dog.

Some men lack finances. Some men lack fidelity. And some men are like Brett—on the surface he has it all. Money. Looks. Personality. Therefore, nothing is out of his reach. His charisma and ambition were a major turn on when we met, but now, since he left the league, it seems to be the bane of our existence.

Well, that and my shift from being his girlfriend to becoming the mother of his child. I admit, I live in mommy-mode until it's time to record a video for my channel.

I open the photos on my phone, looking for the last picture we took, together, without Reese. I scroll until I'm two years into my feed. It's been that long. Since we were just Jayda and Brett and not Reese's parents. I close the app, staring at my phone. I could call Minnie or… go to the party at the address.

Maybe I should give us one more shot. And not for Reese, but for the man I once had feelings for. Some days I think it's love and other times it feels like an obligation.

Neither of us were the relationship type, and now we're struggling to turn it into a family. And I blame myself, I knew the score, and I broke the rules when I got pregnant. But I'm confident I can turn this thing around and make us a real family. One that spends time together, and maybe we can turn into one of those Hallmark couples, all lovey-dovey and picture perfect.

I spend the next few minutes ironing out my plan to send the trick in pink panties packing. I'm about to turn Brett out.

My fingers dance across my screen, first booking a hotel suite and requesting a car. I need to hit up the mall, and when I surprise Brett all heads will turn. It's time I remind Brett of what he has at home.

THE CAR STOPS in front of the address and I peer out the window. I rarely visit this part of town. I ask myself the same question that's tumbled through my mind all day. Who does Brett know here? Maybe one of his friends from the league. The house sits amongst mansions in Beverly Hills.

"Lady…" The man doesn't sound rushed, but concerned.

I glance at the driver. "Right, sorry. Zoned out there for a second. Let me take care of your tip."

I complete the transaction in the app. After a day of pampering, burning a hole through Brett's credit card, I purchased a new sexy black dress, red bottoms, and a clutch. I spend over an hour painting my face with the best that his money could buy, all products I'll use again and share with my viewers.

Tonight's not about my YouTube channel, and it's not about what Brett may have done while I was away in Houston. Tonight's about a fresh start for our relationship. I'm channeling the old Jayda. The baddie in the club.

Sure, I'm a twenty pounds heavier, which became clear while trying to shop today. I can't believe I had to purchase a size sixteen and I feel like I'm breathing through a straw, thanks to my Spanx squeezing me in for dear life. But I paint an image, perfectly beat face, snatched waist, and thighs for days. My dress is long enough to cover my business, but short enough to ensure all eyes are on me.

To pull this off, I want Brett to see me and want me like he used to. I'm having the suite decorated with rose petals, candles, and the works for later tonight. He won't know what hit him.

We used to have long nights at hotels to spice things up. And while running around the mall getting prepared for tonight, I realized my list of "used to dos" is mighty long.

We used to travel. We used to go to concerts. We used to go to football games, and eat out, and party. But now, we're living separate lives, me as a mother, and him as…

"Are you okay?"

I nod and wrap my hand around the handle, as a wave of uncertainty stops me. "Guess I'm more nervous than I thought."

"He'd have to be mad stupid—you're fucking hot." His face turns red for a second. "I apologize. You… are beautiful."

"Thank you." But I hope Brett thinks so. I step out into the cool night. The music from the house spills over and I relax a little.

"Goodnight."

The car drives off and I'm left standing in the middle of the street.

Alone.

I roll my shoulders back. My mother and I never seemed to get along. She wasn't the mother type, and I wasn't the child who handled orders well. I ran away at sixteen and was doing well for myself, and I still am, except in this one area of my life.

My life could be Hallmark perfect. I have the home, an amazing daughter, a growing career. Somehow, I let my relationship slip through the cracks.

I walk up the driveway, scanning the faces for the familiar. Brett and I never traveled in the same circles. I know some girlfriends of his old teammates, but I wouldn't consider any of them friends. Pro ball girlfriends have a pesky way of making their way through the team until they land a husband. Which makes for a very distrusting environment. Fortunately, I have a real friend. Those fake Hollywood ones are not worth my time.

I realize my decision to push away from the Los Angeles life left Brett to branch out and explore without me. And that's something I plan to change. While shopping I amassed a list of To Dos to revive this relationship, along with more sex, not spending my day in pajamas, and finding more time to spend as a couple. I think we have a shot at making this work. But first to find Brett, and figure out whose house this is.

Approaching the front doors, a couple stands off to the side, as the man opens a door for me with a sly smile. I roll my eyes, walking through the large palace-style doors. My head sweeps from the far wall, across the ceiling, and back down the other end of the room. *Breathtaking.*

"Ma'am?" A waiter extends a champagne platter.

I smile, wrapping my hand around the flute closest to me. "Thank you."

"You're welcome." He winks. "Everyone should move to the living room. Mr. Hardin will give the official toast in five minutes."

"Hardin?" The glass destined for my lips stops, but the server moves to another room. Hardin, as in Brett Hardin? Or it could be his cousin or something?

I move through the entryway with purposeful steps. In the sea of faces I search for Brett, unintentionally bumping into a few people. I offer soft apologies they probably can't hear over the loud music.

This is a big ass party with a large DJ booth in the corner of what I think is the formal dining room. Several of the rooms are still bare, so this must be a new house. A housewarming party, maybe?

I dart from room to room until a ringing sound has the crowd moving like a small herd. I follow along, stopping outside a room. The group pushes forward, and I dip to the side, still trying to see into it. And I see Brett.

He looks handsome in a dark suit with the collar of his dress shirt opened by a few of his buttons. The light brown of his skin pairs nicely with the rich blue. A wave of hope moves through me and I'm glad I took this step. I lift a hand to get his attention when he pulls a woman to his side. His head dips to her ear, she blushes, and my heart slugs to a crawl, rattling my chest like the thump of an 808.

My eyes take in the scene like a photograph. His hand wraps possessively around her tiny waist. Her hand draped delicately on his broad chest. The way his eyes soften when he looks down into her upturned face. The look of love passing between them, like the Hallmark couple from the airport.

I can't... I stumble back.

I don't...understand.

This can't be real.

And in a haze, I hear...

"We'd like to welcome you to our home."

I walk backwards, bumping into bodies, forcing my legs to put as much space between me and them as a fire-breathing dragon confiscates my chest.

Vision bloody red, flames flowing through my veins, heart ramped until I slam against a wall. My hands cover my mouth, knees weak, and a pair of firm hands grip my waist tight, holding me upright.

"Jayda?" Whispers through the inferno of my worst nightmare playing out in front of an unknowing audience.

My body spins, not of my doing, and the champagne flute slips from my hand and shatters on the Italian tile into a million pieces. A collective gasp sends a hush over the crowd and I glance back over my shoulder and Brett's eyes lands on mine.

"Jayda?" His voice carries over the crowd, and the woman follows his line of vision until she's facing me too.

Soft hands turn my face from the sight, and for a moment I don't ache so much. Kamal Montgomery. "What is it, Jayda?"

I shake my head. Now's the time for me to act a fucking fool. To show my entire ass. To beat that bitch's ass. But I can't because… Hell, I don't know why I can't, I just can't be here.

"I gotta get out of here."

I pull from Kamal's grip.

"Jayda… wait." Kamal takes a moment to look back over at Brett in a motion I've only seen on the football field. His hand extended, keeping Brett at a distance.

I kick off my shoes, fleeing the scene barefooted, wishing this dress wasn't so damn tight. The moment I reach the door, I glance back and Brett's on my heels, and Kamal's on his.

I stumble down the stairs, running down the driveway when I realize I didn't drive. I whip around and like a super-hero Kamal moves in a blur of superhuman speed, standing in front of me like a brick wall, using his body as a barricade.

"Jayda," Brett huffs, and I glance around Kamal. The entire party stares on. "Look, man, move, this is between me and my woman."

"Which woman?" I don't recognize my voice. "Me or Becky?"

"Jayda, don't do this shit. Go home," Brett yells.

My eyes burn with unshed tears. I drop my forehead against Kamal's back, holding my clutch against my chest. She's the owner of the pink panties.

How do I know? I don't know, but I fucking know.

"She's the bitch you had in your car, isn't she?"

"What?"

"The bitch with the fucking pink panties! Did you have her in our home?"

"Jayda—"

"Did you?" My voice cuts through the silence, and I swear the world hears my heart shatter like that champagne flute. Splat against the concrete. A million little pieces of distorted pieces of love and hope and *pain.*

"You have some nerve, when you show up uninvited with a date. Who are you?"

"Man, you got some fucking balls." I lift my head at hearing the thunder of anger in Kamal's voice. "Go back in the house, so I don't have to Molly Wop your ass up and down this street in front of your guests."

"I wish you…"

Kamal steps forward until they are face to face.

Brett's nose flairs, then he looks over at me. "You better have your ass at home."

"See I told you—" He yanks Brett by the lapel until they're eye to eye.

"Kamal!" I reach for him.

"Threaten her again. Please." The sugary sweet tone is lethal.

Brett snaps his mouth closed. Kamal opens his fist and Brett tumbles to the ground.

"Emmitt, the keys."

A set of keys fly through the air. Kamal catches them with one hand and gathers me to him with the other. This must be what shock feels like. I can't believe this is Brett's house with another woman. And it takes a man I don't even know to defend my honor. And this is what I was willing to fight for? To work out?

"We'll see you back at the hotel."

Kamal tips his head back to the man I'm assuming is Emmitt. His rich dark skin is a direct contrast to the tanned tone of the other man standing off to the side monitoring the situation. Both are striking, and for a moment, I wonder how the three of them must wreak havoc on women when they're together.

"Jayda, let's get you home." Kamal guides me away with a firm hand on my lower back.

"She ain't nothing but a platinum digging thot." Brett points his finger in my direction. I'm sure his guests wonder how this housewarming party turned into a fucking freak show.

"I'm the thot? The woman that cooks, and cleans, and raises your daughter?" I heave, throwing each stiletto for emphasis until all I'm left with is my clutch. Becky gasps, and I face her.

Whether she knew about me is irrelevant. I was in a committed relationship with Brett, and now I'm not.

"Thank you for helping me see that he's not worth my time. Congratulations on your new home, and good luck with your sorry-ass dog." I turn to Kamal. "Which way is the car?"

Kamal studies my face for what feels like a lifetime. "The Escalade."

I fall in step, turning my back on the spectators and the reality of my life. Barefooted in the middle of the street with my ex hollering obscenities.

Then Brett stops, and I swing around. The ground eating pace brings Kamal back face to face with the father of my child, the man I've shared a life with for five years, the man I think I love.

Kamal speaks to him in a hushed whisper, turning Brett's face ashen. The men Kamal received the keys from push the crowd back toward the house, and my eyes lock with Becky's.

I don't know her name. Her name is irrelevant. I meant what I said, this hurts more out of embarrassment, and the time I wasted, but I'd rather know now. How had he bought and moved into a house without me knowing?

We stand on opposite sides of the street. The old fool and the new fool.

"Let's go." Kamal's back at my side.

I nod and he helps me inside with such care that you'd think we've known each other a lifetime. I face him, realizing I don't know this man. But I have to get Reese before Brett talks to Minnie. Then... tears fill my eyes and I swallow them back.

"Where to?"

"I have to get to my baby."

"Baby?"

I nod. "Yes, my daughter Reese. Look, it might be a little late, but you're not a crazy killer?"

He chuckles. "If that dude keeps talking shit, I might be. But other than that, you're straight with me. Call Catrina—she's known me for years. Plug in the address."

Kamal pulls away from the curb the moment I hit enter. I glance out the back windshield. Brett stands. I face the front, falling back against the seat numb.

I text Catrina about riding with Kamal, and seconds later my phone rings.

"What did I miss?"

"Everything." I sigh, leaning my head against the window. "Look, is that room still available?"

"Fresh sheets and all. What happened, Jay?"

I've held back my tears because I be damned if I let Brett see me cry but hearing the concern in Catrina's voice makes it hard to pretend.

"Brett…" I exhale a loud breath, trying to hold it together as the film of my life runs. Scratchy, skipping, ending with the look of love on Becky's face for my man—my *ex* man. And it's not fair to turn my anger on her. Calling her Becky was probably wrong too. Her mom probably spent months naming her.

The weight of feeling betrayed, surprised, and fucking embarrassed is more than I can bear. That's something else I'll have to deal with later because I have a child to think about, and Reese is all that matters.

"I can't talk about it. Because I'm such a fucking fool. How did I let it get to this? I should have… I should have…." The words get stuck.

Don't you dare cry, Jayda.

I'll save my tears for another time. Especially as I stare down my worst fear—being a single mother. The world holds no shortage of heartbreaks and hard times. I guess this is just mine.

This is what I expected, and this is what I got. That we lasted this long is a miracle. But I didn't see the end coming like this. I choke back the wave of emotions by shaking my head, refusing to break down in front of Kamal. The man already had a front-row seat to the worst day of my life.

"Put Kamal on," Catrina demands, and internally I reprimand myself for the slow crack she's forging through my resolve to remain strong.

"I'm good, it's just all hitting me at once, that my relationship is over. Cat, what am I supposed to do now?"

CHAPTER 6

I FOLLOW the GPS directions after she punched in the address, while keeping an eye on her. We're twenty minutes from the destination. She's remained relatively quiet. But the more I replay the night in my head, anger blinds me. I honestly can't imagine how she's remaining so composed. Then she receives a call from Catrina.

I use the time to give her some privacy and to check in with my boys.

I found myself at the party to meet with someone about a business opportunity. Dean, Emmitt, and I invest in several businesses. The last person I expected to see again was Jayda.

This ordeal makes me think of Miya, and how I'm so glad she finally left her last boyfriend. It took one conversation with that jerk for him to realize he had the wrong woman.

I cut an eye to Jayda and back to the road before dialing Emmitt. "Yo, you guys still there?"

"Yeah, since you took my ride. But I have a car service coming, because this was a bust. What's up?"

"Hang around for a minute and keep me posted on him."

"We got you. Who is she anyway?"

"A friend of a friend. I'm taking her to get her daughter then—"

"Cat, what am I supposed to do now?" Her quivering whisper pulls me from the conversation.

"I'll call y'all back."

"Bet." He ends the call.

My eyes dart between the road ahead, the GPS barking orders, and the woman seated in the passenger seat. Then like a before and after picture, I watch her strength melt. And I'm transported to the last time I heard that question, said in that tone after my mother signed her divorce papers from Kenneth. I'll never forget the sound of uncertainty and raw pain.

I change lanes until we're on the shoulder of the highway. The level of strength Jayda has shown is unfounded. Had the shoe been on the other foot, that dude would have gone postal. Yet she's fighting to hold it together, and I'm hoping that she'll let me hold her.

She extends the cellphone in my direction and I take it while wrapping an arm around her shoulders, relieved when she doesn't pull away from me. And Jayda goes from riding in shock to a gut-wrenching wail.

"Catrina, she'll call you back."

I press end, dropping the phone into a cupholder, and I gather her to me. Her face hidden in her hands, pressed against my chest, and I hold her tight.

I've experienced nothing like this. Makes me wonder if I've ever been the source of such pain. In my relationships I pride myself on being honest and transparent, and this is why. Causing this much anguish seems like sowing evil seeds in the world, and I would never want to hurt another human being like this.

Her tears soak through my shirt, and I want to turn around and give her ex a knuckle sandwich. Instead, I keep that thought to myself until the music on the radio replaces the sound of her pain. Her head rests on my shoulder and her champagne-scented breath warms my neck.

"I remember when my mother would come home after a long night of working. We'd sit on the couch with her wrapped in my arms." It's been a long time since I thought of those long nights that turned into long years. "She'd never tell me how hard it was or how bad it was, but she'd let me hold her."

"That explains it."

"Explains what?" I turn my head enough to look down into her eyes.

"Why you're a great hugger." The corners of her mouth curl up. "But it also means you're probably a mama's boy."

"'Til the day I die."

Jayda laughs with her entire body rocking. We laugh

much longer than the joke requires, but it feels good to brush away a little of her pain.

"You'll be all right. Maybe not today, or tomorrow, but in time."

Jayda nods and sits back. "Sounds like personal experience."

"Not my personal experience, but after my mother's divorce." I search the center console for tissues. She takes them, crumpling them in her hands. "I was old enough to watch her work through the transition, but young enough not to fully understand the parts that changed her. You good?"

Jayda nods. "No. But it's not about me."

"I'll get us back on the road."

"Kamal, thank you. You didn't have to do this."

"I know. I'd hope if my sister was ever in a similar situation that someone would do the same for her." The soft glow from the streetlight gives me an unobstructed view of her face. Even after crying, she's one of the most beautiful women I've met. That's the last thought I need to entertain with her world crumpling around her, so I return to driving.

"Was that your sister at your table?"

"My table?"

"When I met you at Southern Soul."

"Oh, yeah. That was my baby sister and my knuckle-head brothers." She smiles a little, and I return it. "So, you're heading to Houston?"

"Yeah, looks like it."

"If you don't have tickets already, you guys can fly back with me." Her mouth drops open. "I'm flying back tonight for a small gathering tomorrow night. It's a private flight, and there's more than enough room for you both."

"I'll pay you."

"Keep your money. It's a gas guzzling plane. I feel more responsible when I have passengers." The GPS says we're at the destination. I glance up at the house. "Need me to go inside with you?"

"No." She turns to the door and glances back. "Thank you for the ride. I'll call an Uber or something to get us home." Her mouth twists. "What time should we meet you at the airport?"

"That's unnecessary, I don't mind waiting, unless you're having second thoughts. I'm sure it's hard to think about the next steps when you have a child involved. Maybe you should decide after a night of sleep."

I force myself to stare out of the windshield. The faraway look in her eyes twists my heart more than the wail of her cry.

Who or what has possessed my body? I wonder, observing the mansions surrounding us. That I jumped between another man and his woman isn't me at all. But the glare of rage in his eyes forced my feet to move, and all I could think was to protect Jayda.

"What would you tell your sister?"

My head jerks to the sound of her voice. "If he can't respect you, he doesn't deserve you. Did you suspect something?"

"Yeah. But men are dogs like that. Most men cheat, but playing house takes it too far." She opens the door. "Tonight was the final blow, and now it's time to move on." She sighs, her shoulders fold forward, then she looks up at the house.

"I'll be here. Holler if you need a hand with anything."

She glances down at her feet, shaking her head. "And those were brand new shoes. I'll be back."

I watch as she travels down the sidewalk, disappearing inside a white house surrounded by a professionally groomed yard. I keep my eyes glued to the door and make a quick call to the airport, letting them know about the additional passengers. Then I dial Emmitt's number.

We speed through the small talk, shifting once I tell them about my change of plans. The three of us spent the week checking in with our business partners. Tonight was the final meeting. Now I need to see if Jayda's Brett is the Brett we planned to meet with.

Dean, Emmitt, and I used a percentage of our earnings from playing professional football to launch an investment firm. We each have our specialties but investing in nontraditional startups is yielding great profits for us.

"Is he the one pitching the talent agency?" I ask.

"Yeah." Dean confirms with me on speakerphone. "I can't believe the man is still hosting this party like he didn't just have the biggest catfish of the year."

"Two women, two households, too much drama," I summarize.

Emmitt chuckles. "According to the whispers, Brett

forgot to tell his girlfriend it was a housewarming party for his side chick."

"And he's still there?"

"Yep. Gotta love LaLa Land. He had the servers bring out the good stuff, and he kept the party going. You should see the smile plastered on his side piece's face," Emmitt adds.

I shake my head. It shouldn't surprise me. A friend from the league referred Brett. Apparently, he's an ex-ball player too. Men in professional sports are known to have more than one relationship, but damn.

"Guess she didn't know about Jayda. Speaking of Jayda, who is she?" Dean asks.

"I met her a couple of weeks back. She's Catrina's friend."

"Catrina?" Emmitt asks.

"The hostess at Southern Soul."

"Oh yeah, when are you going to hook me up with her."

"Never." I shake my head. "We're trying to turn the place around and she's one of our most loyal employees. I can't have you disrupting my situation with your extracurricular activities."

"Hey! I think I should be offended," Emmitt says.

"Yes, sir, you should. You'll have her turned inside out when she realizes you love to play the field. Pun intended." Dean and I laugh. He's the last of us still playing professionally.

Emmitt chuckles. "Y'all act like I'm the only one."

"No, Dean and I know how to keep our encounters free from strings. But you keep finding women expecting a ring."

"My dude, do you know women turn into freaks when they think they can change your mind? Be swinging from chandeliers and shit. Inviting their girlfriends to the mix."

Dean howls on the other end.

"Emmitt, just keep your woman juggling self away from Catrina." I look up at the house. "Is his talent agency legit?"

"Yes, supposedly." Emmitt is back to business. "But he sure made a fucked up first impression."

"And Kamal, the Southern gentlemen, was waiting to swoop up Brett's woman," Dean states.

"Playa… playa…" Emmitt sings.

"Nah… Like I said, she's a friend of a friend. You know I don't date women with kids. Too much baggage, as we witness tonight."

"So, why'd you step in?" Dean asks.

"I'd bust a dude's ass if that was my sister. His shit was foul."

"So… you see her as a sister?" I envision Dean leaning into the phone.

"I didn't call to talk about Jayda."

"Well, Jayda is mighty sweet on the eyes. Thick in all the right places," Emmitt recounts with too much interest. "How about you give her my number? I'm in town, I can look in on her from time to time. A *friend* of yours is a *friend* of mine."

"That shit ain't happening."

The line falls silent. Then Emmitt hollers. I know he's testing the boundaries. The dude is a player with all capital letters. But nothing compared to the stunt Brett pulled tonight.

The front door opens. I need to wrap up this call.

"I'll park the SUV at the hangar and reach out when I land in Houston. I need y'all in H-Town no later than six and invite some friends."

"What about Trish?" Emmitt asks.

"Man, she's boujee." We hung out after she turned her nose up at Southern Soul. She's cool. A low-key party girl, but dateable.

"Boujee women have fine ass friends."

"Emmitt, how is it that you're getting worse every year?" Dean asks.

"Look, you don't want a party full of men. Women bring women. It's basic party etiquette."

"Spell it," I demand, and now Dean's dying on the other end.

"Black card *bitches*."

We laugh until I'm brushing tears from my eyes. Then Jayda steps out juggling a large bundle and a car seat.

"I'm out."

I disconnect the call with the sounds of their laughter on the other end. We might shoot the shit, but together we've built a billion-dollar business. I plan to make Southern Soul our next success story.

I walk up and relieve Jayda of the car seat and the overnight bag.

"Jayda, who's that?" A woman calls from the front door. The sound of a phone ringing inside the house captures her attention for a second before she turns back, cupping a hand over her eyes trying to see me better.

"A family friend. I'll talk with you later, Minnie. Thanks again." Jayda moves faster. "Hurry. He hasn't called her yet."

I fasten the car seat inside, and she slips a sleeping little girl in the chair.

"Mommy?"

"Hey, honey, I missed you."

I toss the bag in the back behind the driver's seat while Jayda places kisses all over the little girl's face.

"Mommy..." She giggles.

Jayda kisses her once more before climbing back in the passenger seat.

"Where to next?"

"Drive a little." She glances back at the house, fastening her seatbelt. "I'd like to grab a few things from the house. Do we have time?"

"They're on my time. Input the address."

AN HOUR later we enter a house large enough to swallow the previous house whole. Not an item seems out of place. I imagine one day I'll settle down enough to buy a house, but this place feels more like a museum.

"Reese, I'd like to introduce you to my friend, Mr. Kamal."

I glance down at a miniature version of Jayda in purple

pajamas covered in puppy dogs. She wraps an arm around her mother's leg.

I crouch down. "Nice to meet you."

She giggles, scurrying behind Jayda.

"Reese…"

"Hiiii…." she sings, peeking around her mother.

"Hi, back." I look up at Jayda, who softly runs a hand over Reese's cornrows. All traces of the night are replaced by a serene glow. "Honey, can you go to your room and pick five toys?" The slight shake in her voice sends my eyes back up to her face.

"Yes, ma'am."

"Okay, quick, sweetie, and just this one time you can run, but be careful."

"Yes, ma'am." She runs with her arms moving faster than her legs. Then she stops at the foot of the stairs, placing one hand on the rail, inching up the stairs in a *step, together, step, together* cadence.

"Jesus, we will be here all night," Jayda whispers, and I hide my smile.

"How can I help?"

"Can you help me grab some of my equipment?"

"Lead the way."

Minutes later, she flicks on the lights in a room. "You're a photographer?"

"No, a YouTuber."

"That's a thing?" I look around. There are several cameras mounted on tripods facing a vanity and a decorative background.

"Yes, it's a career for some people. Grab those black bags over there."

I see the stack on the shelf in the corner. "And you?"

"I have the audience and the interactions. I'm still working to build my brand connections. Oh, and grab that clear tub."

She moves, draping camera bags on my shoulders, and bins of makeup in my hands. "You need all of this."

"Yeah, if I plan on making a living to support my baby. This won't be too heavy for the flight. Will it?"

"No, you're straight. I'll take this out to the truck." The guys and I invested in a twelve passenger jet to move around the country.

"I'll throw some clothes in a bag. We'll be ready by the time you get back."

I travel the hallway, passing Reese in the hallway. Her little arms stuffed with two dolls, a coloring book, and a few other things. I'm stunned by the thought of a child having to select their favorite toys and leaving the rest behind.

Man, I never considered that. After my parents divorced, we lived in the same house thanks to my mother's hard work. Truthfully, very little changed for us. She made sure of it.

I make the trip, and when I return, the pair are waiting. Jayda is makeup-free wearing colorful leggings and an over-sized sweatshirt. Reese added matching bunny slippers with floppy ears.

Jayda scans the living room as if taking a panoramic picture with Reese on her hip.

"You sure about this?" I pick up the last bags.

"Yeah, trying to decide if I'll miss this place. Let's get out of here. *He* called, and I'd rather be in the air by the time he gets here."

"Ladies." I gesture to the door.

Jayda locks the door and while Reese hops down the stairs like a bunny rabbit, I load the bags in the back. It's after two in the morning and we're on our way to the airport.

Reese is asleep within minutes. Jayda has been quiet. For an unknown reason, tonight makes me curious about how it all ended with my parents. Was it minor issues bubbling beneath the surface that finally boiled over? Was it infidelity? Because I never got the feeling that either of them stopped loving each other and knowing they loved each other while "moving on" has created the greatest conundrum in my head concerning relationships. How one could love one person yet engage in an intimate relationship with another?

I steal glances. Jayda changed from walking temptation to a comfy mother. Her beauty is rare. Whether fully done up or with her bare face no one would peg her as an ordinary woman. But it's her strength that has me wondering about her life.

How did she get here? Not in my rented SUV, but here in life? How did she meet Brett? How old was she when she married? What's her favorite flower? Does she believe in fate?

I hold my breath, surprised by the last thought, and I

look over at her. There's something about her that makes me think about my mother. It could be my conscience since I'm hours away from opening Southern Soul, without her consent or the support of my siblings. Or it could be I can't recall meeting a woman as strong as my mother until tonight.

The late-night hour makes driving through Los Angeles a breeze, almost relaxing until I draw lines of comparison between Jayda and my mother. The reality that I probably won't see Jayda again after tonight doesn't sit well with me.

"I bet this isn't how you expected to spend your Saturday night."

I glance over at her, grateful for the interruption.

"No, can't say that I had this planned."

"What do you do, Kamal?"

"I'm an investor and part owner of Southern Soul."

"Investor?"

"My business partners—Emmitt and Dean—hold joint ownership in a venture capital firm. We started before I retired from playing ball."

"Football or basketball?"

"Football."

"Did you know Brett before tonight?"

"No, he's acquaintances with a friend." I glance over. "Mind if I ask about tonight?"

"Yeah, sure."

"Did you know?"

"That I was crashing their party? No. It seems I got all dressed up for the surprise of my life."

"Damn." I glance back, making sure Reese is still asleep.

"Damn, is right. I saw the party in his calendar, and I thought I'd surprise him."

I nod, deciding to shift the topic. "Tell me more about YouTube. How'd you get started?"

"I was bored…"

I could listen to her all night. She talks about products that are vaguely familiar to me. It's the soothing sound of her voice that lures me in, has me asking more questions until we park at the airport.

"All right now." Jayda leans forward, staring at the jet." She's a beauty."

I smile, finding it hard to pull my eyes from her until a light hits that massive rock on her finger. The fact is she has a man at home, and she's here with me. I feel compelled to address it before she boards my plane.

"You sure you want to do this?"

"I told you—"

I hold up a hand to cut her off. "Is he Reese's father?"

Her neck snaps in my direction.

"No judgment, a simple question. Is Brett her father?"

"Yes."

I nod. That makes this situation complicated. "You have reason to be pissed. I can't imagine how it feels for either of you. Dude is fucking wrong, but don't you think you should talk to him?"

"You don't have to help me." She stiffens.

"My offer stands, I'll take you both anywhere you want to go." I hold her gaze in the haze of a night filled with emotions. "Look, you packed your bags, took the man's child, and you're fleeing the city. The moment you board that plane you're sending your husband a message you can't take back."

"You're absolutely right. That he can kiss my ass, and I don't need him." She falls back, staring out the windshield.

"Jayda, I don't agree with the man, but I can't imagine returning home finding my family gone." I look at their daughter. "What about Reese? Divorce ends a relationship, but it alters the lives of children forever."

"But so does living a life of complacency. It's more disruptive because it eats you up from the inside out, all while putting on a front for the world." She curls over, hiding her face in her hands. "Kamal, you think it's easy to walk away? I'm trading a mansion for a single bedroom. A life where I don't pay a single bill for what, I honestly don't know." She sighs like a woman with the weight of the world on her shoulders. "I have my channel and a little money saved but beyond that my life is pitch black. Men..."

"He doesn't represent all men."

Her pain vibrates through my chest like thunder, although her features are hidden in the shadows. "I bet you're second guessing jumping in the middle of this mess."

"No, I had to ask. I know you think you won't change your mind, and I believe you, but if you do, just say the word, and I'll make sure you get back."

"Why?" Her venom-laced tone makes me feel bad for the next man.

"For her..."

Jayda's head darts to the back seat. "He forced my hand. I knew his ass was messing around. But I had no clue he bought, furnished, and planned a life without us." Her voice cracks, then the SUV rocks with the shake of her head. "I can't, and I won't. Returning would give him permission to have us and her. *I* deserve better. I just hate it took looking like a fucking ass to get it. Tonight he made his choice," she whispers.

I hear her. However, the man in me knows this is far from over. Brett's side chick doesn't have half the fire of Jayda, and tonight it showed. It's only a matter of time before Brett realizes he chose wrong.

Is that not the story of my life?

Kenneth left Mom and had women of every shade, size, and ethnicity. Twenty years later, he realized there's only one Jacqueline "Jackie" Montgomery. All the good men Mom dated over the years fell for her just like Kenneth and she had five kids. None of them stood a chance. But it didn't stop them from trying.

That's why I refuse to date women with kids. Too much baggage. To fall for a woman, and her child, only to learn you're keeping the bed warm for her husband, and the father of her child to return.

"He'll come looking for you."

"How do you know?" She looks over at me.

"Because I would."

CHAPTER 7

Kamal dropped the conversation the moment he stepped out of the SUV. He locks gazes with the pilot and with a discreet nod, the crew moves around him with silent precision.

What will Brett do when he returns to the house and we're gone? Will he follow us? And do I want him to? I shake my head. He's made his choice, and it wasn't us.

The plane is in front of me, my past with Brett is officially behind me. That is wishful thinking since we have a child together.

It's easier to watch the crew move like focused ants. Loading our luggage and within minutes the crew moves, Reese and I moved from the SUV to the jet.

The stewardess closes the door. She secures the overhead cabins. I tighten the seatbelt around my waist, and Reese in the seat beside me. I watch, trying to assemble the pieces of my wreck of a life.

I need to review my bank account balances. Revisit the budget I made yesterday at the airport. It seems like weeks ago. How had it all changed in a matter of hours?

Houston is affordable, unlike Los Angeles. I need to find us a small place. A two bedroom—a room for me, a room for Reese and her toys.

What toys?

A slug hits my heart. Her princess-themed bedroom with the painted walls and pink lace canopy bed was stripped to five toys.

Five fucking toys.

Reese doesn't deserve this, and I feel awful for putting her in this situation. This is exactly why I stayed all these years.

I lean forward, determined not to fold to my doubts and uncertainty. The sound of the wheels locking beneath the airplane mimic an iron lock. That's that. I had a one-way ride to Houston, and I took it. I look out the window. I guess this is goodbye.

Kamal moves in my peripheral vision and I look at Reese, avoiding his questioning gaze. She's cuddled into my side, sleeping through a night that will change her life forever.

"You have to turn this ship around, Jayda," I whisper. The cool air drags through my nose, expanding my chest.

Reese doesn't ask for much.

Love, hugs, and hot chocolate with marshmallows.

Protection, strawberry lip gloss, and lots of kisses.

Quality time, coloring books, and bubble baths.

I can give her these things. *I can.*

The truth is, I've been raising Reese on my own her entire life while Brett floated in and out of our lives. But this time is different.

There's no turning back from this. He and I had a shot when the women were faceless. But I can't unsee what I saw.

What choice did I have?

None.

Right?

Right.

Brett stripped me of all options when I saw him huddled up with *her*. The woman without a name—and her name doesn't matter. Brett was off starting a new life in a professionally decorated home.

Did he think I'd never find out? How long had he been living a life with her, while coming home most nights to me? To us.

I rub the fleece fabric between my fingers. The fluffy texture soothes the unnamable emotions as the scene replays through my mind.

The decor I'd admired while drinking the expensive champagne. The house full of guests. Who were all of those people, anyway? But it was the look of *oh shit* on Brett's face that jerked me back to reality, and I collided with Kamal Montgomery.

I don't want to imagine how my night would have ended if Kamal, and his friends, had not been at that party. What would have happened if he hadn't been there?

I stare across the aisle at the man reading an iPad, the

man that rescued me tonight. A stranger. The bits and pieces I know about him seem unmatched to the kindness help's offered us tonight. I could assume he's using it as a gesture to get close to me. Men have tried, even guys Brett considered his closest friends.

But nothing about Kamal and those other men belong in the same category. And just when I thought I'd crack from the pressure of my night, he took the phone talking with Cat before we boarded the plane, assuring her he'd deliver us safely and in one piece.

Am I foolish to believe him? It doesn't matter. My child and I are at the mercy of his crew, and for an odd reason I feel safe, maybe because I had to leave on such short notice. Or maybe because Kamal's been nothing but a gentleman.

No flirting. No attempts to cop a feel. No innuendos about ways I could pay him back. Which is a direct contrast to the high voltage electricity I felt when I met him. Tonight, his presence feels as comforting as this Princess Tiana fleece blanket tucked around Reese.

"How old are you?"

Kamal lowers the iPad, hitting me with his penetrating gaze. "Thirty-three. And you?"

"Twenty-seven."

"And Reese?"

"Four." I glance down at her to steady my breathing. "She'll be five in a few months. Do you have any children?"

"No."

"A wife."

He chuckles. "No, I'm not married."

"And that's funny?" My head pops up and I catch the slight shake of his head. I know that laugh, the kind that mocks the absurdity of my question. I know, because I once found the thought of marriage and children absurd. A waste of time. Only for the insane.

Why tie myself down? When I can see the world doing me.

"Oh, you're the no wife, no kids, no responsibility type?"

"I have plenty of responsibilities. Family, friends, employees."

"I see…"

"What do you see, Jayda?" His eyes squint, and I realize I've crossed a line.

"Nothing."

Kamal holds me captive with his dark eyes, sharp and intent. "Do you make it a general practice to keep your true thoughts to yourself?"

That made me laugh. "Had you not witnessed tonight blown up in my face, I would have said no, but holding my thoughts to myself landed me here."

"Where's here Jayda?"

My inner chatter rumbles to life. Manless, homeless, jobless land squarely at the top of my list, but that's not the issue. Is it?

I look straight ahead. I wanted to get rid of Brett, and apparently the feeling was mutual. The feel of those judgmental eyes that watched Brett call me platinum-digging thot and watched me leave.

"Honestly, I'm embarrassed, fleeing my home and my life in the middle of the night, with a stranger, like I'm the one that's wrong." I shrug.

"Is that how you feel? Embarrassed? Ashamed?"

"Maybe it's shock."

"Or maybe it's a second chance." Kamal sets the device aside, pushing the lap table away. He leans back in the seat, turning his body toward me. "Jayda, you make your reality. You can see it as crawling away in the middle of the night or you can see this as making the right decision for you and your daughter."

"Then what?"

"Anything you want." He opens his arms as if offering me the world.

"It's not that easy."

"Are you sure about that?" There's an air of a challenge in his request. "Because tonight I saw a woman walk away when it would probably be easier if she stayed."

His assessment hits pay dirt. I drop my head, unable to hold his gaze.

Reese stirs and her head pops up from under the blanket like a little turtle. She sweeps the area, surveying her surroundings while scrubbing a balled fist across her eyes.

"Mommy, I'm Thursday."

"Thirsty," I correct.

"Yes, ma'am."

"Liz." Kamal calls out and Reese leans forward to get a look at him. "Bring the service tray too."

"Yes, sir." The stewardess disappears behind the curtain.

Reese sits up, and I gather the blanket. She yawns with her mouth wide open, then she covers it.

"Such a big girl." I smile my approval, kissing the top of her head. "How'd you sleep?"

"Good." Her eyes slide back across the aisle, leaning closer to me. I look up at Kamal and he's smiling at her. Reese turns her face until it's buried in my side, before glancing back.

"Reese, Mr. Kamal is taking us to see Auntie Cat."

That's all I had to say to wake my sleepy princess. My baby's smile covers her entire face. "Today?"

"Yes, baby, today. We're going there now."

"Yay." She bounces around, then stops suddenly. Looking up at me. "Where's my coloring book? I want to show her my coloring book."

"Remember, honey, we had to leave it. But we'll find another one. Okay?"

"Okay." Disappointment clouds her features and I add her coloring book to my list of items we need as the stewardess passes a bottle of water. She politely waits while Reese drinks.

"That's good, sweetie. Want a snack?"

She eyes the tray and back across the aisle.

"He's…" I'm stumped at what to call him. My child has an immaculate memory. "Mommy's friend. Can you say Kamal?"

Reese nods. "Mommy, can I call him Kamal?"

I chuckle. "No, ma'am. You can call him *Mr. Kamal.*"

"I have a niece about your age." Kamal takes the seat closest to us. "How old are you, Reese? Ten?"

"No…." She giggles, facing him.

"Twenty?" He wrinkles his nose up.

"No…" She laughs, rocking over until she's leaning back against me.

"I'm four."

"Four. Man, I was off." His eyes dance with humor. "Who did your hair? It is really pretty."

"My mommy." She rubs it, as if checking to see if it's still there. "Who did your hair?"

Kamal laughs—that one caught him off guard. "My barber."

Reese turns to me for confirmation. "Huh… a barber cuts hair and sometimes shaves faces. Mostly for boys."

"Oh." She nods in understanding.

"What do you like to do?" Kamal asks.

Reese warms up and falls into rare form. She's always animated with me, her Grannie Minnie, and Auntie Cat, but this is the first time I've seen her like this with a stranger.

Kamal asks questions, makes funny faces, and laughs at her stories. I nod along, letting my mind float in and out of their conversation, thinking about the days and months ahead.

I'll need to find a job, but that means I'll need to find a daycare. I wonder if Brett will pay for her preschool, when I feel the light tap of her hand on my arm.

"Yes, honey." I blink.

"Can I?"

"Can you what?"

Kamal is holding his iPad out. "She can use it to color."

"Reese, be careful."

"Yes, ma'am." She reaches with eagerness in her eyes, not listening to a single word I'm saying.

"Sit up and hold it with two hands. Only coloring, no videos."

Her face beams with excitement. I place the device on her lap.

"Lift the pencil from the top." I cut my eyes to Kamal, then back to Reese as she follows his directions. "Use it on the screen."

"On here?" Reese points, and I'm just as curious.

"Yeah, it's like paper. Try it." He flicks his wrist in a writing motion.

Reese looks up at me, and I shrug. I've never used an iPad before. I lean closer to see what will happen. She tentatively taps and stares at the mark it makes.

"Here, let me show you."

Reese passes it back and Kamal moves closer. The scent of his cologne fills my nose when he stops, stooping next to us. I get a good look at the man who swooped in and saved the day like T'Challa. Since boarding the plane, he removed his jacket, and rolled up the sleeves of his shirt, revealing tattoos on his forearms.

He drags the pencil across the screen, acting silly, smiling the more Reese laughs. For a moment I allow his beauty to distract me, the diamond stud in his ear, his curly hair cut in a clean fade. The man's a beauty.

Kamal winks, catching me in the act. I turn away.

The peanut butter-colored leather seats, and the soft lights highlight the plush interior of the jet. Reese and I sit on a couch like chair while Kamal occupied an oversized chair. I count at least twelve seats, and I wonder what he docs for a living. He mentioned investing in companies, but that could mean anything.

Kamal has no wife and no kids, flying around in a private plane. He didn't mention a girlfriend, but it's none of my business. We're bumming a ride to Houston and then we'll be out of his hair.

He's the type of man I would have enticed without a second thought. That's how I ended up with Brett. I groan, and Kamal's eyes land on mine. No more football players for me.

Kamal returns to his seat as Reese happily colors on the device.

"You're good with kids."

"I'm the oldest of five and my niece is about her age. I have several apps to keep her entertained."

"Smart man." I chuckle, tilting back my seat. The night hits me, and I'm exhausted. "How much longer do we have?"

"Over an hour. What's next for the two of you?"

"That's what I keep asking myself." I stare up at the ceiling. "Start over, I guess. Thankfully, we have a place to stay."

"Do you have family in Houston?"

"No, just Cat." My lids drop and I force them open.

"You've had a long night. Take a nap. I'll wake you when we're about to land."

"I'm fine. Do you live in Houston?" I gather the blanket around Reese, who's coloring and smacking on crackers.

"No, I bounce around spending most of my time in New York."

"New York, New York. I've visited but never spent much time there. The hustle felt overwhelming."

He chuckles, appearing more relaxed. "LA is the same."

I think about his statement. "I guess. But it's spread out."

"Where are you from?"

"Everywhere and nowhere." This time when my eyes close I can't force them open.

"Mommy…"

"Let Mommy sleep, Reesie." Kamal's use of her nickname quiets her.

A blanket of warmth surrounds me and the mumble of their voices fade away. I'll rest my eyes for a few minutes and then sleep takes me.

"Jay…" My body shakes and I can't peel my eyes open. "Jay… I got Starbucks."

I blink. The rich timbre of her laugh is too close and warm to be a dream.

"Mommy, Auntie Cat said I can have hot chocolate. Can I?" Reese wiggles beside me. I limit her sugar intake for a reason. My Reesie Piecie goes from zero to one million with the smallest amount of sweets.

"Is it a small? And what time is it?"

"Fifteen 'til six."

My eyes fly open and land on Kamal. "What are you doing here?"

A smile that could complete with the sun God made spreads across his face. "It's my plane."

"Right. How did I forget?" I toss back the blanket and the night floods back. It wasn't a nightmare, but my life. "Wait, what are you doing here?"

"I'm here to take you to my house. I'm scheduled for work until eleven-thirty. Which reminds me?" Catrina digs around in her bag and passes a folded document to Kamal.

"For me?"

"Yes, it's the contract. You can bring it with you tonight," Catrina says.

I fold the blanket after giving Reese permission to start her hot chocolate. Where's my phone? I pat around and find it. Then I turn on the power. The damn thing sings and vibrates, taking us by surprise.

"The donor," Catrina states with a *sister-girl*-eye roll.

She's right. Over thirty missed calls, twice as many text messages, and one voicemail. I tap the screen to listen to the message and Catrina snags my phone.

"Wait until you've had breakfast and rested before you entertain his *bullshit*." The hiss of the curse word draws the attention of Reese.

The adults stare at the phone hanging between us, and I

glance up at Kamal just over her shoulder. I take the phone and drop it in my purse.

We gather our belongings while the crew loads our baggage in Catrina's trunk. Kamal fastens the car seat in back seat then steps back, giving me room to place Reese inside.

"It was nice meeting you, Miss Reesie." He reaches inside, squeezing her nose between his knuckles. She giggles, fluttering her feet. No doubt from having hot chocolate before six in the morning.

"Bye, Mr. Kamal," Reese says with a busy wave.

I swallow, not wanting to get emotional. Then I shut the door and glance back, realizing we're alone. Kamal stares down at me and I don't want to say goodbye. It's nothing romantic, *I don't think*. But I guess we shared something tonight.

"Last night could have been hella awkward, but you made it… better. Thank you isn't enough but it's all I have. I owe you one."

"I'm glad to help. All I want is for you to take care of Miss Reesie, and yourself." His words trail off and the sincerity in his eyes grab my heart. "I'll be around for a few weeks. Here's my personal cellphone." He passes a card. I flip it over to see a number scribbled in ink. "Call me if you need anything. But something tells me you'll be just fine."

"How do you know?"

He shrugs a shoulder and leans against the car. "You remind me of my mother. When my parents divorced, she had five kids to raise, while running a business." He smiles over at me. "You have that same fire I see in her and Miya. All you have to do is trust it."

"You must be an excellent salesman."

Kamal laughs, stepping back a little, and rocking forward closer than before. I join in because he has that type of effect. "What makes you say that?"

"Because I believe you."

"Don't believe me, trust yourself." He glances down at his watch. "I need to get out of here."

I extend my hand. "Thank you again."

"Oh, no you don't." He pulls me until I'm cocooned in his arms with his chin on top of my head. My face presses against his chest, and the mean old world quietens. I wrap my arms around his trim waist and exhale, listening to the thump of his heart. It feels safe here compared to the unknown of moving and starting over.

I'm scared. Not scared enough to run back. But scared to the point of not wanting to let Kamal go.

The moment I get in the car and ride away, I'll have to wrestle with knowing my life is royally fucked. But it won't stay like this because I won't let it.

Reese and I have a place to stay. We'll have to tap into my rainy-day fund, which should give me a few months to figure it out. The logical option is to use what I have in my bank account and to finally use my makeup skills. But I don't have the luxury or financial backing to wait for my channel to grow. It's time to stop playing around and go pro.

The only thing that matters is my daughter, building my

brand, and making sure I never depend on another man the way I depended on Brett.

"Call me, if you need anything."

"You've done more than the nature of our relationship requires." I step back.

Kamal slips his hands in his pockets, holding my gaze. I force myself to look away instead of letting my mind focus on the comfort I felt in his arms.

I can't let myself fall into another handsome trap. My attention is best reserved for creating a new life for Reese and me.

Ninety days.

The clock ticks in my head, neither confident nor defeated. But the arbitrary number chases away the numbness accompanied by the reality of leaving my entire life behind in Los Angeles.

I promised myself the moment I decided to have my baby that he or she would have a home. That my baby would be loved and nurtured. However, my actions tonight feel like a broken promise. I can't let her feel the blows of my poor judgment.

Ninety days. I turn the words over in my head. Three months isn't too bad. Push some sponsored videos, reach out to the boutiques I met with in Houston. Then I'll have the cash flow to move from Catrina's house and start a chapter for us. I'll just pretend we're having a ninety-day pajama party.

I glance at Reese in the car. The animated gesture of her hands tells me she's talking, and after a cup of chocolate my baby will be wound up like the Energizer bunny for a few hours.

"You're not going to call. Are you?"

I blink, almost forgetting Kamal is here.

"Thank you for everything." I reach for the door and slip inside before he can stop me. "Drive. Please."

CHAPTER 8

THIS IS A TEST. The day got away from me with fleeting thoughts about my trip to Los Angeles intercepted by my desire to check on Jayda and Reese.

"Kamal…"

"Yeah." I glance over at Ebony, my publicist and date for tonight. She runs through the flow for the night.

I had several opportunities to call this gathering off, and I considered it after reviewing the contract from Catrina. However, the wheels of this shindig are in motion. Ebony arrived an hour ago from New York.

The list of recipients for the press release, the celebrities, and the organizations invited sounds substantial, at least enough to project the potential earnings I can share with Mother and my siblings.

But the cloud threatening to rain on my excitement is knowing Mother is out of the country this weekend. I know she wouldn't approve of opening, however, I'm certain I can persuade her with solid evidence. Which means we have to pull in impressive earnings tonight.

The driver cuts through town like a native, ensuring we'll arrive on time. To help with the revenue, I canceled the food items and opted for the full kitchen to remain open for the night. Yet I'm still forking over ten grand for the staff, the supplies, all without my siblings, and I'm wondering if testing my idea is worth the discord.

"What are you not telling me?" Ebony interrupts the rollercoaster of my thoughts.

"We have to win tonight. An L is not acceptable."

"I've known you over ten years. You don't host parties and you've never asked me to serve as your date." Ebony lowers her phone to her lap, facing me. "Feel free to fill me in at any moment. Because I can't help you if I'm in the dark. What are we really doing here?"

"I invited you to the team Christmas banquet," I remind her.

Ebony rolls her eyes. "That was to piss Emmitt off."

"I told you not to date him or Dean. My boys are—"

"Off limits." She finishes the second rule on my list. "I know, I fell for his sweet words. Sue me. The man is lick*able*."

I plug my fingers in my ears. "This is worse than talking about sex with Miya. Sex complicates things, and it makes working together difficult."

I hired her on the strength of my agent's referral when I joined the league. Our relationship is strictly platonic, and I'll keep it that way because I value her loyalty. People have come and gone, but Ebony's rolled with me like my boys. She's another sister to me.

"The three of you run through women. Do you ever stop to look back at the casualties?"

"There are no casualties if women take us at our word. Did he not have the talk with you?"

"He did. But—"

"No buts. A real man knows what he wants. I tried to protect you." I shake my head. Being stuck in one place with one woman is the definition of insanity when I have the world to explore.

"What about love?" She bats her eyes like a caricature.

"What about it?" I snort a little. "You didn't want love with Emmitt. You wanted what he gave you."

Dean, Emmitt, and I became closer when we realized neither of us wants the traditional life. We dedicate ourselves to our families, business, football, and the community, in that order.

"You're starting to sound like an asshole."

"I sound honest. A real man tells you like it is and let you accept or decline the offer. Did Emmitt tell you he wanted more?"

"No."

"Did Emmitt tell you he sees other women?"

"Yeah, but—"

"But what?"

"But when you sleep with me, we go together?"

"What kind of fifth grade shit is that? *Go together*." I

laugh because I can't help it. The look on her face tells me she's dead-ass serious.

Is this how women think?

"Dating is recreational, not permanent."

I've sat on the front lines watching brothers get burned, and I'll pass. The one time I forgot the shit came back and bit me in the ass. We all have a game we play, except Sharron didn't do me the courtesy of telling me her rules. And like a lovesick puppy, I freely gave her everything until it I learned I was temporary.

A stand in.

A pawn in her game.

I was wet behind the ears and learned with skin in the game—my heart. Now, I treat the woman on my arm like a queen and when the night is over, it's over until we kick it again.

"You better be glad I'm your friend. You and your *hoe* squad," Ebony shoots back.

"He's a hoe now?"

"He is and now I know to not associate with any of your friends."

"No, you should *associate* with my friends. Your PR agency would cross the million-dollar mark, easily, if you associated with my boys. Don't fuck'em. Some lessons are best learned with some skin in the game."

"Skin in the game?"

"Business and sex don't mix like clear and brown liquors. I bet you'll remember this a little lesson every time you meet a man at a business function." I chuckle, leaning back into the seat.

"More of your player advice?"

"Call it what you want." I shrug. "When people show you their true colors, you—"

"Paint that shit in ink." She air quotes with her nose wrinkled.

"You can scrub off that stank face. You wouldn't be salty if you followed the rules. Listening only works with action."

"Kamal, rules are to officiate games, not relationships." She flicks a dismissive hand. "So, will they be here tonight?"

"Yes, but not for long. Dean is heading to oversee another project in New Orleans and Emmitt's driving home to Dallas."

"Which confirms my suspicions that this isn't a DEK Ventures event." I shake my head. "Why are you really having this party?"

I glance over. Ebony and I joke around, but she's a vital component of all my business moves. She's another set of eyes and ears to balance the competitive edge the guys and I possess with DEK Ventures.

Dean, Emmitt, and I transferred our desire to win from the field to a privately held investment firm. Ebony offers a sound, softer side compared to the guys.

"Tonight's about Southern Soul and whether opening on Sundays is something we should consider. I want the place full with a line waiting to get in."

Details about the financial state of Southern Soul stays between the Montgomerys. Thus, not a project for DEK

Ventures. This one I'll have to handle myself. The guys agreed to attend tonight on the strength of our friendship.

I glance at my phone. Should I call my siblings? No. They made their stance clear. They didn't agree with my idea, and I've kept the plans for this evening to myself. There's no point in telling them now.

"Why are you rushing it? Trying to throw something like this last minute will skew your numbers. Plus, you're holding it on a Sunday evening. Sundays are usually reserved for church, football, or family."

"Yeah, well, tonight it's reserved for Southern Soul."

What my siblings fail to realize is we're on the same team.

Team Jackie Montgomery.

Team keep Kenneth out of her bank account and out of *our* family business. He lost the right twenty years ago, and tonight I'll show them how my plans help us all. I have a plan to line Mother's pockets and to successfully shift ownership of the family restaurant to us.

Once the night is over, I'll have what I need to usher in the new phase of Southern Soul.

I push thoughts of my family and friends aside, focusing on the matter at hand. It's game time, baby.

The lineup includes Ebony, Catrina, and the current staff. The challenge of hosting this event with half the staff needed gives me pause. What choice do we have? We must make this happen.

"All right, Kamal. I got your back. I called in favors,

emailed your database, and called some local celebrities. You've explained the party, what's with this date pretense?"

"A buffer."

"Oh, you trying to use me to sidestep some chick. Who is she?" She crosses her arms with a twinkle in her eyes. You'd think she's waiting for me to walk into a trap. This is when Ebony slips into Miya zone, like another kid sister.

"I'm not sidestepping. I need you to focus. I'm running solo on this."

"Solo?" Her spine stiffened.

Damn. I didn't mean to bring it up.

"Why are you running solo in Houston?" The little frown between her brows appears.

The SUV rolls to a stop outside Southern Soul, and I'm at a loss for words. My heart rate drags in slow motion as I survey the sight. I glance at my watch.

A line wraps around the building twice the length from Saturday morning. I scan the cars in the parking lot, noticing more people. I feel the smile spreading across my face. The taste of victory tickles my taste buds.

I have a lot riding on tonight. But a profitable weekend will keep the doors open, ensure Mother's financial stability, and prove we don't need Kenneth to make it happen.

I open the door, extending a hand back to help Ebony out.

"Here comes the hoe squad," she whispers.

"Ebony."

She nods, "I'll meet you inside."

I wrap a hand around her elbow. "You're my date

tonight. The last thing we need is for this to get awkward. We're a team."

"Don't do this…" she grinds through her teeth.

"The best way to kick a man in the balls is to show him he's a non-factor."

Her eyes snap to mine. "More of your player rules."

"No, more of my truth."

The guys and I don't share women. But Ebony can't run every time she sees him. We have too much ground to cover. Especially if I can get the guys on board to help with turning this place around.

"Fellas, I wasn't expecting you guys until later tonight."

Dean and I lock hands first with a one-shouldered hug. Then Emmitt with his eyes on Ebony. Dean kisses her cheek before whispering a greeting, and Emmitt pauses.

Ebony moves forward, executing the same friendly greeting she shared with Dean.

"You guys ready to work the room tonight." Ebony opens her notes. "I extended personal invitations to a few chefs, Dean, and for you, Kamal, the board members from some local little leagues."

Dean and I share a look when I hear my name called. We look in the voice's direction.

"Jennifer…"

"What happened to Trish?" Emmitt teases, standing back with a hand in his pocket.

"Jennifer happened to Trish," Dean answers on my behalf.

We laugh and Ebony wags her head, hissing about the hoe squad.

Then a thought ceases my retort, *Jayda happened to them both*.

I drop my head, ignoring their laughter, forcing Jayda and her curvy body in those colorful leggings from my mind. I don't know what came over me this morning. The thought of watching her walk away had me contemplating ways to extend our time. I didn't realize the mistake I'd made until it was too late. Pulling her into my arms, smelling her perfume, feeling her body pressed against mine.

A sharp poke in my side regains my attention. I look down at the source and Ebony tips her head.

Jennifer stands in front of us. She's a fun night on the town. A corporate attorney with no drama and no attachments. But unlike before, I'm not interested. I introduce her to the others.

"Thanks for the invite." Jennifer runs her tongue over her glossy bottom lip, and Emmitt snickers.

"I said I'd hit you up when I got back. I'm glad you could make it. I'll catch you inside."

"All right." She turns, meandering to give us ample time to check her out. The guys shake their heads catching drift of her act and Ebony rolls her eyes toward the sky.

"Please tell me you didn't invite your groupies."

"I told you I'm filling the room. Standing room only. Groupies, ex-girlfriends, fans, business associates, whoever it takes to make tonight a success."

. . .

THE INSIDE of Southern Soul is almost unrecognizable. The music fills the gaps of the conversations flowing through the room. The transformation of the dining room reflects my sketch. I used the entry walkway and the dual sections of the dining area to segregate the attendees. The socializers from the diners.

The guests inch inside, filling the restaurant. The right side cleared to standing room only with a DJ area in one corner and the open bar in the other. The waiters dressed in classic white tops and black bottoms weave through the crowd.

Across the walkway on the left side we left the tables and chairs to allow for intimate conversations, sit-down dining. But at the moment, it's empty.

I work the room, take pictures with fans, connect with childhood friends. Ebony stays at my side unless she's introducing Dean and Emmitt to key people in the city. Having my team beside me makes tonight feel like any another business networking event, but a part of me wishes I'd called my brothers. I need them to see they can trust the plans I have for the business. That our legacy is secure.

"Kamal." Catrina slips up beside me.

"Excuse me." I step away from the others. We walk to the hostess station near the center of room. I glance down at my watch. It's been few hours. "How's it looking?"

She shrugs. "The open bar and appetizers are flowing, but no one is ordering."

"What?" I scan the crowd, as if seeing them for the first time, and every hand holds a cocktail and mini plate. I look across the divide and the left side of the dining hall is nearly empty. A waiter sits at one table scanning her glowing phone and others use the tables for private conversations. But there's not a single plate in sight.

"Everything okay?" Ebony joins us.

"No one's ordering food," I relay Catrina's report.

"Why would they? You have a room full of groupies," Ebony teases, and her joke rings louder than I'll admit.

"Ebony, you're here to help," I remind her.

"Mind if I invite a few people? Maybe have the waiters do the same."

Emmitt calls out to me from across the room. He flicks a hand toward some people we need to talk with. I look back at Ebony and Catrina. "Sure. What do we have to lose?"

They nod and I set off to join Emmitt. He and Dean have made several local connections tonight. I join him and the president of a local little league football team. She shares the hardships of the team to gain donors for uniforms, equipment, and their desires to find a permanent location.

"It would give our kids a boost to have a visit from you guys." The president smiles up at Emmitt, batting her lashes. My conversation with Ebony resurfaces and as if she reads my mind, our eyes lock from across the room. She gives me the *told you* look and I shake my head. I'm staying out of their shit. I told her to leave him alone.

"We'll be in touch," Emmitt says, and the suits disappear into the crowd. "Think we can schedule something before Dean leaves?"

"I'm down. What are you thinking? Sending a donation?"

"We could. But what about that camp we discussed last year?"

"A summer football camp?" I turn, getting a drift of where this conversation is going. "I forgot about that. That would make sense. I'm here for a least a few months. What would you do? Stay here for the summer."

"I could." He takes a drag of his beer. "It's easier to join an already functioning league."

"We could fund the camp, update their equipment…" I reason.

"Bring in a few guest coaches, some surprise players…" Emmitt adds.

Dean stops beside me. "What are you two planning?"

"Summer football camp." Emmitt answers and glances back over at me. "How much do you think it'll take?"

"A fraction of the cost if we come in as a donor instead of starting something on our own."

I fill Dean in while Emmitt stares in space. This is why I fuck with these guys. We shoot the shit, but at the end of the day we get money and we take care of the people around us.

"When do you have to be in New Orleans?"

"Tomorrow, but I'm popping in visiting a few of the local restaurants. I can be back in a few days," Dean responds, his eyes roaming the room from the floor to the ceiling. "What plans do you have for this place?"

"Man, get us out of the red."

Dean nods. "How do you plan to do that?"

"My first step is opening on Sundays to take advantage of our weekend crowd."

"Then what?" Dean places his empty bottle on podium facing me. He stopped playing football first. Then he opened a few restaurants, flipped them, and over the years he has built a full-service consulting service.

"Man. This place needs a total overhaul."

"Give me a tour."

"Bet. Emmitt?"

"I'll be here."

I fall silent, watching him stroll through the kitchen. Dean opens doors, inspects the equipment, all while chatting with the staff. He's always been a man of few words, but he's the best at what he does. Clients wait months for this type of treatment.

"Take me outside." He completes the same surveillance, scanning the exterior, picking at the chipped paint. "Will this be a DEK project?"

"No, this is family-owned, and we plan to keep it that way."

Dean nods, walks to the end of the parking lot and inspects the street. He does a sweeping glance up and down the street before returning to me. I'm not a fool. I know I'm not a restauranteur. But I don't have to be to turn this place around.

"What type of turnaround?"

"Couple of months."

Dean laughs. "You're crazy."

"Facts."

He shakes his head, not surprised. Then he stares at me. "Kamal, this place needs a total overhaul. You have an old diner competing with fast food, high-end steakhouse, and you don't even have a fucking paved parking lot."

"Are you telling me it's impossible? You're supposed to be the *restaurant whisperer*." He hates the name and I know my deadline is bordering on insanity, but I want what I want.

"Man, fuck you."

We laugh. He looks between the restaurant and me.

"I'm willing to pay your fee plus a bonus to get this place in order."

"Your money's no good here."

I freeze. We've always split everything equally, tackling projects as a collective unit. But I've never approached the guys with a personal project like this.

"Man… that's unnecessary."

"Your family is my family. But I'll have to squeeze you in between clients. How long will you close the place for renovations?"

"We can't close."

"Kamal." The pique of his voice sounds like a shout in the quiet of night. "You can't do a project of this size without closing. It's impossible."

"Impossible? What's that?"

Dean runs his hand through his hair. "Scratch what I said. Get your checkbook ready."

I laugh, dropping a hand on his shoulders leading him back into the gathering. "Let me get you a drink."

"I'm going to need more than a drink." He asks more questions about the schedule, the staff, and our plans for the space. "Look, I'll help, but cutting down the delivery time will cost you guys."

"I figured as much, but it's time for us to move into the next phase of Southern Soul."

"All right, man. I'll work on the proposal and construction plan."

"I like the sound of that. Think you could have it when you return." I smile so hard my face hurts.

"Shall I bring you a golden calf too, King Kamal?"

"Nah."

We laugh, walking back into the party. I stop, startled by the double in occupancy. I survey the room and both sides are fully occupied.

"Looks like you're off to an impressive start," Dean comments.

"Looks like it." I exhale, pleased at the sight in front of us. My gaze darts across the tables. A warm sensation travels through my body. The left side of the room holds the bulk of the guests. People line the wall while several couples dance in the middle of the space. The fully occupied tables on the right side give me a sense of relief. I've never been so excited to see white plates on the tables.

I inhale deep and slow, and my stomach growls thanks

to the fragrant scent of fried chicken. I drop a heavy hand on Dean's shoulder to get his attention.

"Want something? I'm about to place an order." I reach for a menu.

"Hey… isn't that Jayda?" I stop short at Dean's question. I follow the tip of his head. And there she is, sitting at a table near the wall. Reese sits beside her, scribbling on what looks like a napkin from here.

"Yeah. Looks like it."

Dean nods, and Reese's head pops up as she notices me. She waves with a huge smile on her face. I chuckle and wave back.

"Who's that?" Dean asks.

"Reese, Jayda's daughter."

"She has a kid?" I hear the shift in his voice over the boom of the music.

"Yeah. She's a cool kid. I holler at you."

"Do you need me? I think I'll head out. The sooner I leave, the sooner I can get back."

"Nah, I'm good. How about we plan to get together Wednesday morning?" I have a hotel, but I might need to get Rashaad to find me a house to lease. "I'll text you the location."

"All right. Congrats on the crowd. I'll find Emmitt, then hit the road."

"Thanks, man. Hopefully, it's the first of many. Travel safely and he's over there sniffing behind Ebony." I point across the room.

Dean shakes his head. "You better watch it. He'll run her off."

"He better not." I take another look at the two of them dancing near the DJ table.

We grip hands and hug with one arm.

"I'm out," Dean says, and I shift toward Jayda and Reese.

I tuck the menu under my arm and then duck under the hostess podium for a color sheet and crayons for Reese.

"Kamal."

I stand straighter, staring into my mother's eyes. "Hey, Mother."

"Don't hey Mother me." I swear steam's rising from her ears.

"Baby, let him explain."

"Kenneth, I don't need your help." My eyes snap from my mother to my father. The disdain I have for this man runs deep and wide, disintegrating my explanation.

"Don't speak to your dad…"

"He stopped being my dad twenty years ago," I grate through my clenched teeth.

My heart slams against my chest harder than the sound of the bass through the DJ's speakers. My gaze lands on my mother's. She steps forward and I step back. Then I notice Rashaad, Demetrius, Quan, and Miya.

Them standing on the other side of podium.

Me over here.

The noise of the crowd absorbs my chuckle. *Isn't that fitting?*

The not-so-silent silence hangs between us. Why did I come back? The plea in the depths of Mother's eyes is better served elsewhere, and I tell her without words. She takes another step back, and Kenneth gathers her in his arms, whispering in her ear. She nods, not taking her eyes off me.

I shouldn't let her decisions affect me, and I wouldn't if it wasn't *him*.

Mother's drawing a line. They all are. I grind my teeth as if hearing chalk scraped across a chalkboard.

Fuck this. I turn to leave.

"Hi, Mr. Kamal!"

I glance down, and her smile melts away the ice freezing around my heart. She stumbles forward as if she can't control her little feet.

"Honey, you can't interrupt. I'm sorry." Jayda grips Reese's shoulders, inching her back.

I turn my gaze toward Jayda, and she flinches but doesn't look away. And instead of walking away, she steps closer. Then I feel her hand on my arm, as she faces my family.

"I apologize. We're heading out and I need to steal Kamal for a few minutes."

I slip my hand in hers, dragging her past my family.

"Byeee," Reese sings, shuffling beside us.

I don't stop until we clear the door and I'm outside, commanding my racing heart to calm down.

"Everything okay?" Catrina asks.

"Yeah, Cat, can you watch Reese for a second?"

"Come on, Reesie Piecie," Catrina says.

I hear them, but my attention is on my next move. This is why I stay away.

The door closes behind them, and I look down at Jayda. She's wearing a white blouse with an animal print skirt. Her high heels bring us closer in height.

"You want to talk."

I glance through the glass at my family now talking with Catrina. "Not really. You didn't have to do that."

"I owe you and you looked like a man that needed a lifeline." She crosses her arms, shielding herself from the unusual cool in the air. I remove my suit jacket and drape it over her shoulders. "Thank you."

I nod. "I thought I wouldn't see you again."

"That was my plan." She stares up at me, hidden in the darkness of the hour.

I experience the second shock for the night. "Then why are you here?"

"To apologize." Her voice drifts off as a few people stop to say their goodbyes to her. I find it odd but wait for them to leave.

"I'm listening."

"I didn't mean to behave so ungratefully this morning." Another group of women call out to her. Jayda waves with a bright smile, and something in me wishes I could make her smile like that—heartfelt, relaxed, happy. "Drive safely. Thanks again for coming. Don't forget to tag me."

I wait for her to turn back to me. "I'll accept your apology if you let me take you out to dinner." She rolls her eyes, and I clarify. "As a friend."

"Kamal, people like us can't be friends."

"And why's that?" I smile despite feeling like shit. Somehow the success of filling Southern Soul with customers isn't rewarding. I glance over my shoulder at my family, then back at Jayda. A beautiful distraction.

"We have too much sexual chemistry."

"Damn. I always love a straight shooter." My hollow chuckle stretches between us. Her decline stings.

I feel the chemistry she speaks of and the strength of it is stronger than the hate I feel for my father. This only makes me more determined to learn more about this woman, but it won't happen tonight. Thankfully I have Catrina.

"I need to get Reese to bed." She glances over my shoulder. "I hope tonight wasn't an adult only affair. I didn't have a babysitter."

"Reese is fine. She really is a cutie. Did she enjoy herself tonight?"

"Other than complaining about only having four crayons. She loved the chicken and waffles."

"Ahhh… my kind of girl. Tell her I'll handle the crayon situation." I promise to see Jayda smile.

"She'll be a happy customer when you do." She steps closer to me, bringing the scent of her perfume. "I came tonight to tell you thank you and to celebrate your home-coming. Last night I needed a friend and you…" Her voice cracks.

I see through the tough exterior she's displaying. Life played a fast one on her, yet she's here. A simple leopard skirt rides the curves of her body. Her hair pulled away from her face with a chunky necklace and matching earrings. But it's the way she holds her head high, even as she brushes away a tear, like the queen she is.

"I've vowed to stop crying." She pats her cheeks. "You probably think I'm…I don't know."

"It's been less than twenty-four hours. Give yourself a break. Crying is like a palate cleanser for the soul."

"That was very poetic." Her sultry voice entices me closer. I stop when I see the streetlight reflect in her brown eyes. I inhale, filling my lungs with her scent.

"My mom used to tell us that."

I want to touch her, to catch every tear, and instead I search her eyes for the source. Why can't I seem to see this is a mistake waiting to happen?

Movement in the entry captures our attention. I face the double glass doors. They walk down the walkway as a unit—a family—without me, and it hurts more than I'll ever admit. I open and close my hand to relieve the mounting tension. I returned to Houston, the place I used to call home, but it doesn't feel welcoming or safe or familiar.

My family standing in the middle of my unauthorized party intensifies the consequences of tonight. The last thing I want is to upset Mother, but the unsettled hostility between Kenneth and me weighs heavy on the family. The result leaves me estranged from them, unsettled about the next phase of my life, and now I'm concerned if remaining in Houston has the potential to make matters worse.

"Need a wing man?"

I move from the vision of my family closing in on us to Jayda. Her offer says to the torn man in me—*you're not alone*. A piece of me, the piece I keep hidden from the world, draws closer to bask in the warmth of her.

"Why would you do that, Jayda?"

"That's what friends do, and to return the favor."

"So, we're friends?" I ask, taking another step. "Friends have each other's numbers." I slip my phone from my pocket.

Jayda laughs, and it fills me like air. Taking this chemistry of ours up several notches. "You are such a player. How many times have you used that line?"

"Never. I don't beg for numbers."

Her eyebrow lifts in a challenge. Then a flirty smile crosses her face. "You call this begging Kamal? It might be good for you."

"Nah, I'm starting to think your laughter is good for me."

"Don't…" She exhales with a groan. "Don't make this about anything other than friendship." She grabs my phone, nibbling on her plump lower lip, taking me from intense to aroused in a second, and I like it.

This woman sports a fat rock on her finger, and she has an adorable daughter. She's the type of woman I avoid because I'm not the type of man to play second to no man. I have a room full of options and yet here I am, standing in the middle of the night, waiting for her to give me what I want and that's to satisfy my curiosity.

What makes her laugh? What's her favorite foods? Does she listen to the sound of the ocean with her eyes closed? Has she ever made love in the rain? But am I willing to pay the cost?

I cup the side of her face and my world shifts. I suck in and she gasps. She feels it too. "Jayda, I want to get to know you better."

"We don't all get what we want." She returns my phone.

"I do."

The whites of her eyes glow, and I thrust my phone in her direction again. The door opens and my family exits, and Jayda slips away.

I watch her retreat. She's only here for a limited time, just like me. Maybe it's for the best.

CHAPTER 9

"Kamal, I want these people out of my restaurant." Mamma steps forward.

I open my mouth to respond and stop. Miya grabs my hand. I look down at our joined hands and up into her eyes. She winks before we face our mother. Then I see Demetrius on the other side of her. Rashaad and Q stand to my left.

"Yes, ma'am." I face my mother, knowing I owe her an apology.

"Be at my house in the morning."

"I'll be there at ten with breakfast," I offer.

"Goodnight." She and Kenneth disappear into the night, leaving me alone with my siblings.

"Who told?" I scan them.

"Instagram," Q answers.

"What?"

Q passes his phone, and I press play. Jayda smiles, yet in

the depths of her eyes I see the remnants of the last twenty-four hours.

Hey, Gems! Your girl's in H-Town about to slam at Southern Soul. Why don't you join me? You buy the food, and I'll get the drinks. Smooches!

She blows a kiss at the camera and the video loops.

"Since when do we go rogue?" Q asks.

I give his phone back, looking at the building. Is that how we packed the place? That explains the clusters of women bidding their farewells while I talked to Jayda.

That woman saved my ass twice tonight. And after seeing her little video…

"Kamal?" The tone in Miya's voice asks for an explanation.

"Y'all made your stance clear." I gesture to the inside. The place is still packed. "I knew this was possible, and I needed the numbers to show you."

"Kamal, we called you home to help. Not because we can't do it but because we want to do it together. Which you would have known if you stuck around," Rashaad adds.

"My bad."

"Shit, I'm glad he did it *all* on his own. That's exactly what I'm telling Mamma in the morning," Q blurts out.

"Man, whatever. Y'all act like she will line us up and whoop our asses."

"She might," Miya says.

We stare at each other and burst out laughing. I wouldn't put it past Mother. She raised four men that towered over her before our preteens. She ruled with an iron fist and a leather belt, and it worked.

We head back inside. I search the crowd for Jayda and she's gone. Once the gathering winds down, we all chip in and get the place back to normal.

"Catrina, let me holler at you," I call across the room once she rejoins us.

"You invited Jayda?"

"Yeah, you said employees could invite friends."

I nod. "How much would you estimate her little party contributed to tonight's numbers?"

"About seventy-five percent." Then she quotes the figure, placing the printed receipt in my hand. "Goodnight, y'all." Catrina gives a parting wave, leaving us alone.

I flip through the pages without seeing the words.

Q whistles. "I need to hire Jayda for the club."

My head snaps to Q. "Little brother, that might be a good idea."

I sit on the edge of a table. What's my next move? I roll the paper in my hands, scanning the room. Tonight is more like a win by default. Had Jayda not made that video… I push the thought aside.

I unroll the receipt, scanning the numbers. A profitable Sunday at Southern Soul. The question now is can I do it again, but with actual clients and without Jayda.

My chest burns.

My heart grips.

My siblings glance at me.

I stand to my feet, exhaling the pent-up energy. No

point in playing around with what-ifs. The result is exactly what I need. Numbers.

"You guys wanted numbers. I have numbers." I hold up the receipt.

"Now, to convince Ma," Q says, and the others nod.

"I'll convince her. But am I going in there solo?"

"You're never solo as long as air's in my lungs. But this isn't the time for showboating or hosting private parties. This is about *our* family. We want this as much as you do." Rashaad steps forward. "You want to run point on this? Cool. But do it on the up and up, and you'll have my full support."

I nod. "Demetrius?"

"I'll there."

"Me too," Miya adds.

"Q?"

"I'm down. But what about your girl? The video? Seventy-five percent of the revenue? This all boils down to traffic. Asses in seats and not Club Kamal." Q stands, tucking his helmet under his arm. "Look, I need to get back to the club. What time are we meeting at Ma's?"

"Nine. I'm cooking."

Their heads snap in my direction.

"Aaah shit." Q smiles.

"Need a sous chef?" Miya offers.

I gather her to me, kissing the top of her head. "I'd be honored."

"I'll bring my secret weapon." Rashaad slips his jacket

on. "Mom can't resist Lillian and she thinks her Uncle Kamal is infallible."

"That's because he spoils her." Miya chuckles.

"Leave my favorite niece alone."

They laugh, and I exhale.

"Let's get out of here," Demetrius suggests.

We move toward the doors. The five of us walking in a tight cluster. Rashaad flicks off the lights. The simultaneous conversations start. We stand talking in the parking lot for hours.

"First round's on me," Rashaad offers.

"Bet," I counter. Ebony left to fly back to New York. Then I remember I didn't drive.

"Shotgun!" Miya says, bumping me with her hip. I stumble, but I'm quick on my feet.

It was a game we played as kids, and I take off running for the passenger door of Rashaad's SUV.

"You got those million-dollar feet moving. You better be careful, old man." Q lowers to his bike, slipping his helmet over his head.

"I got you, old man." I shift my weight, spin dodging her grasp.

Rashaad hits the locks and I jump inside. "You gotta do better than that, Baby Miya."

"Cheater!" She climbs in the back seat.

"Where did we go wrong with her?" Rashaad teases, slipping behind the steering wheel.

"That's low." Demetrius shakes his head.

Miya sticks out her tongue. The robust laughter swirls between us and this feels like the old days. I toss the receipt in Rashaad's glove compartment, ready to kick it with my siblings.

The passing hours include five rounds, each of us picking the drink and paying the tab. Q's club is packed with the type of beauty found only in Houston. Black, white, Hispanic. Thick, tall, tempting.

A woman across the room locks gazes with me. She stands, spinning around. Waves cascade down her back and she looks back at me. I see the invitation in her eyes from here.

This is a single man's dream to have financial stability, charm, and a recognizable face. However, tonight none of these things compare to the woman I let slip through my fingers again. I tip my head to the woman and she mouths, *Maybe next time.*

"Yo man…" Q yells over the music, holding up a glass. "Stop thinking and get to drinking."

"All right, man." I lean forward, picking up my shot.

"Four gentlemen and a lady." We touch our glasses. I throw back the shot and then slam the shooter on the table.

Tomorrow, I'll convince Mother. Then I need to identify why Jayda Dallas is wiggling past my defenses and slipping away.

I stop in front of my childhood home, slamming the gear into park with my mouth ajar. She's added to the previous renovations, and everything from the paint to the new front door makes the place unrecognizable. But the thick grass has me wondering if it's Bermuda or Zoysia. The vibrant green makes it appear fake, and the rose bushes…

Definitely with the help of a landscaper. I twist in my seat, scanning up and down the street. It's the best-looking lawn on the block. The others don't come close.

Rashaad said the evaluation of the place had increased. I see why the curb appeal draws me forward. The soft tan paint with the dark brown lining the windows and panels of glass. Are those new gutters too? Then I notice the sign from the homeowner's association designating this as the yard of the month.

Way to go, Mother.

I rest my hands on my waist, taking a deep breath as the sound of flowing water fills the air. It makes me want to sit in one of the rocking chairs on the porch. This is the calm before the hurricane. I know Mother will fight my plan— she's kept us at a distance from Southern Soul, wanting to do it her way. Now, she's sitting on a good business that will be great when I'm done with it. All I need is her keys and a few months.

I open the door, eager to get a closer look. I couldn't sleep and standing right here, right now, is calming. I've had a grand total of five hours of sleep over the past three days. So, between my thoughts about Mother's reactions to my private event, and my growing, and unexpected, curiosity with Jayda, I couldn't sleep. It's like I have some sort of hellified insomnia thanks to these two very different, yet similar women.

I rub my eyes and stoop to run my hands over the grass. I need to get the landscaper details should I buy a place while I'm in town. The hotel is a temporary fix since I don't want to invade on my family's privacy. But hotels remind me of my days of traveling as a professional quarterback. I told myself once I retired, I would spend no more than five days in a foreign bed. I have worked hard enough and amassed enough, financially, to sleep in my own bed, under my own roof. But all of that changed when Mother remarried Kenneth. Her decision had me crossing Houston off my plans and I've floated from city to city, trying to find a place to plant myself. A place to call home.

I yawn behind my hand and glance at my watch. Time to head inside before my brain checks out. I hit the knob on the keychain and gather the groceries.

This morning I'm armed with two plans, thanks to Dean. After tossing and turning, I called him up. We sat on the phone for hours strategizing about how to multiply the success from last night.

I didn't tell him about the part Jayda played or the fact that I had to get her number from Catrina. Dean and Emmitt would laugh me under the table. I shake my head at the irony of it all. The fact is, I have no business pursuing a woman like that, and I know it. I've never been the one to break my own rules, but…

"Everything all right?"

Kenneth. I glance over and he's standing in the doorway with the screen door open.

No lie, this man is the last person I want to see.

The courtesy I show him is on the strength of my mother *only*. He lived his life for twenty years across the country. He missed football games, dance recitals. He never chauffeur Q to gigs, Rashaad to competitions, Demetrius to New York to shop his book, Miya to father-daughter dances.

I did.

Then he pops his ass back up the moment they've graduated. Everyone has amnesia. But not me. I'm not about to step aside and pretend the shit's all good.

Because it ain't.

And it won't be.

I put that on *everything*.

Our gazes hold. Sleep deprived, I don't possess an ounce of patience. This is why I sleep eight solid hours a night without question until I stood between Jayda and that ignorant *boy*.

A man willing to walk away from his woman and children is less than a man in my book. Just like Kenneth.

But this is about my mother and apologizing to her. The happiness of Jackie Montgomery trumps my dislike of the *boy* waiting for my response.

"I'm good." I call back, slamming the truck with my elbow. He closes the door.

I walk up the driveway and peek inside the sweet silver Porsche backed into the space closest to the door. I struggle with the door a little before entering the house.

A warm, unnamable feeling washes over me. I haven't

been home in so long my eyes dart around the room, unsure what I'm looking for. Everything is different.

The floors, the furniture, the curtains.

The warm feeling turns cold. All traces of our lives growing up are gone. The wall of pictures, the lopsided ceramic pot Mother turned into a plant pot. Suddenly, home doesn't feel like home.

I drop my chin to my chest. My heart is pumping. I'd take being anywhere but here alone with Kenneth, however, I kept Dean up all night creating this plan.

Thank God for amazing friends because he helped me get a solid budget for the renovations and relaunching Southern Soul.

The figures from last night and the rough sketches from Dean should smooth things over with Mother, and if that doesn't work, my breakfast spread will.

I need to hurry if I want to have the food ready by the time the others arrive. That I'm still alive shows my mother's not the mother I grew up with, and the rage-filled eyes that haunted me last night moved me to get here early with a trunk full of groceries.

All I need is her agreement to give us three months to turn the place around my way. Fully determined, I walk through the house to the kitchen, ignoring the man I used to call Dad.

But the kitchen isn't how I remember. The dishes, not where they've always been. I open and close cabinets, looking for a skillet. I stop and scan the area beneath the sink when the sound of metal hitting metal startles me.

The skillet.

I look at Kenneth and nod my thanks. I turn on the fire and start washing my hands. I search the area and see the paper towels, and Kenneth unloads the bags.

He smiles.

Food is how we communicate. When we're happy, we eat. When we're sad, we eat. Apparently, we eat when we're pissed too.

I chuckle and start cracking eggs.

"Did you get turkey sausage?"

"Naw, Italian pork."

"Puddin' can't eat it."

"Since when?" I ask.

Kenneth shrugs. "A year, maybe two. I think there's some in the other refrigerator. I'll be right back."

Mother can't eat pork. Not knowing that makes my insides twist. Maybe she told me and I just forgot.

"I found some." Kenneth drops it on the island next to the ingredients for the omelets.

I take it. "Thanks."

"No problem." He passes me an apron. "You take the stove and I'll prep."

"Huh… yeah."

The sound of the knife tapping the cutting board and the fork scraping the inside of the metal bowl seems to eat at the tension between us. He chops vegetables while I start the pancakes.

Memories of the time he and I made Mother's Day

brunch surface. I force the moment back. That was long ago.

It doesn't take us long to have a full spread on the island. Kenneth places a glass pitcher of his signature hand-squeezed strawberry orange juice near the glasses.

I smile, pleased with our work. The front door slams, and minutes later Mother stands looking back and forth between us.

"Hey, baby."

I turn, smiling in her direction, blocking the food. But her greeting is for Kenneth. She kisses him on the lips and then faces me with a frown on her face. I step aside.

"You're early," she says, crossing her arms.

I guess this will be harder than I thought. "I'd like to apologize about last night and talk with you before the others arrive."

"Okay." She sits at the island beside Kenneth. "I'm listening."

"Alone." The word hangs between us.

"Kamal, y'all need to stop avoiding each other."

"I'm not avoiding him. We worked together to make this breakfast. Now, I'd like to speak with my mother alone."

"And I want my husband—*your father*—to stay."

The faint tension ratchets up. Kenneth stands to leave, but Mother stops him.

"I came to talk with you about Southern Soul, not to do this."

"Do what, Kamal? It's obvious your plan is to disregard

my wishes about everything. You know we don't open on Sundays. And you wait until I leave town to open *my* restaurant."

"Our restaurant. Last I checked, there are six names on the books."

"Kamal Frederick Montgomery." Mother stands like a giant with her fists on her hips. I've towered over her since I turned twelve years old, but it never stopped her from commanding the respect she deserves.

This is the mother I know.

"Enjoy your breakfast, Mother." I spin around. "Let's have this discussion after I rest." But she blocks my exit.

"When, Kamal… are you going to stop having a tantrum like a toddler and realize this is *my* choice?" Her words sound like a broken record, repeatedly force feeding me her choice. Then I notice the tears in her eyes.

"Mother, I accept it now."

"Then stay." She walks back to the island, and Kenneth gathers her to him. She hides her face in his chest. Kenneth's arms enclose her until she's almost invisible.

The soft grumbles of Kenneth's whispers in her ear and Mother's muffled cry make me feel two feet tall, or better yet two inches tall.

This was a mistake.

I take a step back and Kenneth's eyes stop me. I'm not looking at my father by my mother's husband. I know the look. I've seen it a time or two in my life and now I can add today. And for the first time in years, my sense of respect for him halts my departure.

He holds Mother's face and kisses her until I'm forced to look away.

"We're listening," Kenneth says, placing a plate in front of Mother. He loads it up with her favorites and pours her a glass of juice. Then he extends a plate to me.

I step forward. But before I can address Kenneth, I wrap my arms around my mother. She sits unmoving. I kiss the top of her braided head and she holds me tighter.

"I'm sorry," I whisper in her ear.

"Just try, Kamal, for me."

I look at Kenneth and take the plate.

It feels forced, but I'm trying. Kenneth asks a few questions until Mother joins the conversation.

I tell them about my reason for opening last night and the numbers. Then I unfold the sketches I printed on copier paper from the hotel business center.

"How are we supposed to cover all of this, Kamal?"

"I'll cover it all. The salaries of the new employees, the renovations if…"

She slides the sketch back in my direction. Her hard-set features tell me she won't approve my request. It's the same face I got when I wanted to attend football camp out of state or I wanted to do things like a regular teenager, not a parent.

"If what, Kamal?" Kenneth asks, taking Mother's hand into his.

"If you give me full autonomy for three months," I request.

"Three months isn't enough time to do all of this and

get solid traction," Kenneth says. "You'll need at least six months."

"I'm not you. I can turn Southern Soul around in sixty if I want."

We stare at each other. One step forward twenty years back.

"I have no doubts that you can do it." He glances over at Mother. "How about you do it in three and use the other three to give Puddin' the time to test-drive retirement?"

Her head whips in his direction.

"You keep toying with the idea. Give Kamal the keys and let's pretend we're old farts," he teases, and she laughs.

"What will I do?" Mother asks.

"Everything. Nothing. Sleep in, hang out with Lillian. It will be up to you. Except you won't interfere with the restaurant."

"Cold turkey?" she asks.

"Cold turkey."

Kenneth is helping me, but I don't like it. I still want to be an asshole because I don't need him to get this done. But I leave my comments to myself while watching them. The sense of wonder in Mother's voice, the calm control in Kenneth's.

A voice in my head whispers, *Look at her*. She's beaming. Shining a light on her wouldn't make her shine any brighter. I've never seen her look like this.

Never.

Actually, the glow in her eyes, the soft smile on her face. I saw her like this at their wedding.

They talk as if I'm not here. This is worse than I thought. Kenneth could be everything my mother missed or the man he was for twenty years—a deadbeat who left his family to fend for themselves.

I clear my throat. "I'll stick around for six months in exchange for the master keys."

"Kamal, promise you'll take care of my baby." Mother gathers my extended hand in hers.

"I'll take care of Southern Soul…" *and you*. Because I still don't trust Kenneth.

"Ma," Q says with the close of the front door.

"We're in the kitchen." Mother walks over to her purse. Then the sound of her keys captures my attention. She lifts my hand and drops the cold key in my palm. "Thank you for breakfast. I need to get to the restaurant—I'm working this morning. I guess I'll tell the others about this change."

I nod, holding the master keys like a lifeline. "I'll be there before the end of the lunch rush."

"Okay." She twists to face Kenneth, then looks back at me again. "Just promise me you won't fire the staff and you'll let me bake on Saturdays."

"Jackie, you're missing the point of retirement." Kenneth leans forward.

Mother rolls her eyes. "This is my retirement and if y'all want to force me into it, I'm doing it my way. That includes baking and spending time with my grandbaby since no one else will give me grandkids."

"Is that all you think about?" Q strolls into the dining room, swiping a slice of bacon from my plate.

I slap at his hand before looking over at Kenneth. "What about you? Will you stick around?"

Q and Mother exchange a look. I feel their stares, but I think it's time to reacquaint myself with my mother's husband. The best way to judge a man is by his actions, and other than the blood running through my veins, I don't know Kenneth or the *real* reason he's back.

"No, I only work at the restaurant to help Jackie. I look forward to getting back to golf and traveling with my lady." He smacks Mother on the backside.

Q chokes on his bacon. "That was gross."

"Gross? I know Mr. Playa, Playa is not trying me this morning." Mother snaps. "How'd you think you got here? Immaculate birth? The stork?"

"Need me to tell you about the birds and bees, little brother?" I laugh behind my hand.

"And don't you start, Kamal. You boys act like I'm not human. Like I don't enjoy the company of my man and…"

"I think I'm going to be sick." Q folds over the back of a chair.

"I'm going to work. Bye, babe." She kisses Kenneth and pops Q on the back of the head in the same swift move.

"Dang. She's still got it." I burst out laughing, dodging her quick hands.

"Love y'all," she calls over her shoulder.

"Love you too," we say in unison.

Q takes the chair beside me and tips his head toward Kenneth, hidden behind the morning paper. I open my hand and show him the keys. His mouth drops open.

It's on! I mouth, then face Kenneth. "So, how's your store doing?"

"Good. I travel back a couple times a month to check in, but my staff is strong." He folds the newspaper, dropping it on the table. "Look, I'll stay out of your way. But if you upset Jackie, then expect to see me."

"Man, whatever. You don't put any fear in my heart." Heat burns my skin. He couldn't wait for Mother to leave to show his true colors. "All I know is you won't see one red cent of her money or touch anything she owns. You'll have to go through me first."

"Kamal, I don't need Jackie's money. We don't have to be on opposite sides."

"What you fail to realize is there's no we with us. I'm here for Mother. That's it."

"But I'm your father, Kamal."

"Since when?" I wait, not out of respect but because he doesn't have shit to say. "You left us. And now that you're back, I'm supposed to pretend we're cool. Well, we're not."

"Kamal, there's more to what happened," Kenneth says. The sincerity on his face is almost convincing, but he's not playing me for a fool.

"I don't give a damn." I stand up, dropping the keys to Southern Soul in my pocket. "Kenneth, stay away from me and I'll do the same. And keep your weak ass threats to yourself. Q, I'll holler at you later."

CHAPTER 10

THE SOFT CARESS of a hand runs down my cheek, soothing the constant tension in my chest. I smile, wrapping my hand around his wrist. A thick chuckle vibrates through my chest, but it's not my own.

How can a heart beat this fast and not explode?

I turn to see his face, eager to taste his lips. I'm stopped short by a trail of slow kisses from my shoulder, up my neck, a moist lick suckles over my pulse.

I moan.

His chest is firmer, and his hold is tighter than I recall. I twist around the tingle between my thighs, wanting to taste him. For him to tell me he'll make it better. The lazy brush of his lips makes me plead for more.

"Kiss me," I demand.

"Jayda."

My eyes open, forcing the aroused air from my lungs. "Kamal?"

It was another dream.

I stare at the ceiling, gripping the damp fabric over my chest. The damn man is haunting me. Each dream feels more real than the last, and this one. The images and sounds of Brett have been replaced by the tatted caramel-skinned man with curly hair.

This has to stop. I heave upward, scanning the dark room and letting my eyes linger over the other twin bed.

Thank God I didn't wake Reese this time. But I don't see the familiar lump of her body beneath the covers.

"Reese?" I snap into mommy-mode and I'm flying across the room. Patting around the unmade bed.

"Yes, Mommy." I twist to see her over my shoulder, standing in the doorway.

"Oh, you scared Mommy." I drop to the bed, relieved. "What are you doing up, honey? What time is it?"

"Time to… go to the zoo." She jumps with her little fists, pushing to the sky. "Zoo… zoo… zoo."

I laugh while she dances around. "Silly girl. Is it Sunday already?"

"Yes, ma'am." She stops brushing her hair from her face. "Mommy, can I be a princess today?"

"You're a princess every day." I reach for my phone to check the time. It's almost nine—I slept through my alarm. Then I see his name.

Kamal called again, and Brett too.

Brett's gone from calling every fifteen minutes to every hour. Now, after being here a month, he's settled on calling once or twice a day.

"Mommy… please."

I clear the missed calls and face my child. "Did you brush your teeth? Wash your face?" She nods and I chuckle. "Such a big girl. Is Auntie Cat still here?"

"Yes, I am, but not for long. Training starts today." Catrina appears dressed in her Southern Soul t-shirt and jeans.

"That's right." I make up Reese's bed.

"What do you two have planned today?"

"It's our inaugural New Memories day. Right, Reesie?"

"Yes, ma'am." She bounces on the bed I just made while I move to make my own. "What time, Mommy?"

I think about it. I need to record a quick video for my channel. Maybe an everyday makeup look. Then it will work double duty. I smile—I'll tackle two tasks at once. I turn back to give her the estimated time when my phone rings.

"I'll get it," Reese offers.

"No, honey. I'll get it." I silence the phone before tossing it aside.

"It's been a month. Don't you think it's time to talk to him?" Catrina says, sitting at the foot of the bed.

It took weeks of watching Netflix, eating junk food, and spending my days in pajamas to decide Reese and I have to make Houston our new home. Like an angel spoke, something Kamal said came rushing back the other day—*Jayda, you make your reality.*

I can do anything I want. By the end of this week I pieced together a budget to get us back on track and get me out of the funk, starting with getting back to what I love my fans.

Brett cheated, no surprise there. He's moved on, it's time I do the same.

"What's New Memories day?" Catrina asks.

"We plan to tour the city and get to know it. To make new memories together in Houston. Today, we're visiting the zoo, grabbing lunch—"

"And ice cream," Reese adds.

"And ice cream," I confirm. "But first I need to record a video. So, we can get out of here. Reese, pick your dress while Mommy jumps in the shower."

Reese is off. The bulk of our clothes are in the closet in the guest bedroom. I watch her until Catrina clears her throat.

"I think you have an admirer."

I roll my eyes, reaching for my planner, and toss it onto the desk. This room is smaller than we're used to, but it's more than I expected. Catrina transformed her entertainment room into a bedroom. But the more I think about it, it seems like the original owners had two master bedrooms minus the walk-in closet, or maybe even an office based on the fixtures and mounts around the room.

Reese and I have our own beds, a desk, a large tv, cable, Wi-Fi, and a gracious host. I set up my mini office on one wall with Reese's area on the other end.

Kamal left his first message the Monday after seeing him at Southern Soul, which told me Catrina gave him my number. I haven't returned his call, and he didn't call again until this morning. I thought he realized I'm not interested. But apparently not.

"Did he tell you to tell me?"

"No, but he asks about your guys every couple of days." She wiggles her eyebrows.

"I'm not looking for a replacement man. I still have to deal with the one I *had*."

"I'm surprised he hasn't popped up."

"It's hard to pop up when you're playing house."

The words sting, and I hate that it still pisses me off. I sit on the floor beside my desk. My makeup supply is low. I need to update my contact information with the PR companies. Yet another thing on my growing list. I select the makeup I plan to use for today's video.

"It's time for us to move forward and I have a list of places for Reese and I to see. I figure we'll be out of your hair in a few months."

"There's no rush, Jay. I have plenty of room and I enjoy having you guys here."

"Thank you," I croak out, overwhelmed with emotions. But I'll get through this. I always do.

I fill Catrina in on my plans. Yesterday I called a few summer programs to find a place for Reese until school starts. She's always gone to a daycare for a few days a week to give me time to record, edit, and handle the business side of my channel.

The first step to obtaining a sense of normalcy is getting time to shuffle through how to relocate my business from

Los Angeles to Houston, and for that to happen smoothly, I have to talk with Brett.

"Until you find a program, you got me. Anyway, I thought you'd want to know the restaurant is hiring."

"Really?" I return to bed and sit beside Catrina.

"Yeah, Miss Jackie turned over management of the restaurant to Kamal for the next six months."

"Huh."

That night at Southern Soul was intense. I could feel the tension between them. But it was the guarded look on Kamal's face that thrust me into action. A part of me felt the need to protect him. I still don't know where that came from, and the more I think about it I think it's because he saved me. Most men would have used that moment to whisper their sweet nothings. But not Kamal.

He called and his voicemail wasn't to ask me out again but he said he had a business proposal. What kind of business could he want with me? He's not in the cosmetics or fashion industry. So, I didn't return his call, and I won't.

"Want me to put in a good word for you? The pay is probably less than what you're used to, but it's consistent and a good place to work."

"No," I say with more force than I intend. "There's no way I can work with Kamal."

Saying his name brings back images of this morning's dream. I ignored his call. But I can't make the dreams stop. And that's after one freaking night. Yeah, there's no way I could work with him.

"You sure about that? Because this morning…" Catrina lays back, draping her hand over her chest.

"Cat!"

"Kamal… Kamal," she moans, tossing her head side to side.

"All right, I got you. Keep playing with me." Her hearty laugh fills the room. "The man won't let me sleep."

She rolls over to her stomach. "Maybe it means something."

"That I'm sleep deprived. I'm done with relationships." I shake my head.

"He's not really the relationship type. He's the have a good time type. The wine and dine to chase your blues away type. But that man must be hypnotic."

"What?" I snap my neck, facing my friend.

"Girl, he's dodging women left and right. They come in just to watch him drink water," she teases, but a part of me thinks it's closer to the truth than she realizes.

Kamal has the swagger of ten men. There's no way he doesn't carry it into the bed.

"They can have it and him. Speaking of men. I left a message for Rashaad yesterday."

"Dang! You said a few months." Her expression changes at the mere mention of his name. She told me about him over years, here and there. It was usually by phone, so all I had to go on was her tone.

"I have to know what I'm working with. I need to find a summer camp for Reese, a car, and save for a deposit on our own place. Unfortunately, my rainy day fund only accounts for a light drizzle, not typhoon."

Catrina bumps into me, laughing, and I drop my head on her shoulder.

"I guess we're more alike than I thought. We're both in the position to take control of our lives. I've been thinking about asking for a promotion at work."

"You should. You've been there forever and if they're hiring new people, your responsibilities will increase." I wonder how much Rashaad has to do with her staying at Southern Soul. She could work anywhere for more pay and yet she stays.

"Kamal has plans to turn the place around."

"You think he'll do it." I sit up.

"Yes. He showed me the plans yesterday. Southern Soul will be a whole new restaurant when he's done with it."

"Huh." I guess the family worked out their differences. I'm not versed in the workings of large families. Since I was sixteen, I survived on my own until Brett and Reese.

"Maybe he could remake you too."

"You keep trying to throw Kamal on me. What about you and Rashaad?"

Now that I have a face to put with the name, all her past stories make sense. I can't help but wonder what's up with the man? And why he can't see the obvious? Catrina is the type of person you want beside you. Just her willingness to open her home to us will leave me forever in her debt.

An image of Kamal flutters across my mind. Another debt I'll never be able to repay. My heart upticks and I swallow around the boulder in my throat. Maybe moving to Houston can do more than get my life on track. What if it could help my best friend too?

Catrina fronts like it's mere attraction, but I'm putting two and two together. She loves Rashaad. And if my hunch is correct, it would explain all the changes she's made over the past few years.

"Our situations are different. You might want to date a little before moving on. I'm ready for more now." She sighs.

"So, why not tell him?"

"We've known each other since we were kids. I was the wild child then, and I guess he never took me seriously. But I didn't either."

I nod. That makes sense. It took becoming a mother to change my life and old ways of thinking.

"That must suck. To make all of these changes and not get the thing you want most. Buying a house, settling down, and you're building a career you love. I always wondered if him getting married was the trigger."

Her back stiffens and her mouth falls open for a second. Then she snaps it closed. "I guess. I had this feeling of, why not me? Then I took stock of my life and realized I was the hookup girl. Not the forever girl."

"But there was something about working and saving to buy this house that proved I could do anything I put my mind to. Not for him, or anyone, but for me. I went from not wanting to look like a loser to building a life I love."

... building a life I love.

God. The words penetrate my chest and slam into my heart. I swipe at the tears, tired of crying.

"What's this about, Jay?" Catrina grabs my hand.

"This week I kept staring at my list. Thinking about the budget. Thinking about what's next for us. Thinking about all the sacrifices I've made to give Reese the life I never had, only to end up in the same space."

"And where's that?"

"A single mother." I drop my head, not wanting to embarrass myself.

"Being a single mother isn't a death sentence. My mother was a single mother. My grandmother was a single mother. I don't want to have children until I'm married, but I'm not scared of being a single mother. I'm scared of…"

"What scares you, Cat?"

We scoot closer together until we sit shoulder to shoulder with our backs against the wall.

"Not being loved." Her voice tapers off, then she continues, "In all the women I've known, I only know one who is truly loved by a man. The right kind, you know?"

I nod. But I wouldn't know "real love" if it walked up and introduced itself. My mother drifted in and out of my life. My grandmother raised me and my grandfather died before I was born. I never knew my father.

"I think that's a tall order. I can't think of anyone."

"When you see it, you'll know it," Catrina says with such authority that my heart knows she's right.

We sit in our own heads. I can front and act like I'm done with relationships. That's just my pride talking. I'm not in love with Brett, but I have love for him. We have a child together, and for her, I would have stayed with him because I thought we were in a committed relationship. But knowing he had an entire life without us severed any chance of us having a family.

The sound of the TV surrounds us, and I look over at Catrina. This is why I love her. She's hard and soft. A riot and the epitome of peace.

"So… how will you find this unicorn of a man if you don't put yourself out there?" I ask.

"I don't need to find him," Catrina whispers. "I need him to see *me*."

"Help him!" Her dismissive gesture rubs me the wrong way. "You can't get the man riding the bench. Do something."

"Like what?"

"Take off that old t-shirt. Put on your pushup bra. Do something with your hair."

"Jay, that's not me. That's you."

"No, Cat. Men are visual. Give him a reason to look twice."

She chews on her bottom lip a little. "I don't know."

"What the hell did you do with my best friend?" I look around, up at the ceiling, and I lift her weathered shirt.

"You know I don't get down like that."

"*Bish* please… you wish." I laugh. "I need to get ready. What's it going to be? Want to be my face for the day?"

"Your face?"

"I need to record a video. It's been over a month since

I've posted. Moving on means getting back to business. So, you ready for a little glam?"

"Fine. But don't put a pound of makeup on me."

"Oh, no you don't. My chair. My rules." I jump up and pull out everything I have. "I think we wear the same shade. Are you okay with me recording?"

"Yeah, maybe I'll be IG famous too."

I laugh. "You're crazy. Come on. Let's do this."

I stand back, making sure I blended everything in. I flick the brush over her cheekbones.

"Girl, hurry. I can't ask the man for a promotion and arrive late for his first staff meeting."

"I'm done." I drop the brush to my desk. Can't have her at the restaurant shining like a Christmas tree. I step back and motion to the mirror.

She gasps, eyes round. "Oh, my… Is that me?"

"Pretty. You need lip gloss, Auntie." Reese offers her strawberry gloss with a smile.

"Tell her what you think, Reesie."

"Gorgeous!" Reese says with a sassy snap of her fingers.

"What are you doing to my niece?"

We laugh.

"What do you think?" I bend to look in the mirror with Catrina.

"I look the same but…"

"Polished."

She nods, batting her subtle eyelash extensions. "I have a half-pound of makeup on my face. Can I sleep in these?"

"No, you don't." I elbow her. "And yes, they'll last about a week to ten days."

She stands up. "What if I sweat? Or he stares at me? I've never had my makeup done like this." She looks back in the mirror. "Have you ever thought about doing this professionally?"

"This is what I do on my channel."

"No, you do your own makeup, which I can't do because I don't have the tools or the skill. I mean doing people's makeup for events, interviews, weddings."

"As in a makeup artist?" I step back, giving her room. "I'm not licensed."

"So?"

"I wouldn't even know where to start."

"I can tell you that." She heads for the door. "Google."

"Ha ha ha… Next time I'll draw your eyebrows up to your baby hairs." I laugh and she rolls her eyes.

"Think about it, smartass."

"Auntie!"

"Sorry, Reesie."

"I can't go back to school. I barely made it out of college alive."

"You and me both. Think about it. Nowadays people know makeup artists by name. And you already have a following. What would it hurt?" She shrugs, then turns to Reese. "Give me a kiss. I need to go."

Catrina darts out of the room while I remove my

memory card from the camera. I've never considered free-lancing as a makeup artist. I never had time or the resources.

"Will you need the car today?"

I blink, processing her question. "No. We can Uber around town and maybe take the train to the zoo. I'll figure it out."

"I don't mind, Jay." Her exasperated expression should make me take the offer, but we've imposed enough. "You're trying to save for your place. Right?"

I nod.

"Then take my car."

"Fine, let me throw on some clothes." My phone rings again and I stare at it, wondering if it's Kamal again. But it's not.

"I think you should at least talk to him. Get it on the table and hear what he has to say."

"You can't stand the man, but now you're rallying for me to talk with him?" I wiggle into some jeans and I can barely breathe. No more ice cream for me.

"I can't stand his *ass*," Catrina mouths, covering Reese's ears. "The best way to start over is with a clean slate."

"I'll call him later. Let's get you to work."

We dash around the house and out the door. Thirty minutes later she jumps out of the car. I glance around for what I don't know since none of the cars are familiar.

"What time do we have to pick you up?" I holler.

"Six. Love you both. Bye, Reesie Piecie." She blows kisses at my baby and my baby throws them back.

"Bye, Auntie!"

I glance at my baby in the back seat in her yellow princess dress and black sneakers. I could go back and get dolled up but we're already out and if we hurry, we could make it to the mall.

"Ready, honey? Where do you want to go first?"

"To the zoo!"

"All right. The zoo it is."

CHAPTER 11

I LIFT my shirt and take a long drag. I smell like grass, the Houston Zoo, and McDonalds fries. But today was the perfect kickoff to our tour of Houston.

We stop by the trolley, and I rent a cart for Reese. She sits inside content with a Happy Meal in her lap while I rush us through the mall with three stops on my list— Sephora, Ulta and MAC. It's important to stay on top of makeup launches.

I walk down the aisle, talking with the staff about the most popular brands over the last month. The beauty advisor names a few, when an idea hits.

"Looks for under $20." I spin around. "Think we can pull a few combinations for every day, office, and glam?"

"Sure." She gathers the makeup, tossing it in a basket.

Reese and I continue our stroll down the aisle, chatting, when I hear my name called.

"Hi, Jayda, I'm a Gem."

I smile and a small crowd gathers around. We talk about trends, affordable products, and selecting foundation. I take pictures for Instagram without a lick of makeup on, and when the small crowd wonders off, I feel exhausted.

"That was fun," Reese proclaims with a smile on her face. They wanted pictures with her too.

"It was, honey. But we need to hurry and get your Auntie from work." We rush to the register when the manager, a sister, steps outside her office.

"Please call me if you host another gathering. We'd love to serve as a sponsor."

"Thank you…" I take the card, shocked. Then I think about my channel. "Would it be possible to get some samples? I'll shout you out."

"I think I can handle that."

I leave the store invigorated, ready to record my new series.

"Mommy, Apple."

"What do you know about Apple?" I stop in front of the all-white store. Reese is climbing out of the cart.

"Can we go in there?" She points, and we don't have time. But she waited patiently for me.

"Five minutes. Okay?" I park the cart and sling the makeup bags on my shoulder.

"Yay."

We enter the store. I'm not much for electronics besides a good camera. Reese stops in front of a table of iPads, and I know exactly what she wants.

She climbs up on the stool and taps around on the

screen. I stare at the price tag and choke. Who pays this much money for a tablet?

Reese picks up the pen. "Look, Mommy."

She points at the icon. It's the same one Kamal had. *Oh, brother.* I watch her and scan the table for something more affordable. That she's fully occupied would seal the deal if the price tag wouldn't wipe out a chunk of my savings.

I think about the account I share with Brett. If he was here, he'd buy it for her. I glance at my phone. Maybe I should call him first. But that means I'd have to talk to him.

I'm torn.

Reese looks up at me, swinging the pencil in her hand. "Mommy, please. Can I have this?"

"Baby, this is way out of our budget. What if we think about Christmas?"

"Okay." The light in her eyes dies. She glances down at the iPad and sets the pencil down, not stopping until she's standing beside me.

"We'll put it on the top of your Christmas list," I say as we walk back to the cart. "You ready for your ice cream?"

"No, ma'am." She climbs inside the cart and I feel like a loser. I know kids aren't supposed to get everything they want. But any other day, any other time, she'd have that iPad without a second thought.

We start back across the mall toward the car. I glance down at my baby and I'm crushed. I stoop beside her.

"Reese, honey, if we get that tablet that's it. Nothing else until Christmas." I count the months across my fingers, but she's already bouncing up and down. "Do you understand?"

"Yes, ma'am."

"You have to take care of it, it's not a regular toy." She nods in the way that makes my soul happy. "No throwing it around… No getting it wet."

"I will, Mommy. Thank you… thank you."

"We haven't bought it yet." I huff. "Come on, let's go get it."

We rush back to the store. The mall is about to close, and I have to get back to Southern Soul. The Genius makes quick work of getting the iPad from the back. He asks for my form of payment and I remove the hidden card from my wallet.

He scans it, and his eyes jumps between mine and the little device in his hand.

"Everything okay?" I motion for Reese to calm down as she wiggles around.

"I'm sorry. The system shows this card as stolen."

My heart drops. "Stolen? I assure you it's not stolen. My name is on it. Try it again."

He does and hands the card back. "Maybe there's a mix-up. Do you have another form of payment?"

I look down at Reese and at the card. Then it hits me. *Brett.*

"Just a second."

"We're closing in ten minutes."

"I only need five." I tap his picture because like an idiot, I still have him in my favorites. I hear half a ring.

"Ahhh… now you call."

"Did you cancel my card?"

"Hello to you too, Jayda." His cheerful tone makes me stop in the middle of the store. I stare at the phone. This man has lost his mind.

"Brett, answer the *fucking* question. Did you cancel my card?" I feel lightheaded, so I take a deep breath, using the closest table for support. "What kind of man are you?"

"Come home and your problem's solved."

"Whose home? The one you're sharing with Becky?"

His gut laugh plants a seed of hate for him. Then I feel her arms wrap around my waist. I glance down at my baby.

Thoughts clash. The irresponsible option is to buy it, but the total will wipe out a third of my savings. I'll need to either find a job or get some brands willing to pay me directly to create content to replace the money. That will hurt. But not more than telling Reese she can't get the iPad.

I pull out my wallet and give the man the card for my savings account and turn my attention back to Brett.

Why would he want to put me in this situation? It's not like he's hurting for money. *Damn.*

My hand aches with the tight hold I have on the phone. His actions are yet another slap in the face. Yet another truth of who he is and how much I overlooked for the sake of financial security. Now, this jerk reports my card from *our* checking account, stolen.

I shake my head, wanting to call him everything but a child of God. I want to tell him to rot in hell, to forget my number, to forget he ever met me. But for my child's sake, I can't lose my cool again. Not in front of her, because a part

of me still hopes that he'll see how important our relationship is for her stability.

She squeezes me tighter and I let her love ooze through
me, calming the simmer beneath the surface. I glance down
and find her inquisitive eyes waiting. She's depending on
me, and I won't let her down. I can't afford to.

"Goodbye, Brett." I smile and disconnect the call, then
drop the phone in my purse. Reese squeezes tighter. I close
my eyes, resting my cheek on her fresh cornrows.

"Mommy?"

I open my eyes. "Yes, honey."

"Can I dance?"

I stand upright. An elated smile spreads across her face
and the rays of her sunshine breaks through the dark clouds
of doubt hovering over me. To push them away, I nod my
approval and she doesn't miss a beat.

Reese spins around with her arms wide, yellow fabric
swishing left and right. Her happy dance is infectious,
taking on a shuffle and a complicated twist in the air while I
laugh.

"Dance with me, Mommy."

I give it my best, I add a little poplock to it and she tries
it too. I rock my hips to inaudible sound of my baby's
happiness. I'd buy her a million iPads for this dance of
victory.

We will be all right. Just the two of us. I kiss the top of
her head with a fresh surge of courage.

The Genius returns with a giant white bag. I stop
gasping for air.

"You're all set." He extends the bag and I motion to Reese.

"Thank you," she sings.

"Hold it tight, honey."

"Yes, ma'am." I help her adjust the straps on her shoulder.

We leave the store. "Let's hurry—your Auntie Cat is waiting for us."

She climbs in the cart and we're running across the mall to get to Southern Soul.

"Can we have chicken and waffles?" Reese asks while I buckle her in her booster seat.

"I don't think they're open today. Maybe next time."

She nods. "Can I play with my iPad?"

"Yes, sweetie." I sit behind the steering wheel.

Thank God I kept my private savings account to myself. I shake my head, still in shock that he canceled my card. What a fucking… *Wait, our joint account.*

My shaking hands fumble with my phone, swiping until I see the bank app icon. I tap it, holding my breath.

"Mommy…"

"Just a second, honey."

I log in, praying all he did was cancel my card. He wouldn't… He wouldn't…

He did.

The balance is zero. The swishing sound from my lungs emptying fills the car and my phone slips from my sweaty hands. I open the door and hop to the ground, searching the floorboard for my phone.

Not a single cent.

Not a single fucking cent.

He can't do that. Can he?

"Honey, I'll be right here." The quivering tone of my voice sounds like desperation.

"Yes, ma'am." She doesn't look up for the glowing device as I dial Brett's phone.

I close the door behind me, pacing beside the car. A text message comes through. I don't stop to check it.

"Brett, you motherfucker! How could you?" I try to take a deep breath, but it's lodged in my throat. "How will I take care of our daughter? Tell me that. How? While you're playing house!" My voice echoes through the near vacant parking lot.

A text message chimes in my ear.

"Call me back. I swear or you'll wish…." I spin around, trying to compose myself. "Call me. Tonight."

I get in the car and slam the door. The sinking feeling contradicts the cadence of my heart. I grip the steering wheel at ten and two, dropping my head with my eyes squeezed shut.

"Mommy…"

"I'm fine, honey," I lie. Another text message chimes, and I gather the phone in my hands.

Where are you? Everything okay? Should I get a ride home? Catrina's text messages keep rolling in. Stopping with, *Call me.*

I respond, *On the way.*

That I'm driving is probably not safe. Not when everything is a blur. All I can see and hear is: *What now?*

There are only three cars in the parking lot. Catrina is waiting in front, talking with Rashaad. Now, that puts a smile on my face. I park, ready to turn over the wheel.

"Mr. Kamal, look!" Reese shouts and my head darts to her and then outside the car. He's locking the front door, talking with the others.

"Honey, he can't hear you with the windows rolled up." Then I see him waving. Reese giggles, waving back. I lower the window and she leans forward.

"Look, Mr. Kamal."

Kamal doesn't stop until he's kneeling beside the car next to her window. "What's that?"

"A apple."

He chuckles. "An iPad."

"Uh, huh, an iPad." She corrects. "But it doesn't work."

"Why not, honey?" I ask, confused.

She shrugs.

"Let me check it out." Kamal offers, and Reese passes the device out the window. "Ahhh I see what's wrong. You need to buy the app." He taps around. "You can start with this and I'll tell your mom which one to get."

"Thank you," she sings, retrieving her iPad.

"You're welcome. Hey, Lillian, come and meet my new friend Reese." Kamal rests an arm on the car and our eyes hold for a moment. "It's nice to see you, Jayda. How are you?"

I look away, unable to hold his intense gaze.

"She's sad," Reese offers.

And my head snaps back. "I'm not sad, honey."

"What do you think we can do to make her happy?" Kamal asks Reese, but his eyes are on me.

"Pizza. Pizza makes us happy."

Kamal's head falls forward in a chuckle. "My kind of ladies. How about you ladies join us for dinner?"

"Yay!" Reese cheers and Lillian joins her.

"Reese, honey, we can't impose." And I can't afford to buy another thing until I fix this problem. Not even pizza.

"It's not an imposition. I insist, since I can't get you to return my phone calls." His eyes see right through me and he won't let me go. In my current state I'm liable to cry through the entire night or spill my guts and both are equally embarrassing. "Jayda, it's cheap buffet pizza. You'll probably demand a date because they give you more sauce than cheese."

The corner of his mouth tips up and I feel butterflies. But his statement has me curious.

"Then why go?"

"Lillian loves the arcade."

"You'll love it too, Reese," Lillian adds, and the two of them talk.

Kamal walks around the car and squats near my window. "Want to talk about it?"

"Talk about what?"

"What's on your mind?"

I twist in my seat to see him better. His dress shirt is open at the collar with complementing dark pants. All seems exactly the way we parted except his eyes. "You look exhausted."

"I am. It seems running a restaurant is a twenty-hour ordeal. Between the staff and renovating, I'm constantly moving."

"How did the orientation go?"

He laughs and I lean against the door with my chin on my arm. This type of conversation is easy. Nothing like the one I expect when Brett returns my call.

"Man, they went through a box of dishes. But it's a step in the right direction. I guess I expected it with a new wait-staff." He stands and opens my door. "Grab your stuff and I'll drive."

"I didn't say yes."

"But you will. There's more room in my SUV. The girls can talk and you can tell Mr. Kamal all about your day."

"Oh really?" I laugh.

"Yeah. Does she need a car seat?" He walks back around the car to Reese. I guess I'm going for pizza.

"She has a booster." I pop the trunk and toss my makeup bags inside. Then I look over at Catrina.

"We'll see you guys there," Rashaad calls out to Kamal.

"Power off, Reese." I reach for the device and put it in my purse. "Thank you, honey."

The girls jump inside, talking like they've known each other a lifetime. They start with the princess dress and move to cartoons when I tune them out.

Kamal climbs inside the SUV. The vehicle shifts under his weight. He's not a big guy and from the way the fabric clings to his body, he's rock solid. His head falls back for a second.

"Kamal…"

His head rolls in my direction. He rewards me with a toe-curling smile, and I wonder if I'm making a mistake. Kamal has my Spidey senses ringing the alarm because this man is fine from the top of his head to his designer shoes. The type of fine that has trouble guaranteed with every smile, and I've had more than my share of trouble. Hence my empty bank account.

"I'm starting to think this isn't a good idea," I whisper because for the first time in over a month Reese has someone to play with and I am hungry, even for bad pizza, and after the drama with Brett I don't want to be alone blaming myself for yet another bad decision.

"I just want to kick it with you." He glances into the back seat. "I'll feed my little ladies and return you home safe and sound."

"Fine," a face forward fastening my seatbelt, "but for the record, I can't date you."

Kamal turns over the engine. "Okay."

"I'm serious, Kamal."

He chuckles and says nothing more. I keep one ear on the girls and my eyes on my phone, checking every app.

Chase.

Capital One.

Discover.

Brett closed all of my accounts. I jump at the sound of

doors opening and closing. The girls play on the sidewalk, and Kamal waits outside my door.

"Lillian, stay where I can see you."

"Yes, sir."

He leans with his back against the SUV. "I'm a good listener."

"Why? Because you have a thing for single mothers?" I glance at the back of his head. He must think I'm a nutcase. That he's seen it all makes me question his sanity.

"Far from it." Kamal looks over his shoulder, holding me captive. "But I'm starting to think I have a thing for you."

"Another day, another time, maybe. But my life is falling apart at the seams and I'm determined to hate the male species."

"Is that right?" He faces me. "That sounds like a challenge to me."

"No, Kamal. It's not a challenge, but me being brutally honest. So, you can stop the flirting and calling." I drop my phone back in my purse and wait for his response. "Why are you looking at me like that?"

"Because you're beautiful."

"Now I know you're lying. Get me out of this truck. I'm hungry."

He opens the door. "I'm not lying."

"Kamal, I have no eyebrows."

"Okay… see I noticed that," his finger flicks back and forth, "and I didn't plan to bring it up but—"

I burst out laughing.

"What?" The man turns up his palms.

I can't stop laughing. Tears roll down my face and I can't breathe.

"See, isn't that better?" His face softens, and he opens my door. "I plan to keep a smile on your face. Nothing is that bad, Jayda."

I'm in trouble.

"Ready for some basic pizza and some bangin' margaritas?"

"Lead the way."

I believe him and I shouldn't. Men know how to put on a front to get what they want. Tonight I'm only here for the pizza. I follow them inside but before I cross inside, I turn my cellphone off. I've had enough drama for one day.

CHAPTER 12

"Cheap pizza and margaritas from a slushy machine. You sure know how to treat a lady." Jayda sits back with her legs extended across the bench. Catrina and Rashaad came and left. I'm glad Jayda agreed to stay a little longer.

"And tokens… you can't forget the tokens." I laugh, unloading the fake gold tokens with enough noise to make them laugh.

"Get some, Reese." Lillian jumps up, sliding handfuls of the tokens into a plastic cup. "We put them in the machines and play games. And we get tickets for toys and candy over there."

Reese looks over at the little shop in the corner with glass cases filled with all the cheap stuff kids like. Then she looks to her mother for permission. Jayda nods her approval and the two run off to play.

Lillian and Reese talked more than they ate, and now it's game time.

"She's a sweetheart." I sit back and stretch out. The weight of my day is heavy, but tonight makes it worth it.

"Thanks. I can't ask for a better kid. What about you, Mr. Uncle of the Year?"

"Well, what can I say?" I pop my collar and Jayda laughs from her gut. It took two margaritas and more cinnamon rolls than I could count to warm her up. Few women would find a place like this fun. "How are you adjusting to H-Town?"

"I'm not. I've successfully become acquainted with every flavor of Blue Bell Ice Cream."

"And your favorite?"

"Butter pecan. My jeans aren't happy, but I think they added a slice of heaven in that ice cream." She plays with her straw before turning to face me. "It's been a month and I'm numb, I guess."

"Give yourself time. Marriages experience rough patches. Maybe one day you'll be able to look back and laugh."

"Marriage?"

"Yeah."

"We're not married."

The room falls into a haze. I take in her features to see if she's joking. "Either you got a divorce in a month or you're lying."

"Neither. We're not married. I considered us engaged, although he never really asked me. I sort of assumed…" Her words trail off.

"So, he's just your boyfriend?"

"My ex-boyfriend and Reese's father."

"Huh…" I struggle for what to say next.

Keeping my distance for a month was a test of my will. The only reason I called was to offer the job because I don't mess with married women. But I couldn't stop my thoughts from worries about her and Reese. How they were doing? How were they adjusting? Had her man came to Houston to patch things up?

I drop my legs, sitting in front of her, not sure how I plan to move forward.

"What about you? How are you adjusting? Catrina said you're turning the place around."

"I'm a month in and we've barely scratched the surface of what I want to get done."

"What's on your agenda?" She folds her hands.

"You're not interested in Restaurant 101."

"Says who? I'm not the most business savvy, but the thought of owning something to pass on to the next generation fascinates me."

"But you run your beauty channel business."

"I do, but it's not the same thing. I record videos and post them. There's a whole other world behind it that stifles me."

"In what way?" I ask.

"The business stuff. Contracts. Brand deals. Collaborations."

"All that takes is a lawyer and an excellent manager. Do you have a manager?"

"I don't think so."

"That's a bad answer." I glance over, checking on the girls and see them at the Wackamole machine. Then I focus on Jayda's confused expression. "Either you do, or you don't. Which is it?"

"I never signed a contract, but Milton said Brett's my manager. He made a few calls for me and connected me with a few brands. But we didn't sign a contract."

"It sounds like you need a lawyer."

"A lawyer…" She clears her throat and fiddles with her straw. She's nervous again.

"I could refer you to one."

"Thanks, but I'll work it out. So, how does the whole family business work? Do you all split the responsibilities?"

"Are you changing the subject?"

Her eyes round and she snaps her mouth closed. Our gazes hold until she answers, "Yes, please."

"There's nothing wrong with just talking with someone to explore your options."

"I realize you're used to getting your way. But there's nothing wrong with me wanting to keep my personal business personal."

"Fine."

"Thank you."

We sit quietly, assessing each other. She shifts from quiet as a lamb or vicious as a wolf, and I won't see her beyond tonight if I don't change my approach.

"Southern Soul is owned equally by my mother and siblings and myself. She handled pretty much everything until last month."

"When you took over?"

"Yes." I sit back. "I'm working to… I guess revive it and get people back in the doors, like they used to."

"Is that why you guys were… tense?"

"You remember that?"

"It's hard to forget."

"That's part of the reason."

"And the other part?"

I sigh, shifting in my seat. "We've been off since our parents remarried."

"Most kids would love that."

"I'm not most kids."

"Huh…" She takes a drink of her margarita.

"What does that mean?"

"It's interesting. You're an adult. All of your siblings are adults. It'd think you'd be happy to see your parents together."

"I'm not."

She nods her head without breaking eye contact. "Then how did you get the keys to the restaurant if you object to how she wants to live her life?"

My mouth drops open, and I close it. Then I tell her everything from before I left from Los Angeles to the time she and I stood on the breezeway of Southern Soul with my family. It feels good to lay it all out.

Jayda nods but doesn't says a word. The more I share, the more her face twists, painted with her displeasure.

"What?"

"Nothing." She drains her glass, sliding to the end of the bench.

"I tell you all of that and you have nothing to say?"

"I asked a question, you answered."

I search her eyes. The icy glare staring back surprises me. "What are you thinking, Jayda?"

She swallows and looks over at the girls, then back at me. "I think you're a bully."

Jayda walks away and I follow.

"How can you say that? I'm protecting my mother."

"Sounds like someone needs to protect her from you."

"From me? I'm not the one staying around for her money."

"How do you know that?"

"Because I know Kenneth."

"That's what you call your father, Kenneth?" She grips her hip and her beautiful eyes narrow.

"That's his name."

"Unbelievable." She stomps off, and I'm on her heels. I stand, watching as she inserts a token into the classic Asteroids game.

I lean against the machine, walking a fine line. For some reason, I care about what she thinks.

"Jayda, help me see what you see." I glance over at her, and I swear I see rage in her eyes. "I've protected my mother and my family since I turned thirteen years old. As a man, and her son, I can't sit back and watch Kenneth weasel his way back into her life."

"Forcing her to turn over the keys to her restaurant—"

"I didn't force her." I fight to control the anger rising inside me. "Why does everyone see me as the bad guy? I wasn't the one that walked away. He did."

Jayda faces me. "Kamal, your actions forced her to choose between her children and her husband. What about what she wants?" She crosses her hands over her chest and I see the tears in her eyes.

"Let's step over here." I guide her away from the girls. "We'll be right over here."

I turn her body to face me with the girls in sight. "What's this about?" She shakes her head, but I'm not backing down. "Tell me, Jayda. You have me spilling my guts. Level with me because I know this isn't just about my family drama."

She swallows and takes a deep breath. "Brett is trying to do the same thing to make me return to LA."

"What do you mean?" She doesn't miss the growl in my tone. "Do I need to fly back and talk with him?"

"No. This is exactly what we're talking about. Stop trying to force people to do things your way."

"What if my way is better?" I tease to see her smile.

Her head snaps in my direction. "You really are a piece of work."

We share a laugh before she drops her head.

"Is that why you won't see a lawyer?" I ask.

"Brett is trying to use his money to get me back."

"Is it working?"

Jayda shakes her head. "I'm not going back."

I pray it's true. There's something about her that makes

me want to know more. But the thought of her ex-man waiting in the wings doesn't sit right with me.

"What's different this time?"

"I'm different. Working and taking care of our needs isn't easy, but it's not as hard as I thought." She sits on the edge of the table watching the girls play. "It's like walking into that party and seeing him with her was the picture I needed to close that door."

"And that's why you left?"

"At the time, no. I was shocked and embarrassed. I was running from the reality I tried to ignore."

"And now?" I ask.

"Now, I understand that he was always that man. He didn't change. I did. That night he showed me who he really is, and I've decided that's not what I want for my life. And me trying to force him to comply with my expectations is as much at fault as his cheating. We both carry some part in the breakdown in our relationship."

"What will you do now?"

"Eventually I hope we'll find a middle ground for Reese's sake. She deserves it." Jayda stands back at the video game.

I watch her play for a while, thinking about all she shared and how I'm handling the business transition with my family. I see myself as protecting my mother, but what if she feels the same as Jayda? There's only one way to find out.

"Mommy, look!" Reese calls out, shaking a handful of tickets in the air.

Jayda claps and I smile at the sight.

"Head over to the ticket counter. I'll be right over." The girls skip off with their paper tickets waving in the air. I stop behind Jayda, placing my hands on either side of her. She slowly faces me.

"Thank you for listening." The scent of her fruity breath makes me pull closer.

"Let me take you out."

She searches my eyes, and when she looks away, I gently turn her chin.

"I'm not ready to date."

"As friends."

Her mouth twists and I suddenly have a taste for margarita. I step closer. The heat from her body fills me with warm desire.

"You and I can't be friends."

"Yes, we can. We've successfully navigated our first disagreement. We've had pizza, drinks, and tokens. I've been a perfect gentleman."

"Is that what you call this?" She wiggles and her breast brush my chest. The fire in her eyes makes me close that last inch. Not caring that we're in the middle of an arcade.

"Mommy, can I have candy?" Reese calls out.

"One piece," Jayda answers and her mouth tips toward mine.

Our lips touch and I exhale. Playfully nibbling on the lips that teased me all night. The tension building since the first moment we met collides into a perfect kiss. Her hot little hands run up my chest, circling my neck and her sweet tongue fills my mouth with the flavor of mangos.

"What about one Twizzler and one lollipop?" Reese asks.

I force myself to step back. But I want more.

"Mommy?"

"One or the other, Reese," she croaks out, her hand travels to her lips and I know I'm not alone.

"We'll take it slow," I offer.

"I didn't say yes."

"But you will…" I gather her hand in mine and lead her to the ticket counter, plotting on the next time I can taste her sweet lips.

THE GIRLS TALK in the back seat, and my mind keeps replaying our kiss.

"Kamal, is Southern Soul still hiring?"

I wait until I stop at a light to look over. "Yes. Why, you know someone who's interested?"

"I might. But I can only work shifts opposite Catrina."

"I need a hostess." The thought of having her around makes my long days seem more bearable.

"You gave Catrina the promotion? I knew you were a smart one."

I laugh. "So, you're asking for the job?"

"No, I'm asking for an interview."

"I can interview you right now." My eyes slide over her body and stop when I see her wagging finger.

"No, sir. I'm asking for help, but not like that. I'll come to the restaurant in my interview clothes, like everyone else."

"But you're not everyone else."

She stares at me and I hate the shadows of the night that keep me from seeing her facial expression.

"Kamal, we're just friends."

"Uh-huh, as long as you don't kiss all of your friends the way you kissed me."

"See…" She snorts a laugh, shaking her head.

"I was innocently standing when you were all over me. I knew you couldn't resist me." I laugh. "I had to remind you there were innocent eyes in the room."

"You keep on…" she teases back.

"You don't have to ask me twice."

"Hush, man, and drive." She faces forward, I don't need a light to see her smile. I hear it in her voice. "When do I need to come by?"

"You can *come* any time."

"I try to give you a shot and you're about to blow it."

"Blow it? Really?" I howl, struggling to keep my eyes on the road.

"Kamal."

"I'm just playing. My bad." I look back at the girls. They're not paying us any mind. Thanks to a cheap Slinky. "Just come by tomorrow since Catrina's off. Then if it all works out, you can talk with her about the schedule."

"Thank you, Kamal." The slight quiver in her voice

captures my ear and my eyes. "I need to ask you something and keep it straight with me."

"That's the only way I roll."

I cut the engine of the SUV in front of Rashaad's place. The faint snores from the back seat give us a moment of privacy. I turn off the headlights and lean into the door to face her with the taste of her kiss still lingering on my lips.

"Are you expecting something for your help?"

I laugh, staring out the windshield. The shit isn't funny. Here I am feeling this woman and she thinks I'm trying to smash.

"Is that what you think about me, Jayda? That I'd take you for some fake ass pizza and expect to have sex with you?"

"Don't curse at me, and I didn't say sex."

"You don't have to." The porch light flicks on and I see Rashaad walking in our direction.

I climb out and pick up Lillian without disturbing her restful sleep.

"Uncle Kamal does it again," Rashaad says, taking his heavy bundle from my arms.

"They had a blast. Wait, let me get her bag of junk," I joke, ducking back inside and I see her bag of trinkets and candy on the floor.

"Jayda, we'll have to plan a playdate with the girls," Rashaad offers.

"Reese would love that. She doesn't know any kids her age here. I have your number. I'll call and set something up, maybe a sleepover."

"That's cool." Rashaad takes the plastic bag from me and throws a wave back at Jayda. "I'll see you Saturday."

"Oh yeah, that might change if I start a new job." She glances at me.

"Uncle…"

"Yes, love." I kiss Lillian's head.

"Can Reese come to the spa?"

"We'll talk about it later. Goodnight, love you."

"Love you too," Lillian whispers.

"Tell Uncle K 'thank you.'"

"Thank you, Uncle. I had fun." Her eyes dip closed. "You're the best uncle ever."

"That's what I like to hear. I need you to tell your Uncle Q and Uncle D that." We laugh at the sound of her soft snores.

"Quit trying to get her in trouble." Rashaad pats my back and turns to the house. "Night."

"Goodnight." I watch them leave before returning to my seat. The space between us is tense.

I stare at Jayda. I can tell she wants to say something. Her apprehension irritates me. My night with her was refreshing. It's been a while since I had this much fun with a woman.

No one complained. The kids behaved. We laughed, talked, and even kissed. That was unexpected, and her lips were softer than I imagined.

I thought we clicked.

But what else should I expect from a woman who leaves her man in the middle of the night? She had just cause, but it's another sign of her relationship—whether she's married or not.

It's a sign.

I need to let go of this unexplainable desire to know everything about her. That I let it get this far shows I'm not in my right mind. The woman has a man and a child. Those are some red—*fucking*—flags.

That man is probably chilling with his other lady, giving Jayda space to cool down. When he's ready, he'll spit a little game and she'll run right back to LA like nothing ever happened.

Red flag number three.

"Kamal. I'm sorry if…"

"Nah, don't worry about it. We're good." I turn over the engine. "Let's get you two home."

CHAPTER 13

KAMAL WAS a perfect gentleman last night. *Again*. And my reaction to this uncontainable attraction between us makes me feel like a total bitch for pushing him away. I've sort of shoved every man, including Kamal, into the Brett category.

Frustrated, I yank off the coral blouse.

Catrina stops in the doorway. "Want to talk about it?"

I settle on the last blouse I have after changing a million times, which should be impossible since I only have a single suitcase of clothes. But I want to look perfect today.

"Brett cleared our bank account and reported my bank card stolen."

Her eyes register her shock. "I told you he was a no good loser. What kind of man would leave you to care for his child with no money? Can he do that?"

"I can't stop him. It was his money."

She clears a spot on the bed and sits down. "But it's a joint account?"

"It's the account he used to give me a monthly allowance to cover our expenses. He gave it and he took it back."

"That's a bitch move."

"Yeah, well, it worked. I have less than five thousand dollars. Summer camp is two grand a month. I don't have the new makeup releases to record fresh content and he knows it."

I sit at the vanity, opening an eyeshadow palette, prepared to spill my guts.

"What makes this situation worse is I built my plan on increasing my income with brand deals. However, those deals came through Brett. So, not only did he clear out the account, but he's suffocating the possibility of me earning more through PR companies and product placements."

I laugh, but nothing about my life at this moment is funny. "I have to give it to him. He's trying to force my hand, and he has successfully knocked me flat on my ass."

"Call him. Get a lawyer. Fight him."

"With what? My good looks?" I stare at her. "Brett doesn't play ball anymore, but he has enough money to drag it out."

"What if you talk with his mother?"

"I thought about that too. Minnie and I are cool, but not that cool. We're amicable because of Reese."

"So, what do you need? Makeup? Camera equipment? I got you if it means you don't go back to that jerk."

"No, right now I will retire my makeup brushes until I get back on my feet. So, I'm getting a j-o-b."

"I don't think moving away from what you love is the answer, Jay. And how are you going to work a regular job with Reese?"

"Kamal agreed to interview me today for your old job. He okayed me working opposite your shifts. That will have to do until I figure something else out. By the way, congratulations."

"Thank you." She beams. "I was wondering when you were going to mention him. How'd it go last night? Y'all were all booed up."

I shake my head. "I'd be surprised if he doesn't kick me out of the restaurant today."

"Why would he do that?" Catrina asks.

"Because I asked him if he was helping me to sleep with me."

"And?" She laughs, stretching out alongside my clothes.

"We went back and forth. I think I offended him." I turn around and face her. "I called last night to apologize, but he didn't pick up."

"What made you ask him that?"

"I don't know. He was just being extra nice."

"Since when is it a crime to be nice, Jay?"

"It's not a crime. I just don't know what to do with it." I turn back to the mirror. I can't let myself get caught off guard again.

Brett's betrayal exposed parts of me I thought had died. I knew he did his dirt, but I never questioned my place in his life, that Reese and I would be provided for. Him cutting me off, financially, is the last act for us and I'd be a fool to willingly let myself depend on another man. That and the chunk it took from my pride. There's a difference between walking away and getting replaced.

"I want to do this on my own. Kamal already helped me back in LA. Now he's offering to give me get a job. I don't want it to turn around and bite me in the ass."

"Kamal's not like that. He seems to enjoy a variety of women, but he's not the snake type."

"Why do you think that is? He's a cool guy, and he's great with kids. He's loaded. He must have a woman in every city."

"He might." She shrugs. "But I think the divorce rattle them all. Kamal and Q avoid monogamous relationships. Miya and Rashaad fell fast and hard for the wrong people. It's like their desire for love left them blind."

"And Demetrius?"

"He lives his life through his books."

I nod. "What about their mother? Kamal said I reminded him of her."

"You'll meet her. Miss Jackie and Momma were best friends. Miss Jackie is one of the strongest women I know. She stayed by my side through everything when my mother passed away. I'll never forget it." Catrina quiets with a serene look on her face. "What else did he say?"

I walk over and grab my shoes. "Nothing really, just that he believes I'm capable of running a business."

"Huh..." A slow smile spreads across her face.

"It's not like that."

Then I remember our kiss. I brush a hand over my lips, tingling with the memory of his touch. How could a stranger kiss me like that? It was warm and familiar, like he'd kissed me a million times. I exhale and focus on finding my shoes to keep Catrina from reading my thoughts.

"Aaahhhh… What was that? What are you not telling me?" She flies across the room.

"I can't tell you."

"Oh, that means it's good. Come on, Jay tell me. I'm your best friend."

"Tell *you*? No. No. And hell no. Cat, you can't hold water. And I've already accused the man of wanting to sleep with me."

"He does. Kamal's eyes could have set the place on fire last night."

"See. This is why I can't tell you." I slip past her and sit in the chair to put my heels on.

"Oh, come on, Jay. My life is boring, and you're withholding the juicy details. Besides, who am I going to tell? I don't talk to anybody but you." Her empty hands open, reminding me of Reese.

"Your trifling butt would go straight to Kamal."

"What did you guys do? Get a little nookie at the pizza parlor?" Catrina squeals.

I'm going down, like Mary J, because she's not about to let this go. I know because if we swapped places, I'd demand to know every tantalizing detail.

"What?" I ask.

"You did! Just nasty."

"No, I didn't have sex with him. Didn't we just put that to rest?" I stand to my feet, inspecting myself in the mirror. "We kissed."

"You kissed Kamal?"

I glance toward the living room where Reese is watching a movie. "Please tell the entire world, why don't you?"

"What kind of kiss? A kiss like…" She smacks the back of her hand. "Like you're my little sister. Or did you get all those lips?" Her eyes sparkle like diamonds and I can't believe I'm having this conversation with her.

That's a lie.

Catrina is a freak waiting to get buck wild. In her pre-I'm-in-love-with-Rashaad days, I lived for her wild sex tales.

Me? All I've had is basic, boring—we're doing it because it's been a while—sex.

Nothing in my life ever compared to all the nasty freaky borderline porn stuff she's done. Therefore, I leave the sex conversations to her. I had absolutely nothing to tell.

That's probably why Brett was sexing everyone else but me.

"Cat, please don't say anything."

"I won't."

"No. Promise me because you said it too fast."

"I… won't… tell… everybody… that *you* kissed Kamal. Okay?" She pops her tongue.

Oh hell, she's going to tell. My face is on fire. I should have taken that kiss to my grave.

"So, tell me, Jay, was it PG-13 or Rated R?"

"NC-17. But..."

Catrina runs in a circle like a dog chasing its tail. I want to hide behind my hands, but I can't mess up my makeup.

Why did I tell her? My only solace is knowing she won't tell *everybody*. However, she's known to go directly to the source, and that's the last thing I need.

This is why people question our friendship. Catrina's the life of the party—loud and extra to keep the laughs rolling. While I'm pretty to look at but I'm digging to have more going for myself than my face.

Which makes last night an anomaly. Not once did I care about my lack of makeup or my favorite leggings. I had a great time. Kissing Kamal seemed right.

I laughed and had more cinnamon rolls than I needed. I could take another night like that with zero pressure and maximum fun. For a few hours, I forgot my ex cleaned out my bank account and that I'm jobless and homeless. And it had nothing to do with that old pizza parlor and everything to do with Kamal.

"Listen, Jay, whatever you do, don't tell those girls at the restaurant. Those new chicks are pulling straws to see who will bag him first. Did he ask you out?"

"He did, but that was a onetime occurrence. I'm still trying to get rid of the Brett. Speaking of which..." I slide the promise ring off my finger and drop it in my purse. That chapter of my life has ended.

"You sure about that?" Catrina asks.

"About taking off his ring? Absolutely."

"No, about kissing Kamal being a onetime occurrence." She looks from my bare ring finger to my face.

"Yes, Catrina. He barely spoke to me last night." But what if he asked me again? Would I say yes? Maybe.

"He will when he sees you in that dress." The assurance in her voice makes me stare at myself in the mirror.

The extra time I spent on my hair and makeup shows. I'm wearing my favorite pencil skirt. It accents my curves and makes me appear a few inches taller. Paired with this quarter length sleeve top, I have an executive appeal.

"Stop being messy, Cat. I need a job and he needs a hostess. That's it." I fluff my hair. "Mind if I take your car?"

"No. Don't mind at all. Can you bring us back something to eat?"

"Yes, text your order." I add on an extra coat of lip gloss.

I'm rocking my good hair today with my red bottoms looking like old money. Black girl magic mixed with a splash of Black excellence on deck. Then I remember Catrina's makeup look yesterday and her having dinner with Rashaad last night.

"What happened with Rashaad?"

"Nothing." She drops to the bed. "It's like I'm stuck in the friend zone. I got two numbers at that old rundown pizza parlor, probably somebody's baby daddy, and Rashaad was unfazed."

I spin around, confused. They sat huddled up most of the night. "What were y'all talking about?"

"Houses."

I snicker. "Houses?"

"Yep. Condos, townhouses, single-family homes. HOAs, subdivision, ordinances, escrow. I could sit for the real estate exam," she rolls her eyes.

"He'll come around." I grab my purse.

"I was all in and it's like I'm invisible. I had my girls all in the man's face." She flicks a dismissive hand. "Anyway, speaking of coming around, did you check into the freelance makeup gig?"

"I didn't."

"Let me know what you decide. I had a few people ask about my makeup yesterday."

"I'll keep that in mind."

Working as a hostess for fifteen bucks an hour won't get me the dough I need to gain my independence. But it will be consistent income if Kamal is willing to still give me the job.

"I'm out."

"Good luck!"

Luck.

What would that look like? Not fighting with Brett. Not wondering how I'll financially provide for my child. Not questioning if every man is like every man I've known —present but unavailable, never satisfied with the woman they have at home, always using their peckers to search for a new model.

A replacement.

Her face is etched in my head. Her blonde hair, long legs, blue eyes. The model type. And I have to stop crying, because his ass isn't crying over me.

I yank down the visor, checking my makeup. My relationship is over, but it doesn't mean my life is over. The man who proclaimed to love me cleared my account, yet he believes I'll take him back.

I sit outside Southern Soul scanning the near empty parking lot.

I'm not going back, and I don't need Brett to take care of Reese. All I need is a new plan starting with getting this job. I love my makeup brushes, but I don't earn enough from YouTube to support us.

A knock on my window scares me to death. I grab my heart and look up to find Kamal.

"You all right?"

My heart races for a different reason. Kamal stands over me with his hands on the roof of the car. He's rocking a t-shirt and gym shorts. The colorful artwork of his tatted arms has me praying my mouth is closed.

I can't look away.

God… What's wrong with me? Men are selfish, opportunists, and my number one enemy. But Kamal is…

"Keep looking at me like that…"

"Like what?"

"Like you want more than a job."

This man does something to me. Not like Brett or any other man I've ever encountered. I'd feel in control if it was just his looks. That's explainable, that's natural. The man is a chiseled, tattooed, melanated king. But there's something else, something I can't put my finger on, something that makes me want to say yes to the invitation in his eyes, placing my heart in real jeopardy.

Maybe it's his confidence. Maybe it's his kindness. Maybe… He moves fast and close. I smell the faint scent of his cologne and I'm fascinated by the light brush of freckles across the bridge of his nose.

"Jay, I'm about to kiss you." The words whisper over my waiting lips.

"I know."

His body folds into the car and I wrap my hands around his neck, holding him tight until our lips finally touch. A soft voice whispers, *surrender*, as if I have a choice.

Kamal kisses me. Not in a hurry. Oh no, this man takes his sweet time and I'm thankful for it. He worships my mouth, and I feel cheated because the door is between us. I moan, suckling on his moist tongue until a throat clears and Kamal pulls away.

"Kamal, I…" I ramble.

"I thought you said this was an interview." A voice booms with humor behind each word.

"Q, Jayda, Jayda, my knucklehead brother Quan." Kamal steps to the side with desire swirling in his eyes. "I asked Quan to interview you."

"Why?"

"I want you to feel comfortable. I know you'll fit around here, and we need you." He runs a finger down my cheek and my eyes close. "I don't want to scare you off."

"Who are you and what have you done with my broth-er?" Q asks.

"Man, wait inside the office." Kamal shoves him a little toward the building.

"While you play Mr. Casanova, *nah playa*, let me see you work." Q crosses his arms over his broad chest.

I chuckle as the two size each other up.

"Jay, you can't encourage him." Kamal wraps an arm around Q's neck and they wrestle around a bit.

"Keep on and I'm telling Mamma about you kissing in the parking lot."

I burst out laughing. My makeup will be a streaky mess, but they are hilarious.

"Come on, Jayda." Q opens my door.

"I said interview her." Kamal smacks Quan's hand and helps me out of the car. "I'll walk you inside then get back to the roof."

"That explains the clothes."

Kamal wraps my hand around his biceps, stopping to inspect my ringless ring finger. A smile tickles the corner of his mouth. He doesn't have to say it because I know my decision to ditch the ring pleases him.

"Yeah, the contractors start next weekend. I want to inspect the state of it for myself before they start banging around."

"So, you're a roofer now?"

"I like this woman, Kamal. Beautiful *and* smart. Not like your usual—"

"Q."

"Touchy… touchy. I'll see you inside, Jayda." He winks at me and enters the restaurant.

The moment we're alone, I face him. "I'm sorry about last night."

"About what, kissing me or lumping with the other men in your life?"

"I didn't lump you. I just can't afford another mistake."

"Is that how you see me, Jayda? I'm a mistake hanging around to get in your panties?" He steps back. The man's eyes are like fucking lasers. Shooting straight to my core and I feel compelled to explain.

"Kamal, you don't know me yet, you jumped in to save the day. Not once, but twice. You scoop us up in a private jet. You play with my daughter. You offer me a job. You kiss like a dream. So yes, I think you want something and I have nothing to give." I open my arms wide, laying it all out.

"I kiss like a dream?"

"Kamal…" I roll my eyes.

"What? Men love to hear shit like that."

"What if this is just a rebound? That I'm feeling this because you're merely being a gentleman."

"Jayda, you don't have to know all the answers. I just want to get to know you. Spend some time with you, and when you're ready to slip your ring back on—"

"That's not happening."

"If it does, all I ask is you keep it straight up."

I shouldn't consider his request. This is stupid—running from one man and clinging to the first man I meet. This has rebound written all over.

And I shouldn't have these growing feelings for him

with this stampede of butterflies fluttering every time he looks at me.

But I do.

"And then what?" I ask.

"We let nature take its course."

"It's too soon. I'm barely out of my relationship. What do I look like jumping from one man to the next?"

"I don't care what people think as long as you're good, I'm good."

I stare into the depths of his eyes. "We don't all have that luxury."

"You do, you just don't know it. Most people can't handle their own problems, let alone speak on yours. I'd rather give them something to talk about." He pauses, letting his words sink in.

I drop my head back, staring at the sky.

"Jay, the moment you stop caring and do you, your life will change."

"That's some rich people stuff."

He laughs. "It is, and that's why I'm rich. I do me all day, every day."

"Can we take it slow?"

He wraps his hands around my waist, gently pulling me closer. "Will you throw in a few of those friendship kisses?"

"Kamal..."

"Jay, this is a negotiation."

"This is a game to you." I stiffen, stepping back.

"Must I teach you everything, love?" His words feel like

a cashmere sweater. The one you don't get to wear nearly enough, but you'd never let it go. "Life is a game."

"…with winners and losers?"

"I always play to win." His cocky expression sends a fresh wave of anticipation through my body.

"Kamal, I ain't got all day," Q calls out. Kamal glances back for a quick second.

"Well, I'm not rich… *yet*. So, it means I need to get inside." I spin around just to see his eyes sparkle. "How do I look?"

"Beautiful." He brings my body back to his, kissing me until I'm breathless.

"I'll be back," I promise, stepping out of his warm embrace.

"I'll be here."

CHAPTER 14

I stand in the middle of the dining room. My time alone in Southern Soul is a luxury. Between the construction crew on the weekend and the staff during the week, I don't have a second to think without constant noise and commotion. The highlight has been hanging around to see Jayda.

Q approved hiring her, and Catrina got her on the schedule. Just like I thought, she's blended in seamlessly. I weave through the tables.

Today's no different. Mother should arrive in a half hour to start the breads and muffins for our Saturday rush. I got Dean to stop by and work out the details for the next phase of our remodel.

I move a couple tables together. The place looks better every day. I'm eager to see the inside reflect the changes we've implemented outside. Southern Soul has a new roof and fresh siding. Next is a paved parking lot.

That thought puts a little pep in my step. I walk to the coffee station and stop when I hear a knock on the glass.

"Eh…" I smile. Dean and Emmitt stand on the other side. I open the door, stepping aside to let them in. "Did y'all come straight from the airport?"

"Yes, I thought we could discuss the other projects on our agenda before Emmitt heads to training camp," Dean offers with a casual sweeping glance around the room.

"That's perfect. It would save me a trip. There's no way I can get away, anyway." I hug my boys then lock the door behind us. "Sit over there. I was about to start the coffee. Wait, do you guys want some breakfast?"

"Who's cooking?" Emmitt cracks.

"Me, fool. Come on. We'll meet in the kitchen."

The guys follow. I remove my jacket and put on an apron. Then I lay out the ingredients for omelets and freshly cut ham. I reach for a loaf of bread and change my mind—there's no telling when I'll stop to eat again. It's a grits and biscuits kind of morning.

"You got another apron?" Dean asks.

"Yeah, man, check in the closet over there. Leave the yellow one."

"I'll get the coffee started." Emmitt steps out of the kitchen.

I toss the skillets on the burner, and Dean chops the vegetables. The aroma of coffee fills the air.

I update them on the progress while making the biscuits. My hopes of making this an in and out trip went out the window. This project will cost me close to two million dollars and that's not including the salaries of the staff. But thanks to Dean, we're stretching every dollar and counting every cent.

We move around the kitchen like it's an everyday occurrence. Dean takes over the burner while Emmitt handles the coffee. We catch up with their traveling, Emmitt returning for another season, and Dean's gig in New Orleans. In no time we gather around the prep station with coffee in hand, ready to eat.

I pray over the food. We give a hearty *amen* when the sound of the front door interrupts my first cup of coffee. I glance at the time.

"It's probably Mother. Start with the other projects," I suggest walking to the front. The sight of Jayda stops me. "Good morning, Beautiful."

"What are you doing here?"

"Working." I curl a finger, calling her closer. She complies, and I gather her in my arms, rewarding her with a light kiss on the lips.

"Mr. Montgomery, are you on the clock?"

"I'm always on the clock."

"Then keep those steamy eyes to yourself." She cups my face. "When is the last time you had a full night's sleep?"

I shrug. "Months."

"You can't keep going like this."

"I won't. Now kiss me again before we're interrupted." My hectic schedule and her working opposite Catrina make it impossible to spend time alone. I need to fix that and fix it soon.

Jayda chuckles and does exactly as I ask, resting her breasts on my chest. Hot kisses from her sweet lips have been a daily prize for a job well done.

I reluctantly pull away. "Now, what are you doing here? I thought you're scheduled for later."

"I am. I'm here to prep for Miss Jackie. She has a meeting with her guild."

"Prepping what?" I ask.

"Let me see." She removes her phone from her back pocket.

I lean against a table, appreciating the fit of her jeans. Jayda has more than a handful of ass—and I have big hands—wide hips, and her full breasts make her curves dream worthy.

"Oh, here it is." She taps the screen. "Buttermilk biscuits, banana nut muffins…" Her voice fades as my heart pounds. "Kamal?"

I flinch a little.

She tilts my head until I'm facing her. "You have to stop functioning off of three hours of sleep. What if you zone out while you're driving?"

"I'm using a driver."

"Stop being a smartass. I'm serious."

I nod then try to get a peek at her phone. "Mother shared her recipes with you?"

"Yeah, why is it a secret?"

Secret? Mother doesn't share her top-secret recipes. Family recipes meant to pass through the women of the Montgomery family. We all quickly learned Mother is choosy about who she considers "family" and marriage isn't an automatic in. Which Rashaad's ex-wife learned when Mother didn't classify her as "family." Apparently the sentiment doesn't apply to Jayda and I need to know why.

"Kamal, you're scaring me."

"Uh… you're the first non-Montgomery other than Catrina to know them."

"What?" Her face drops.

Jayda is a thinker. Her mind can spin a thing a million ways before she moves into action. I can see the wheels turning in her eyes.

"We started talking about food and I don't know…" A hint of confusion crosses her face. "She had a meeting and Catrina isn't feeling well."

"Right." That doesn't explain Mother's reasoning. "You're probably right."

"Probably? What are you not telling me?"

"Nothing. I just find it interesting." I smile to mask my concern.

Jayda is slowly coming around to our regular friendship kisses, but she's still on the fence with us dating. Well, technically not dating because we've only been out once and we had the girls with us.

Something doesn't smell right. Mother said she'd retire, but she's been here several days a week. She said she feels off when she doesn't start her day in her kitchen. I've let her because it makes the customers feel comfortable with all the changes we're making.

But if Jayda knew the truth behind those recipes, I'm

certain she'd bolt like a cat with his tail caught under a rocking chair. And her reasons are valid, I guess. Her ex-man didn't appreciate her and now she's watching my every move, waiting for the other shoe to drop.

"*Ahem.*"

Jayda jumps back and I pull her back to me, ready to kiss away the skittish look in her eyes. "Leave us alone."

"No, sir. We have work to do," Dean says. "Save your lip locking for later."

"Hater."

"Work then play. Your rules." Dean spits my rule at me.

"Yeah… yeah… yeah. Give us a second." I get Jayda close enough to nibble on the spot at the base of her neck.

"Kamal…" She giggles.

"Come home with me tonight." I whisper in her ear.

She spins around in my arms. "You promised to go slow."

"And I will…" I run my hands down the curve of her luscious backside. "I promise."

"Kamal!"

"Damn, man, I'm coming." I stand up, brushing my lips over her ear. "I'll pick you up after your shift."

She nods and I suckle on her earlobe. Her heated moan sends my blood racing and I can't wait to have her alone. I take her hand in mine, leading her to the kitchen.

Emmitt stands.

"You met my business partners and best friends, Dean Wellington and Emmitt Booker." They shake hands.

"I'm glad to meet you both on better terms. Thank you

for letting me steal Kamal from your meeting a while back." She glances over at me with a smile.

"We'll move to the dining room," I offer.

"Oh no, finish your breakfast. I need to pull ingredients."

"Have you had breakfast?" I ask, returning to my seat.

"No, I'll grab something later."

"No ma'am. Have a seat." I pat my lap and she stares at me. "Don't worry about them. They're nobodies."

"Don't fall for that player line." Emmitt snickers.

"Kamal's not fooling me," Jayda says, settling back. Her hand brushes my aroused manhood. She startles forward and I hold her in place with my hand against her stomach.

"It's your fault," I whisper over her ear.

"Kamal, she can stay if you'll focus. We're about to approve a million-dollar budget."

"I don't play about my money or my woman. I'm listening." Emmitt and Dean exchange glances and Jayda stiffens. The only way she'll get comfortable with me is to see I'm all about her, and I don't care who knows it. I pull my plate closer. "Eat, babe. I'm listening to Dean."

DEAN AND EMMITT stare at me like I'm a unicorn. I lean forward to leave, but Kamal's large hand stills me. This isn't the first time I've sat on his lap. The last two weeks of working and seeing him daily transitioned us from unfamiliar to friends before I realized I went from Jayda to Jay to Babe.

He has one hand on stomach and the other on my thigh. The proximity of his thumb, lightly brushing my heat, leaves me breathless. I look down at the plate to keep from embarrassing myself.

I take a bite of his untouched biscuit and moan. The men stare at me.

"That good, Babe?"

"Who made these?" I glance over my shoulder, and the heat from his eyes sends lava oozing down my spine.

"I did." His head tilts to the side and the desire I see makes it hard to comprehend that this man wants me.

This Kamal is a teaser. This is the sexual chemistry that had me steering clear of him. But it seems we can't help ourselves.

Every word holds a sexual context. Every gesture reminds me of how long it has been since I've been satisfied. Playing along only feeds into his explicit teasing, but right now I don't care.

I stopped counting at six months in a sex-free relationship. So, instead of acting like I don't want him, I will enjoy it. While it lasts.

"They melt in my mouth," I whisper.

The layers of this man keep me guessing, but never about where his interests lie. And for that reason alone, I play back, discreetly brushing my ass across the length of him. He chokes with round eyes, telling me he's on to my game.

"You all right?" I ask.

He sits forward, cupping my heat with his mouth pressed again my ear. "Keep playing and I'll have you melting in *my* mouth."

Well, hot damn. That shut me up. I settle for eating his orgasmic bread, knowing the calories are headed straight to my thighs. The man can make homemade biscuits, I stare at the fluffy, flaky, lightly browned piece of heaven with new eyes, and I follow the thoughts cooked up by his words. I wonder how he'll heat it up in the bed.

"*Bay-bae…*" Slips out and the meeting stops. "My bad, I didn't mean to say that aloud. Carry on."

Emmitt shakes his head and they continue. I polish off Kamal's breakfast, listening to the three of them discuss their projects. They throw facts and figures around, and my head spins with what I'm witnessing. These men are talking millions like I talk lashes.

"Excuse me." I move to stand, but Kamal tightens his hold.

"I need you to stay for a few more minutes."

I nod and settle back on his lap. Another fact I'm registering is this man holds me like I'm light at a feather. Which I know isn't the truth since Blue Bell and Miss Jackie's sweet potato pie serve as my therapists.

The next project up is Southern Soul. Dean shares the design details for the kitchen and the dining room. I glance around, finding it hard to envision his sketches. The stainless-steel appliances. New floor layout in the dining area. Then I look back at Kamal.

A pleased look covers his face. The man and his dream team. He's working around the clock to make this happen. Catrina said he had plans to turn this place around and judging by this conversation, he's doing it. I have to hand it to him. The man is a visionary. It's hard to be around him and not catch the bug. It makes me wonder how I can remake my career.

"I think this calls for all new everything," Kamal says and all eyes are on him.

"What do you mean?" Dean asks.

"New menu, new logo, new website. I want to make this a huge rollout."

"With a grand reopening?" I ask.

"Yes. What do you think?"

They all look at me, and I face Kamal. "Me? I know nothing about all of this."

"Yes, you do." He challenges.

"No, I don't." I shake my head, glancing back at the guys.

"What would you suggest to a beauty brand trying to relaunch?"

My head snaps back to Kamal. "With the current competition in the beauty industry?"

"Yep." His eyes glisten. "What would you do?"

"What would *I* do?" I think about it. "Well, I think about how some brands get it all wrong. I'd get my products in the hands of the top influencers on each social media platform, but I'd also include maybe ten to twenty up-and-coming beauty gurus."

"Why's that?" Emmitt asks. "Wouldn't that be a waste of products?"

I shake my head. "No, I mean, it might look like that in the beginning, but if they're a natural fit for your products those are the people that sing your praises, if you do it right. They'll buy the products and not wait to receive them free. Plus, you'd naturally build your amen squad."

"Amen squad?" Dean asks.

I nod, looking around at these very rich and powerful men, waiting for me to explain, and my eyes settle on Kamal. He nods, encouraging me to continue.

"They're the ones who will stick by your brand for the long haul. That buy your product before you send it to them. I'm guessing the equivalent in your worlds are the fans you've had since high school and college. Your amen squad are your ride or dies. Like my Gems."

The last part is more for me than them. I miss my Gems. They've stuck by me for years and I need to work and get back to my fans.

"How can we create that?" Kamal asks, looking at us all.

"Use what you have," I whisper. That's how I'll give to them, the way they've always given to me.

"What do you mean, Babe?"

I push my Gems aside and think about Kamal's situation. "If I were you, I'd do all this." I swirl my hand over the plans scattered over the table. "*And* I'd also reach out to your siblings."

"I do." He tenses beneath me.

"Do you?" His face falls serious, and I continue. "Dean

asked you a few minutes ago about an executive chef. Why not ask Miya? And Q runs a very successful nightclub. To do that it must mean he knows the Houston night life. And Rashaad knows this city down to the hole in the wall restaurants and the rare neighborhood attractions."

"So, what are you saying?" Kamal asks.

"I'd rebrand with, I don't know…" I stand up and pace a little. Then I spin around, facing Kamal. "The Montgomery Legacy. This was your grandparents' place, then your parents. Now it's about rebranding with a new generation of Montgomerys. You'll be the same, yet different. Like a 2.0 version."

Kamal zones out a little, nodding his head.

"Can I add one more thing?" I ask.

"Yes, love."

I search Kamal's eyes for the reason. It's a term of endearment reserved for the women in his life. I've heard it during his conversations with his sister Miya or when he's addressing Lillian and Miss Jackie. But never has it been directed toward me.

"Uh… if this were me… I'd make sure you don't rebrand it so much that you leave out the parts that make you, *you*."

A collective gasp rings in the air. The three of them exchange looks without saying a word. The energy in the room feels magical and the hair stands on the back of my neck.

The guys huddle up and I look at the clock.

"I've held you up. Guys, let's move this to the dining

room." Kamal walks over to me. "I have a business offer for you."

"Me?"

"Yes, you. Work with us."

"I'm already on your payroll. Remember?"

"Not as a hostess, but on a contract basis."

"Doing what?"

"Social media."

"Why? You don't need me." I extend a hand toward the dining hall. "You have them."

"Why do you have to question everything?"

"Because everything has a cost, and this feels like more of you wanting to help me. You helped me get this job, and that's good enough."

"Did you not pay attention to what just happened? We could relaunch Southern Soul better than ever and I need you to do it. Why are you hesitating?"

"Kamal, I know men like you. I'm the flavor of the week, and I'm okay with it because I'm not interested in more. But you don't have to do this."

"You know no one like me. And I'll show you, believe me." The rich tenor of his words seeps into my pores. Then he closes the space between us. "I'm asking for your help. Will you help us?"

I tip my head back, searching his dark brown eyes for the truth.

"The best way to do this is by being up front. Let me decide without all the soft words and friendship kisses."

He smiles. "You don't like my soft words?"

I'm not sure how to answer that. I love his soft words, soft caresses, and his soft kisses. But Kamal only plans to remain in Houston for the duration of this project. He's made that known, and I'm less than two months out of a long-term relationship. How serious can we be with one another?

"How about we establish a few rules?"

"Rules? I like rules."

"Keep everything one hundred. No assumptions. No games. Only straight shooting."

"Everything?" he asks.

"Everything."

I don't like the simmering smile on his face.

"I can do that. But I must warn you. I play to win." The scent of sweet death lingers between us and I can't breathe. The blaze in his eyes turns up. "You sure you can handle that?"

"Yes," I mumble, partly terrified of what I'm agreeing to do, while the other part of me is curious about the passion I see in his eyes.

"I'll have a contract drawn up for your services on this project. You'll work directly with Ebony, my publicist."

I nod. He's doing it again. Like the time he had Q interview me, he's making sure I'm comfortable. How can I not take this offer? I'd be a fool.

"I want to keep my job here." I bump into the table.

"Done." He levels his gaze. "Anything else?"

I shake my head. "I need to clock in and get started."

"Sure. But there's one more thing." He braces his hands on either side of me. "Are you ready?"

I feel like I've stepped in a trap and Kamal holds the key. Nothing in my life has prepared me for this man or this conversation. We went from biscuits, to makeup, to negotiating for a social media job, I think.

"For what, Kamal?"

"For me, love."

I shake my head.

"But you said you want me to keep it one hundred. I'm about to keep it a mil because I want you, Jayda, in every way a man wants a woman."

Kamal grabs my legs, wrapping them around his waist. He grips the fleshy part of my ass and with ease he sits me to the edge of the table. The thin fabric of my leggings makes his aroused state rest in the folds of my wetness.

His mouth hovers over mine, and I need him to kiss me. "I have a rule of my own. You're mine."

"That's not a rule, Kamal."

"It's my rule." He rubs against me and I moan. We shouldn't be here, doing this, but what's a woman to do? "Do we have a deal?"

This man is dead serious, and a whisper of fear crosses my heart. I'll recover from Brett. Truth is, I already have. I have love for him, however, I was never *in love* with him.

But Kamal is different. This man could rip out my heart and not only will I be jobless, but I'd be a shell of myself.

I look into his eyes, trying to decide if I can survive

another disappointment. Can I let myself have this moment, knowing it won't last?

"I wouldn't do that," he whispers across my lips and my heart skips.

"Do what?"

"Hurt you."

"Sure you will," I toss back, as if I'm teasing.

"My word is my bond."

His mouth covers mine. Each kiss sends a shock wave through my body. Each kiss communicates a promise of more to come and I'm falling. For this tatted, cocky, ex-ball player. He greedily consumes me and I hope this time will be different. That he'll be different.

He pulls me closer, deepening the kiss, as if he's answering the doubts swimming in my head. And my heart begs, *Please don't break me.*

CHAPTER 15

Jayda ruined our original plan. Thankfully, Dean came back with something better and now I'm waiting on my siblings. Like before Catrina sets us up in the party room with a strict cutoff time since she needs to convert this space into extra seating for guests.

"Good morning."

I twist, standing to my feet. "Hey, Baby Miya. How are you, love?"

"I'm great. I can't believe how much Houston has changed since Hurricane Harvey."

"I know. So, are you settled in your new place?"

"Not really, but I'm not in a rush. What about you? I see so many unfamiliar faces *and* we have a paved parking lot."

I chuckle. "Yeah, it's happening slowly. Wait until you see what I have planned."

The others roll in, one by one. Demetrius and Quan stroll in together. Rashaad enters alone.

"Where's my girl?"

"She's hanging out with Reese today." Rashaad hugs the others before taking his seat. "Jayda will drop her off this evening before her shift."

The mention of my little ladies brings a smile to my face. Lillian and Reese have been joined at the hip since they met.

"When are you starting this thing? I'm hungry," Q says.

"We're waiting on…" I see Mother and Kenneth heading this way. "Here they come."

"They?" Miya asks. She glances over her shoulder, following my line of vision. "You invited Kenneth too?"

"Yes, I don't want to upset Mother and this concerns us all."

"Who are you and what have you done with my brother?" Q jokes and they all laugh.

"Whatever." I ignore their teasing. This morning Jayda's observation about tapping into my natural resources hit home. I stand to greet Mother and I shake Kenneth's hand. I still have doubts about the man, but that's not the point of this meeting.

"Everyone, let's get going. We're on borrowed time." They settle around the table. "Thank you for coming on such short notice. I've been working around the clock trying to prove a point."

I look over at Kenneth and continue.

"I want to show Mother we can turn this place around

and preserve the legacy. But I forgot something, which Jayda brought to my attention this morning."

I open the folder from Dean and give everyone a copy.

"Here's what I have planned for Southern Soul." They review the documents. I have the revised floor plan for the dining area, the update to the kitchen, plus projections for our first five years. "I want to brand this as a pass off from one generation to another and I'd like to bring everyone in on the changes starting with nominating Miya for the acting executive head chef position."

I sit back. I thought about including them before, but dismissed it. I figured they would voice their concerns. It didn't occur to me to ask.

"Now that you've seen and heard my plans. Will you join me?"

They remain silent. I'm not sure if I've stunned them or if they will decline my offer.

Q leans forward. "You got me, Big Boy, if you include a clause to keep Jayda around."

I laugh and the others do too. We stand exchanging hugs, all eager to see Southern Soul move forward, together. The others give Miya a hard time about filling Mother's shoes, but she's an obvious pick. So obvious I almost missed it.

"Thank you, Kamal." Miya wraps me in a warm hug. Then she dances around in true Miya fashion. "This is major!"

"You're welcome. This is only the beginning."

"We'll get out of the way." Mother stands.

I walk them to the doorway and face Kenneth. "Are you free to talk sometime this week?"

"Yeah, man, name the time and place and I'm there." We shake hands. He holds for a moment longer before turning to leave. "I'll be in the car."

Mother faces me with unshed tears in her eyes. "I'm so proud of you. Thank you for what you're doing around here and for giving your father a chance."

"I still have my reservation. But your happiness is all I want, and he makes you happy."

She nods and I gather my mother to me. This woman is my heart, and she knows it. Then she folds a key in my hand. I stare at it.

"I already have a key."

"But it's not the master key."

"You gave me a copy?" I grin. Leave it to her to pull a fast one on me. "One more thing before you leave. Jayda said you shared the family recipes with her."

"I did."

"That's all you have to say about it?"

"She's good for you." Mother stares deep into my eyes. "I never seen you like this. I hoped, but I didn't think you'd get past the pain of our divorce and stop pretending to be a playboy."

"Pretending? Momma, that was no pretense." Her smile softens, communicating more than her words. "What?"

"Nothing. Jayda is good for you and seeing you with Reese makes my heart smile."

"But I'm always with Lillian."

"Lillian's family. Family in your book is an extension of your own body. But I've never seen you with someone else's child the way you are with Reese."

"And that's why you shared the recipes?"

"No." Her face tells me she's not budging.

"And you wonder where I get my stubborn ways."

"I don't wonder, child, I know. Love you, baby." She kisses my cheek.

"Love you too."

"Sunday dinner at my place. Six o'clock." Mother calls out. "Love y'all."

The *love you too*s ring through the air. We hang around for a few more minutes discussing when Miya will step into her new role. In the end, we agree to get through the renovation and meet again to outline the official rollout with Ebony and Jayda present.

REESE and I enter Southern Soul an hour before my shift. We passed off Lillian to her father, and I have enough time to sit with Reese while she has dinner.

I hold Reese's hand while she skips beside me. She steals the show the moment she enters the doors. Staff members stop to hug her as she waves like a princess in a parade.

"Hey, Auntie!" She hugs her around the waist.

"Hey, sweetie. Jay, I can't leave. We're short and I need to stay until close."

"Don't apologize, Miss Manager." I reclaim Reese's

hand, out of a babysitter, and there goes my night out with Kamal. I glance around the dining area—the place is still packed. "Are you going to be okay?"

"Yeah. This is a great problem to have. I'd rather have a packed place than empty seats. What about you? This means fewer hours on your check."

"It's fine." I didn't get to tell her about the contract with Kamal. I'll tell her once I know the details. "Reese and I will head home and relax. Want me to leave the car?"

"How will you get home? I'd hate to have you out late tonight picking me up with Reese."

"I'll call a ride after we grab something to eat." I spot a free table and we snag it. Reese flips through the menu and I send Kamal a text.

Hey! Bad news. The blue bubbles pulse on the screen. While I wait, Reese and I discuss a few dinner options. My child is determined to eat only chicken and waffles from here.

My phone vibrates, signaling an incoming text. I glance down and see a crying emoji.

What happened? Got scared? He adds the emoji with the tongue out and I shake my head.

Just nasty. I shoot back. Then I get his winking emoji. *No. I don't have a sitter.*

I wait for his response and my phone rings.

"Hey, Beautiful."

"Hey, yourself." The sound of his voice invites the butterflies back to my stomach. "How did it go after I left?"

Kamal tells me about what I missed, including the

meeting with his family. I've met them all since working here. Catrina is a solid part of their family, and they've welcomed me as her best friend. But Kamal doesn't talk about his father much.

I point to the corn dog kids meal on the menu and Reese shakes her head. She flips the menu over and starts coloring.

"How's my girl?"

"Fine, except all she'll eat is chicken and waffles."

"Mmmm, my favorite." We laugh.

"We have a menu full of options other than chicken and waffles."

He stalls. "Wait, where are you?"

"Southern Soul. Then we're heading home. Where are you?"

"Behind you."

I twist in my seat, disconnecting our call. It's a Saturday night and Kamal is wearing dress pants and a button-up shirt. He walks over.

"Mr. Kamal!" She sings his name, and he scoops her up.

"Hey, Miss Reesie. How are you?"

"Good."

"I need an extra nose. Can I borrow yours?" He pinches her nose between his knuckles and she giggles.

"No, I need it."

I laugh. "Mr. Montgomery, please tell me you haven't been here all day."

"I took off my tie." He kisses me on the forehead, and I look up, wanting more. He sits Reese in her chair and he takes the other. "We have a nice-sized crowd for a Saturday night."

"When are you leaving?" He's working all day and staying on the phone with me all night. "You can't burn the candle at both ends and expect to be productive."

"Yes, ma'am." He runs a finger down my cheek, but I don't believe he'll stop. His eyes are locked on a goal. "Don't look at me like that. I'm off tomorrow." Then he turns to Reese. "I think I'm in trouble."

"Did you do something bad?" Reese asks.

"No. What about you?" He rolls his sleeves back.

"No, sir. I played with Lillian today." Reese pushes part of the menu in his direction and Kamal grabs a crayon.

"What did my favorite ladies do today?"

Reese starts with the top of the day. Kamal holds my hand under the table and a purple crayon in the other. He asks questions, laughs at her jokes, and comments on her stellar artistic abilities.

This is it. The sounds of their words and the room fade. Reese has her arms open wide and Kamal throws back his head, laughing. This is that *something* about him I couldn't put a finger on. How could Brett be so foolish and miss this? His little girl growing up, piecing together the world. All without him.

I drop my head to our joined hands.

"Babe?" He squeezes tighter and I look up. "You all right? You're about to miss the best part," he teases, but I see the concern in his eyes.

"I am. I'm just happy," I whisper.

"Happy is good." I get his trillion-dollar-killer smile.

"I like happy," Reese adds.

"Me too, Miss Reese," Kamal says.

"Can I dance, Mommy?" She wiggles in her seat, and I'm on the verge of saying no, not in the middle of the restaurant. "Please?"

"Go 'head baby." I'm about to let my baby shine. This is a new day for us both. To go from shrinking in front of her father to opening up with the Montgomery family. It seems we're adjusting well in Houston. Then she starts.

"What is she doing?" he whispers.

"Dancing. She was such an antsy baby. So, we'd dance off the energy."

"Miya's going to die when she sees this."

"Why?" I laugh, a little surprised.

"She does the same thing. She'll stop and bust a move anywhere. No music required." He faces Reese. "Get it, Miss Reesie."

And my baby does, hopping and jumping. Her little body folding and bending. Her skirt is a prop to swing side to side, and her arms are wide, ready to receive.

She stops. "Dance with me, Mommy."

I don't hesitate. I see the eyes of the surrounding people, but their opinions can't matter more than sharing this moment with Reese. I pop my fingers, rocking my hips, swaying side to side. Dancing is the great remedy for the blues. And the delight on Kamal's face makes this dance close to perfection.

I drop back in my chair, laughing. Kamal kisses the back of my hand.

This is better than happiness. This is joy. Pure and simple. I'm no closer to the answers of how I'll get us out of this holding space, and I'm not a dollar richer.

But this is a gift.

"Ma'am, if you have time to boogie woogie come over and help a sista out." Catrina stands beside me.

"I got Reese."

I shake my head. "Kamal, you need to go to bed."

He tips his head towards Cat. "I have Reese now, and you'll keep her tonight?"

"What?" Catrina's eyes round, sweeping from Kamal and landing on me. "Jay?"

All eyes are on me. I sit up. This is a big step, and we all know it. Well, except Reese.

Kamal wants to take our situationship to another level. Catrina sees Kamal as the remedy to get Brett out of my system. I am drawn to this man, but the fear of getting in over my head haunts me.

"Auntie Cat, can I sleep in your bed? Like a slumber party?" Reese stops mid-stroke. "Can Lillian come?"

"Maybe not today."

"What about tomorrow? Tomorrow is spa day. Right?" She turns to Kamal. His eyebrows hit his hairline. I forgot to tell him my baby's a genius.

"It is." He looks at me for a split second. "How about I call her daddy and we'll talk about it tomorrow?"

"Okay." Reese returns to coloring.

We share a common gaze and Kamal struggles to hold back his laughter.

"Well, Miss Reesie, let's get going. We can order dinner from my office." He stands and adds, "You can pop in and check on her."

"You sure she won't be in the way?" I know she won't, but the man is juggling a million balls in the air. Throwing in an energetic kid with nonstop questions doesn't seem fair.

"I'm a pro at this, as long as she doesn't need diapers," he teases.

"I'm a big girl. Right, Mommy?" Reese answers for herself.

"Yes, you are." I help her down from the table and kiss her forehead.

Kamal winks and tugs on her ponytail. "Then we'll be just fine."

"Behave, honey."

"Yes, ma'am." She takes Kamal's hand.

I watch until Kamal and Reese disappear.

"You guys are really about to do this?"

"Yeah, I'm having mixed feelings. I want to, but a part of me feels like it's moving so fast."

"What has you confused?" She sits on the edge of the table.

The restaurant is calming down. A few waiters bus the tables and prep to close this section off.

"The thought of making another mistake."

"Mistakes come with living, Jay. It's got to be more than

that."

"We want different things. I'm planning to make Houston my home. He's here until they get this place settled. I want a family, get married, have another child. He doesn't want marriage or kids."

"That's a lifetime goal. What do you want and need tonight?" Then she leans forward. "Because quiet as its kept, I see some ass smackin' in your future."

I die laughing.

Catrina continues as I gasp to catch my breath. "Stop trying to save the world overnight. I say, let that man love on you from the top to the bottom and from the front to the back, then from side to side. And if he offers seconds, *take it!*"

"Fine. I will."

"Stop acting like you don't want to."

"Oh I want to, I guess I can't read too much into it."

"That sounds better. Now, go get Reese's coloring book and clock in."

"Okie-dokie."

THE HOURS PASS. "Jayda, do you have a few minutes?" I glance up from cleaning menus and see Miss Jackie.

She reminds me of Clare Huxtable, poised, speaks her mind, and *the* example of a Black mother. Her wrinkle-free brown skin would have me guessing she's in her mid-forties. But the ages of her kids and the silver in her salt and peppered hair tell me she must be at least in her early fifties.

"Yes, ma'am. How are you tonight?" I dry my hands and reach in to hug her. She holds me and gives a little squeeze before I stand back. "How can I help you?"

"I'm hoping you'll do me a favor."

"Sure, anything."

"I'd like to invite Reese to join us tonight."

I look toward the back. "Did Kamal call you?"

"Yes, and no. He and I talked about some final approvals and I heard him talking with Reese."

"I… it was a last-minute schedule shift." I'm surprised by the offer and slightly embarrassed. "I don't want to impose on your generosity."

I've kept my financial state to myself since there is nothing there to speak of. Houston has public transportation but it doubles, or sometimes triples the travel time, which doesn't work when I'm depending on Catrina to help with keeping Reese. So, I've shifted my immediate goal from paying for summer camp to getting a car.

Miss Jackie stares at me as if uncertain how to deal with me. "Can we talk single mother to single mother?"

My back straightens, and the walls around my heart lower. I nod, encouraging her to continue.

"I raised five kids alone. I went from having partial support full-time to no support all the time."

I know the look on her face—a struggle between the good and bad inherent in the situation. How it can be equally good and awful at the sometime.

"Jayda, it's a feeling I would want no one to feel, but it made me the woman I am. It made me so strong and independent that I got lost between the restaurant, the kids, and my customers. It wasn't until ten years after my divorce that I realized I had alienated my kids and nearly ruined my business, all because I didn't want to ask for help."

I'm mush. I hate asking for a ride. Limiting the groceries I buy for Reese. Struggling with the necessities. I brush my tears away before they roll down my face.

I'm sick and tired of crying. My tears make me feel like Brett's won. I use the hem of my shirt to dry my face.

"Oh no, dear, let's give you some privacy. Catrina, we'll be back."

We step outside and sit on the bench in front of the building. The night sky is clear, and the street is quiet. For a summer night, the humidity is manageable. The crew shaped up the trees and we have an unobstructed view of the stars.

Miss Jackie wraps her nonjudgmental arms around me, and I crack. An avalanche of emotions descend on me and the tears just won't stop.

"I'm sorry." I hiccup, trying to compose myself.

"Don't be sorry. You let it all out and we'll keep it right here between us. Okay?"

"Okay."

I cry. Snotting all over her beautiful blouse and she holds me tighter.

Tears from my childhood of not having my mother's love. Tears from burying my grandmother. Tears from raising myself. But the tears from the severing of my relationship are raw and laced with a question of my worth and whether it will always be like this.

Miss Jackie rocks me like a baby. I've never had this. It's the hug I've always dreamed about from my mother but isn't possible.

I cry for what feels like hours.

I open my mouth to apologize, but Miss Jackie stops me with a hand.

"Don't apologize for how you feel." She digs in her purse and removes a tissue. Then she dries my tears. "Grief is real. Pain is as real as love. That's what I hate about this whole Black Girl Magic movement. I get the sentiment. But people act like our melanin makes us immune to grief, heartbreak, and disappointment. Well, it doesn't."

I sit back, feeling much lighter. "I'll take care of the dry cleaning."

"Chile, I raised four boys. Tears are nothing compared to dirt, mud, frogs—"

"Frogs?"

"Yes, they went through a season of frog catching. There's a creek back there." She points into the night and starts telling me stories about the little Montgomerys.

"I feel exhausted with one. I can't imagine having five children."

"Neither could I. But we have to do what we have to do. So, take this advice as one you don't want to learn on your own." I turn on the bench, feeling closer to her after this conversation. "Asking or accepting help isn't a sign of weakness or that you can't support your child. It just makes you human."

"Yes, ma'am." I shift under her direct, no-nonsense gaze.

"With that said, I'd like to extend an offer, and I hope you'll accept. I'd like to keep Reese for the summer."

"I…"

"Let me finish. I'm newly retired. With all this upheaval and transition of ownership, I have way too much time on my hands and not enough to do. So, I thought I'd keep Lillian and Reese. We'll visit some museums, take in some concerts in the park, have a few slumber parties. I'll get to do some things I wanted to do with my children but couldn't."

She rests her hands in her lap, and I nearly overtake her with my hug.

"How much?"

"Nothing."

"Miss Jackie, you can't do that. I'm fighting hard to learn to stand on my own two feet. What about something small?"

She leans her head in a manner that reminds me of Kamal. "Okay. How about you cover the snacks for our movie nights? Kenneth just bought me a projector and we can watch movies on the side of the house. It's amazing and no fun alone. So, what do you say?" She extends a hand.

How did I get so lucky? And this means I can work a few more hours and maybe get my channel back rolling.

"Deal." I take her hand and it ends in another hug.

"Let's go grab her. I'm sure Lillian is driving Rashaad crazy."

We walk through the restaurant. It's only eight, but it's been a long day. I get her address and number in the hallway.

"Thank you so much. How will I ever repay you?"

She opens the door to Kamal's office and I'm momentarily distracted by the sight in front of me. Kamal is leaned back in his chair on the phone with Reese knocked out in his arms.

"You already have, dear."

His discerning gaze sweeps between us while talking the phone. Then we lock eyes. I enter his office to get Reese.

"She's fine. Give me five minutes."

Miss Jackie steps into the hallway to call Rashaad. I sit in the chair in front of Kamal's desk.

"What happened?" he asks the second the call ends.

"What do you mean?"

"Your eyes are red and puffy. And your makeup looks wiped off."

"It's a long story." I should have checked my face. "Why are you holding her?"

"She was coloring and almost face planted." He chuckles, looking over his shoulder at Reese.

"What's that on her head? Is it foil?"

"Yes." He chest shakes with laughter. "She wanted a crown."

"So you put foil on my baby's head?"

His head falls back, muffling his laugh. "I had to improvise. What's up with you and Mother?"

"She's taking Reese for the night."

"I like the sound of that." The heat in his eyes returns. "So, we're back on for tonight?"

"If you're not too tired for company."

"I'll never be too tired for you."

I drop my head to hide the way his words affect me. Then I look up. "Is this your doing?"

"What, my mother? No, we talked about it, but her coming was her own doing. What did she say?"

"We had a heart to heart."

He nods. "What time is your shift over?"

"Nine."

"Bet. I'll call the car service and wrap it up."

"Is my girl ready?" Miss Jackie asks, reentering the office.

"No, your girl is knocked out. Let me take her to the car."

The two of them dote on her and Reese is missing it, asleep on Kamal's shoulder. He stands to take her to the car, when Reese wakes.

"My picture."

"I got it, princess."

She nods, her eyes struggling to stay open until she sees Miss Jackie. She waves and with a sleep smile she's out again.

The transfer is seamless. I kiss my baby goodbye.

Miss Jackie sits in the car. "I'll have them ready for your

spa day. I might have to join you guys. I haven't been to the spa in years."

"Then have your bag ready."

She blinks as if surprised. "Goodnight, dear."

I lean inside, kissing her cheek. "Thank you again."

"You're welcome. Enjoy your night off."

"We will," Kamal says, bringing me to his side. The moment her car turns off the street, he kisses me until my toes curl in my tennis shoes. "You have twenty minutes to close out."

"I'll be inside in a second."

Left alone, I sit back on the bench. What a day.

CHAPTER 16

"Do you need to stop by Catrina's place?" I offer, opening the car door. She slides across the seat and I climb in behind her.

"Yes, if…"

I kiss her to erase the hesitation in her eyes. When I pull back, I see a smolder instead. "He'll need the address."

She tells the driver and we're on our way. I lean back in the seat and reach for Jayda. I relax my head against the seat, wrapping an arm around her.

"This is nice."

"It is." She glances up for a second, then snuggles against my chest.

"How was your day?" I kiss the top of her head.

"Emotional."

"Tell me about it, babe."

"That's not why you asked me to join you tonight."

"If it concerns you, then it's exactly why I asked you to join me tonight."

Jayda sits up and stares me in the eyes.

"What were your rules? To keep everything one hundred. What made today emotional?"

"You. Your family. Adjusting to my new life."

"Why me?" I tip my head to see her. Jayda thinks more than she speaks. But on rare occasions like this morning, she loosens up and her sass comes out to play.

A series of emotions cover her beautiful face. Tonight she's rocking big cornrows that hang to her lower back. Earlier she had on makeup and now her face is bare. After waiting for a while, I take another approach.

"What can I do to help you relax?"

"What are you expecting from tonight?"

"To spend time with you alone, away from the restaurant. To hold you. And if we get a few of your simmering kisses in the mix, I'll go to bed a happy man."

She exhales as if relieved.

My feelings for Jayda are outside my norm. She has a child. She's my employee. She has a man waiting in the wings for her return, yet she's here and I wouldn't want it any other way.

"What did you think I'd expect?"

"I'm not sure. You are a hard one to nail down."

"I like the sound of that. Now can I hold you?"

"Yes, Kamal, you can hold me."

I smile, letting my eyes close. Jayda rests against me and the stress of the day leaves my body. I hold her tighter and she adjusts, wrapping an arm behind my waist.

"How are you?"

I open my eyes and look down at her. "Right now, I'm a blessed man. I had a successful day at the office. I hung out with my best friends and my family in the same day. I had my favorite meal with Reese, and now I'm going home with my lady. A man can't ask for more than that."

"Your lady?"

"Yes, I've introduced you to my family, my boys, and I'm about to disclose the location of my bat cave. Woman, I think that settles it. You might as well stop fighting it."

Jayda shakes her head with an amused smile on her face.

"How do you feel about that?" I ask.

"Honestly, I'm all over the place. One minute I'm questioning it and the next there's not a single doubt in my mind."

"I get that. What questions do you have?"

She sits up, and I pull her back to me.

"Jayda, I want to be your friend and your man. The only way we can truly hurt each other is with dishonesty. You said one hundred. Let's do one hundred."

"I will, if you will. How do *you* feel?"

I shrug. "I understand your distrust and indecisiveness, but I don't like it. I've always tried to enter and exit my relationships on the up and up. So, experiencing this with you is different. Your turn."

"I'm scared."

"Of me?"

"No, of getting hurt, of looking like a fool, of trusting an untrustworthy man."

"Do you see me as untrustworthy?"

"No, but we've only known of each other for two months. People change." She plays with the front of my shirt. "You told me you didn't see yourself married or with children. It makes it hard for me to believe you're into me."

"What?" I sit forward.

"I know we're attracted to each other. But attraction is what led me to this place. I'm not ready for anything serious, but when I'm ready for more, I want the real deal."

"What's the real deal?"

Her mouth twists as she sits back. "Someone I can depend on that puts me first. Someone who loves my daughter. Someone I can spend the rest of my life with. Somewhere I belong."

We fall silent.

"So, Kamal, the question is, why me?" She looks over her shoulder.

I think about her question. My gut says, *She's the one.* But I never gave much weight to soulmates. Not when my parents professed to have never loved another person the way they love each other.

"Your beauty. Your smile. Your sass." Imagines of her dancing with no music tonight brings a smile to my face. "I love the mother you are. I've learned so much about you through Reese."

She turns in the seat. "Like what?"

"You have compassion for people. You see beyond the

external. A child who doesn't mind dancing in the middle of a crowded room has a shitload of confidence, and Reese got that from you." I cup the side of her face and kiss her softly on the lips.

"As for the marriage and kids, I don't trust love. Respect, loyalty, family. Those are what I stand on. But love doesn't love you back. People fall in and out of love. And after witnessing the death of my parents' marriage, I knew I didn't want marriage either."

I laugh, but I've never thought about this aloud. "It's like I see family as permanent and marriage as optional."

I stare out the window. "The moment I saw you stare your ex down, I knew I had to get to know you."

"Why?"

I shrug, "I'm attracted to strength, I guess." Then I think about it. "Nah, I'm attracted to you and that added one more reason on my list."

"What's on this list?"

"Your eyes. The way you switch your situation up, from your hair to your looks. Your hips. Your ass."

Jayda smacks my chest.

"If I keep eating at Southern Soul, I'll have two asses."

I laugh. "That shit sounds good to me."

"You're a mess."

"I am. I have one last question."

"Okay."

The car stops outside Catrina's house.

"What about your ex? Where do you stand with him?"

"I told you, it's over."

I nod. "Have you spoken to him?"

"A few times."

"And…"

"I told him the same."

"And his response?"

"He wants me to return." Her words only confirm what I knew. "Kamal, I can't control what he does or what he wants. I'm where I want to be."

"And where's that, Jayda?"

"With you."

For how long? The words hang around longer than I like. I rest my arms on my knees and look over at her. "This is when you decide if you want to rock with me. I'm not perfect, but I'm honest. I don't enter this relationship with the delusion of changing you, which leads us back to the beginning. I want you."

I'm asking for the very thing I've avoided my entire adult life—an unavailable woman. But despite everything I know about her situation, everything I know about the consequences of asking her to be my lady, I still want her. And when it's over, I'll have to move on.

WE ENTER CATRINA'S HOUSE. I quickly pack a bag for both of us since Reese need clothes for tomorrow.

"Do I need to bring robes for the spa?"

"No, they have little kiddie ones too." Kamal sits on the

bed, looking around the room. "How is Reese adjusting to the smaller space?"

"She makes all of this easy. Every day is a slumber party where she gets to see her Auntie Cat daily. Adding in Lillian and chicken and waffles places my baby in heaven."

"That must make you happy." He lays back and I watch as his smile fades into a soft snore.

I sit beside him. I use the time to really look at him. His beard, the slight laugh lines, his lips.

"Kamal…" I shake him a little but he looks so peaceful.

I try a few more times and decide to make an executive decision, sending the driver home. Catrina drags into the house as I head back to my room.

"Hey, Cat, is it okay if Kamal stays the night?"

"He's in there?" She moves to look and I stop her. "What?"

"He sat and the next minute he was knocked out." The man has worked around the clock for two months.

"Just don't wake me up with your ass smacking. 'Night, Jay."

"You and ass smacking. I need you to get a man or something."

She laughs, trying to keep it down. "Whatever! 'Night, Jay."

"Goodnight."

I turn out the lights and return to my room. I'm not sure if he's a light sleeper or not, so I tiptoe around preparing for bed, thinking about all that we said tonight. I take a quick shower and change into my nightclothes.

Kamal Montgomery is asleep in my twin-size bed. I chuckle, removing his shoes, and gently pull his legs up on the bed. When I turn to sleep in the other bed, he pats the mattress beside him.

"I'm holding you tonight," he says.

"We can't fit."

"Then make a pallet on the floor."

"Oh, no… I'm not sleeping on the floor."

"I guess the twin bed it is. Come on."

He lies on his back and I cozy up to his warm body. He grabs my leg, resting his hand on my bare thigh.

"You smell sweet." He inhales, brushing his nose over my shoulder. "Are you naked?"

"No, I'm wearing shorts."

He pats around in the dark, finding my boy shorts. The bed shifts and a light shines. He uses his cellphone to scan my body. I'm braless in a tank top.

"Fuck… You would have let me sleep through all this."

"You need the rest."

He jumps up and removes his shirt. Seconds later, he closes the bedroom door. I wait under the covers, watching him move around in the dark.

The sound of his zipper echoes and I know he's at the foot of the bed. Then the rustle of his pants leaves me wondering if he's naked.

I hold my breath as he lies beside me.

"Come on."

"Kamal…"

"I won't do anything you don't want. But if you ask, I'll

ensure you're thoroughly pleased." His voice drops, and I twist beside him. I stretch out and like before, he brings my thigh across his legs.

All I hear is the sound of our breathing. "Are you still awake?"

"Yes. I can't believe we're doing this," I answer.

"Doing what?"

"Lying here almost naked."

"Almost naked is far from naked." He chuckles.

"I thought you were sleeping."

"I was until somebody crawled into bed almost naked."

I laugh this time. "I didn't think you'd notice."

"Baby, I notice everything about you."

I still. "Why do you say stuff like that?"

"Like what—the truth?" He draws little circles on my thigh. "I notice everything about you."

The circles transform to the strong grip of his hand massaging my thigh.

"You can't keep doing that."

"Doing what?"

"Rubbing my leg."

Kamal sits up on his side, looking down on me. "How about we play a game?" His eyes manage to twinkle in the dark.

"What kind of game?"

"We get to explore one body part at a time for thirty seconds. But no sex."

"No sex?"

"No, you're not ready yet."

"Says who?" I ask. He's right, but having his rock hard body so close has me curious, starting with his tattoos.

"Do you want to play or not? And since I'm a gentleman, I'll let you go first."

I get up from the bed.

"Where are you going?"

"To turn on the light."

"No light. That's part of the fun."

I return and wiggle beneath the covers. "Are there any more rules I should know about?"

"Depends."

"On what?"

"How far are you comfortable with going?"

Kamal leaves the game to me. I could play it safe or I could play to win. Adrenaline rushes through my body.

"I'm in. How do I win?"

"The first one to climax loses." He whispers the words over my lips. "You still want to play?"

"Yes."

Kamal reaches for the blinds, cracking them enough for the hint of light to cast down on the bed. The colorful art covering his chest and arms is more extensive than I imagined.

"Lay on the bed."

"Yes, ma'am."

My heart pounds in my chest as I straddle his body, resting my ass over his cock. I roll my hips, and Kamal holds on for my next directive.

"Mmm… mmm… mmm."

The rumble in his chest vibrates against my thigh. I can't believe I'm about to do this. But the little vixen in me sees this as my nasty little dream coming true. I lick my lips, trying to decide where to start.

"Anything off limits?" I ask.

"My ass. Other than that, just tell me what to do."

His eyes caress my body while his hands caress from the tops of my thighs to beneath the weight of my ass.

"How will we keep time?" My eyes slide close, following the path of his hands in my mind.

"Hell, if I know." I look down at him. "This is my first time playing."

"I like the sound of that."

"Then show me."

"Start counting…" I rock my moist core, letting the friction awaken my body.

He mumbles, "One-one thousand… Two-one thousand…"

I select his luscious mouth as my first body part to explore. I crawl up his body, letting my breast graze across his chest, loving the heat in eyes.

"Five-one thousand… Six-one thousand…"

I assault his mouth. The top lip, then the bottom. My body shifts as Kamal rocks against me.

"Nine-one thousand… Ten-one thousand…"

I take my time devouring his mouth. He bites my lower lip and I moan. His mustache tickles everywhere his mouth kisses.

"Time."

I pull back. Panting. Hot. Sweaty. Ready. "Your turn."

I see the flames of desire staring at me. Kamal pulls my legs, wrapping them around his waist. He leans forward and slowly rolls my shirt up.

By instinct, I cover my bare breasts, and he peels my hands away. He settles perfectly between my thighs, cupping my breasts in his hands.

"Start counting…"

"One-one thousand…"

Kamal takes my nipple in his mouth. The suckling sensation makes me thrust harder against him. My eyes roll closed. He plays close attention to not one, but both. Leisurely, as if he has nothing better to do than consume my hard buds.

"Kamal…"

"You're supposed to count, love."

"Eleven-one   thousand…   Twelve-one   thousand… *Shyte*."

This man laughs without missing a beat, and I'm teetering on the edge.

"Thirty-one thousand…" I scramble from beneath him.

Kamal chuckles. "Where do you want me?"

I'm about to lose and we both know it.

"You can tap out." His finger circles my nipple, and my body remembers the way his tongue felt across my skin.

"I hate losing."

"Don't we all. But for someone to win, someone must lose. No way around it, babe."

I shake my head, suddenly disliking this game. The only way to win is… "Lay down."

I reach of the waistband of his boxers and he stops me.

"I'm good," I assure him and he releases my wrist.

I uncover the magic stick between his solid thighs. The light of the moon gives me a good idea of the length and girth.

This will be fun.

"Start counting…" I whisper, running my hand up his length, cupping the head in my palm. Kamal growls. "I can't hear you."

"Seven-one thousand… Eight-one thousand…"

I find the little vein and follow it from the base to the tip, then I cup him tight. Jerking a couple of times until I get into the right position.

"Fourteen-one thousand… Fifteen-one thousand… *Fuck it!*"

I'm flipped and Kamal wraps my legs behind his back. The length I held in my hands rocks between my folds. His motion has me crawling up the sheets. He explores me with his tongue, I arch off the mattress and suckle on the tender flesh of his neck.

"*I can't scream…* God… Kamal… I…" He adorns my mouth, stroking my tongue in sync with the motion rocking my bed. Pure ecstasy is within reach, filling my veins with fire. Then he thrusts once more and his kiss absorbs my cries of pleasure.

"I won…"

CHAPTER 17

I WAKE in a child's bed with my woman in my arms. The chime of my phone has me searching the floor. I answer without disturbing Jayda.

"Yeah."

"The crew is at Southern Soul to start the kitchen."

"I'm on my way." I disconnect the call and glance down at Jayda. "Babe, I need to let the crew in."

"I'll take you," she mumbles, not opening her eyes. Then she wiggles closer.

I haven't had a sexual encounter without sex since high school. But it was enough to make me ready to get this sexy ass woman in my bed, quick.

"Keep wiggling like that and…"

"Whatcha gonna do?"

I cover her body with mine in a smooth motion. Legs wide, arms above her head, and I'm aligned for business. "Make you mine."

I kiss her with all the sexual ache I have in my body to do more than rub her. I want to be in her, and I kiss her until she's breathless.

Morning breath and all.

"Be ready when I come back and bring your bag." I climb out of the bed.

"Good morning to you too." She turns over on her belly and glances back at me. "I had fun last night."

"So did I. You surprised me."

"Good. Gotta keep you on your toes."

I kiss her goodbye and watch as she falls back asleep. Today marks the first change inside the walls of Southern Soul, starting with the heart, the kitchen.

I step outside and consider what will get me there the quickest. Q is probably still up from last night. I start the text to him and change my mind. A quick cut and paste of the address and I send the message to a different recipient, Kenneth.

Seconds later he responds, *On my way.*

I sit on Catrina's porch watching the street. It's ironic how I used to wish I would see my father drive up to take me to my games or to have long talks with like I saw on tv.

The desire grew so strong that we made a game of it, searching for him inside of every passing vehicle until my hope was extinguished because he never returned.

The silver Porsche I saw in Mother's driveway stops in front of the house. I duck my head and see Kenneth inside.

"Look at this man." I stand, shaking my head, and glance at my watch. He's here might as well talk with him.

"Good morning. Rashaad with you?" He looks around outside.

"No." I shut the door, dropping my head back on the seat. "New whip?"

"I got it for Puddin' for our anniversary. I'm taking it to have the tags added after I drop you off. You know Cat and Rashaad are…"

"Yeah. Jayda's staying here. Wait? How do you know that's Catrina's house?"

"The boys and I take turns looking in on her. Checking her gutters, lawn care, moving furniture. Whatever she needs help with." He pulls off.

We ride in silence.

"What's up with you this morning?" Kenneth leans into the door and looks over at me.

"I thought it's time we talked."

"I agree, I'm glad you reached out." The car rolls to a stop and he tips his head back, greeting a man handling the grounds near the exit of Catrina's subdivision. Then he pulls out into the flow of traffic.

The car purrs like a satisfied kitten, weaving in and out of lanes. I rub the soft leather seats. She's a beauty but doesn't reflect Mother's style. But a gift is a gift.

"I know we've had our differences. Puddin' misses you and I told her I'd do whatever was necessary to mend our relationship. I'm here to ask what it will take to move forward."

"It's not that simple."

"Why not? You guys are grown. Puddin' and I have

squashed all that shit from the past. Why can't you do the same?"

"Because Mother asked for a relationship with you. I didn't."

"Then why did you call me?"

"I've always been curious. How can a man marry a woman and create a family, then turn his back on them?"

"As a man, you know, nothing is ever as it seems."

I laugh around my racing heart. Maintaining my cool is imperative, but a struggle when I've waited most of my life for this conversation.

"I saw my mother working day and night, year-round to clothe and feed us. Then the moment all the kids are up and out, you came weaseling yourself back into her life."

"You don't know what the fuck you're talking about."

"Then tell me what the fuck happened. I raised my siblings. *I did*. I was a child raising your kids. That's what the fuck happened. Now tell me how that shit's not what it seems. *Let me out of this muthafucka!*"

He hits the brakes and I jump out, slamming the door. The glass shatters.

"Kamal, get back in the car."

I don't respect that man as my father, but I won't break my mother's heart by putting my fist in his fucking mouth. I tried.

"Kamal!"

It only takes a few steps to recognize the area. Q's spot is a few blocks away. I move as fast as my legs will carry me.

"Kamal." The car rides beside me, slowing down traffic.

I stop and stare at him, daring him to say my name again. He burns off, turning at the next block. I pull out my phone to call another ride. I'm paying the crew by the hour and I'm out here bullshitting with Kenneth.

Jay's face pops up on my screen. I tap it and bring to my ear. "What's up, baby?"

"Just calling to check on you."

Kenneth jumps out of the car and stands in the middle of the sidewalk with hands motioning for me to stop. "I'm still your father."

"I gotta call you back, Jay." I shove my phone in my pocket. "I don't have a father, *Kenneth*."

"Man, don't do this."

"Do what? Tell you the truth about your actions? Everything I do is for my family. That's what a man does."

"I'm sorry. I didn't want this conversation to go like this." His gaze drops to the ground.

"That's the first truthful thing you've said all morning. Because you're one sorry mutha—"

"I ain't gonna be too many more muthafuckas." He puffs up his chest.

I close the space. Nose to nose. I smile.

I got twenty-five solid pounds and three inches on his ass. I wish he would swing on me.

"Kamal, baby," Jayda pleads with me.

"Listen to your woman," Kenneth grits through his teeth.

I laugh. "It's whatever. You don't put no fear in my heart."

He looks over my shoulder. "Will you take him to the restaurant?"

"Don't start worrying about me now. Just know I'll be here for Momma when your ass bounces again."

"Kamal…" Jayda jumps between us.

Kenneth climbs in the car and burns off, leaving the scent of rubber in the air.

"Jay, I'll call you later."

I walk. Playing the entire conversation in my head. I stop, turning my face to the sky. "I don't have time for this."

"Need a ride?"

I spin around.

Jayda stands in her funky leggings and designer slides.

"I'll be right back." She turns back and I see Catrina's car back several blocks.

Why did I let him get to me? I lost my composure and I let Jayda see it. I jog to catch up with her.

"How did you find me?"

She holds up her phone. "You didn't disconnect. My first thought was to get to the restaurant, and I saw you guys. What was that?"

"Me letting go of the past." I walk to the car and open her door. Then I sit inside.

"Talk to me."

"Nothing to talk about."

"Fine." Jayda drives. "But for the record, calling your father a motherfucker doesn't fall in the nothing category." She air quotes nothing.

"It's complicated."

"Drama usually is. But something tells me that little conversation will not go over well with Miss Jackie."

I watch the city roll by until we're outside Southern Soul. I let the crew in and then I call Demetrius. During the talk about the renovations, he agreed to write here on the construction days to give me the day off.

Jayda sits on the bench out front while we get the crew set up. I walk out and she pops up.

"Want to cancel today?"

"No, I gave the girls my word."

"Do you want to pick them up first or take you to the hotel to change?"

I glance down. "Let's get the girls. Look, Jay, I'm sorry about what you saw."

"Sorry for how you behaved or sorry that I saw it?" She crosses her arms.

"That you saw it. It was a long time coming."

I sit back in the seat thinking about how to make my next move. Kenneth has told no one because my phone's not ringing. I could talk to Mother myself, but I'm not ready.

We arrive at Mother's house and Jayda holds the bulk of the conversation, leaving it about the kids. I kiss Mother's cheek, promising to call her later.

The next stop is my hotel. "Order the girls' breakfast. I'll shower and we'll be out."

Reese and Lillian look at me, then Jayda. Kids sense everything.

"I'll be back," I assure them.

I have to shake this shit off. What did I expect? That he'd turn into the father of the year. No. But at least he could have taken some responsibility. The way he's handled this is foul and acting put out because I'm not calling his shit chocolate pie makes him look sketchier.

I let the steamy, scorching water relieve the tension in my neck. The girls have waited for this day for weeks and I can't spoil it for them, but I'm not in a company kind of mood.

I walk through the bathroom until I reach my bed. Closing my eyes, I fall back. The weight of the bed shifts and I open my eyes to Jayda sitting over me. She gathers the hem of her shirt, pulling it over her head. I check to ensure the door's closed, and it is.

"What are you doing?" I keep my eyes on hers.

"Since you're a fan of games, I thought we could squeeze in a round, as a little pick me up." She winks, tossing her shirt to the floor. "Because I haven't had a day at the spa in ages."

I trace the edge of her lace bra, and she smacks my hand. "Ouch."

"No touching. I realized after you left this morning that you cheated last night."

"How so?"

She un-pops her bra and her full breasts spill out. I cover a nipple with my mouth, and she cups my head.

"You're cheating again."

"This is a practice run."

I roll us over, settling between her warm thighs. "Where are the girls?"

"Watching a movie and eating breakfast. We have fifteen minutes." She glances at her watch. "Correction—twelve minutes."

"What did you do—set a timer?" I insert my hands into her waistband. "Lift up."

Jayda digs her heels into the mattress and I slip the emoji-covered leggings off. "Yes, a 'Mommy Time' timer."

"What's a 'Mommy Time' timer?" I hang over her, plucking her braids out of my way.

"Fifteen minutes and she stays put until I get back, unless there's an emergency."

"Inventive." I go through the same motion with her panties, surprised when she allows me to slip them off. "Did you lock the door?"

"Of course."

"You're a very creative parent. Are you using one of your Mommy rules on me?"

"I am"—she sweeps her tongue across her full lips—"but I can't tell you about it now. Time is ticking."

"What are the rules?" I sit back, reaching for my towel, and she stops me.

She opens it, dropping the terrycloth to the follow. "Your body is amazing."

I thank her with my kiss. "Focus."

"Any rules?" Her eyes twinkle with excitement.

"As long as I get another tour of your wondrous curves."

I kiss across her shoulders and up her neck, ending with a sample of her tongue.

"Thirty seconds. The first one to climax loses. But we can only touch with our mouths."

"Ladies first."

"Such the gentleman."

"I try."

We switch places and she's back on top of me. I could sit in this spot for a lifetime.

"Start counting…"

I lie back, curious about where she'll start this time. She wiggles down my body. "One-one thousand… Two-one thousand… Three-one thousand…"

She places her first kiss on my inner thigh. A part tickling, part erotic sensation covers my body. I groan, struggling to count the moment she nibbles so close that her nose brushes my dick.

I sit straight up.

"What number are we on?" Jayda asks with flames in her eyes. She knows exactly what she's doing to me.

I think and can't come up with an answer. "Fifteen or sixteen."

"Start over."

"Why?"

"Because you lost your place, and you distracted me. Start counting… we only have eight minutes left. Now where was I…"

I start counting again. She works a spell over me with her mouth, and when I reach twenty-nine, she uses her tongue to travel the length of my cock and I almost lose it.

"Oh damn, out of time." She sits back as if she didn't almost have my dick in her mouth.

"You call me a cheater."

"What?" She gives me an innocent smile. "Where do you want me?"

"On your stomach."

Her eyes round.

"Move it. You're wasting my time." She rolls over and I smack her ass, and I've found my spot. I plant my hands on either side of her body. "I'm ready when you are."

She starts counting and I start at the crease where her thick thighs curve into the plump flesh I plan to devour. She moans with every lick and nibble. I bite, running my teeth gently across her bottom. Her body lifts off the mattress and her womanly scent fills my nose.

I'm so hard, I'm scared I'll break my johnson. But I can't stop. There's something about the taste of her scent. The count is muffled in the duvet and her ass lifts just enough for me to make a suggestive swipe of my own. I twirl my tongue, entering her from the back.

"*Fuck*!"

"Watch your language, love." I lick again out of a need to hear her lose it. I French kiss her pussy and Jayda screams. "Game over."

I flip her over and clean my plate. She throws a pillow over her face and the sounds of her pleasure have me reaching for my cock. Stroking it with each twist of her hips and thrust of her pussy on my tongue. Then I join her, spilling my seed and licking her dry.

KAMAL CHECKS us in at the spa. The girls bounce around, too excited to sit. The clerk asks for us to give them a few minutes to set up the room. I keep an eye on the girls at the magazine table and the other on Kamal. His heated eyes remain trained on me, as if he's expecting me to say something.

"What?" I ask.

"Nothing."

I exhale, looking around, and the place is beautiful but empty. He drops a magazine over his lap to hide his erection and I fight to keep from laughing.

Is he thinking what I'm thinking?

I've lost this little game of his twice. Today, I played to get his mind off this morning, and thought I'd catch him off guard, but the moment I felt his moist tongue I was out for the count.

"What are you smiling about?" He sits on the couch beside me.

"You," I admit.

"Mr. and Mrs. Montgomery," the masseuse announces from the doorway.

Mrs. Montgomery?

Kamal stands and the girls follow hand in hand.

"Jay?"

"Coming." I shuffle to catch up with them.

"Wait… wait for me."

I turn around. "Miss Jackie?"

"Momma?" Kamal and I share a glance.

"I'll get the girls." I run off to wrangle the girls, hoping Mr. Kenneth didn't tell Miss Jackie about this morning.

The masseuse gives us a series of instructions and everyone receives a key to lock up our belongings. The girls have backpacks with swimsuits and two changes of clothes. We decided on massages first and the pool second.

"Put on your tank top and shorts for the massage."

"Yes, ma'am." They say in unison, followed by a fit of giggles. I'll be giggled out by the end of the day.

I'm almost done and Miss Jackie walks in with her key and locker assignment.

"Hey, Jayda." Miss Jackie hugs me. "Why do you look so surprised? Kamal said I could join you. I thought you'd like to have some alone time with him." She winks and walks right past me.

I exhale. Maybe he didn't. I shrug, following my party inside the women's dressing room. The all white decor with gray marble stones pairs beautifully with the natural wood and bamboo. The girls ooh and aah.

"I got the girls. Bye." They turn off and I'm ushered through a side door where I find Kamal stretched out on a massage table.

I climb on the free table, and the moment the masseuse leaves, I lean over. "Are you sure this place is reputable? It's empty."

I jump down and peek around corners and in the cabinets.

"It's the best in Houston." Kamal rolls to his side, propped up on his elbow.

"Then where are the people."

"I booked the place for the day."

My mouth drops open. He pulls my table closer. The scratching sound has me looking around for the workers. He pats the table.

"Come on, we have lunch scheduled, then another round of treatments this afternoon."

We lie on the tables, and I exhale. The soft music and dim lights infuse an air of relaxation and after my morning I need it. The masseuse and masseur work out every kink and knot, and I keep my eyes on Kamal.

The rage I saw in him shows me the depths of his anger toward his father. And I wonder why?

"Kamal?"

"Yeah, babe." He turns his face.

"What happened?"

He opens his eyes, searches mine, and I don't look away even after seeing his raw pain looking back. He starts at the age thirteen and walks me through his life.

Football games, recitals, the lean years with his mother, the height of his football career, ending with giving away his mother to the man he blames for it all.

I leave my table and join him on his. This little table is about the size of the bed we shared last night. He flips over on his back and gathers me close and tight. I rest my chin on his chest and I spy the words, "Put it in ink."

"What's this one?" I point to it.

He doesn't budge to see it. "It's my motto. Put it in ink."

"What does it mean?"

"It's my version of when people show you who they are, believe them."

Pain pierces my heart. "So, that means you don't give second chances?"

"No. I'll only play the fool once."

"I'm confused."

He looks over at me. "About what?"

"Kamal, you extend himself to the point of physical exhaustion, caring for the future of your siblings and their unborn children. You made my baby a foil crown and held her until she fell asleep to keep her from sleeping in a chair."

"Jay, that's not the same thing. He chose to leave. He left us and started a new life, leaving us to suffer. That's unforgivable."

I rest my head over his heart. Feeling his pain as if it were my own.

"Kamal, we all need a redo every now and again. An opportunity at a fresh start."

He shakes his head. "Nah, not him."

I sit up enough to lean over his body. "I don't believe you. That's exactly what you gave me, which means you

have the capacity in this oversized heart of yours to extend
that same compassion to your father."

I SIT POOLSIDE with my shades on, reading a book. I
needed today. Kamal's said next to nothing to me since the
massage.

"That meeting with you and the guys got me thinking."

He glares at me.

"If you're sending a curse down on me, can you please
include some Blue Bell ice cream? And maybe that I'll
shrink to a size six with some butt-length Malaysian hair?"

He laughs and laughs. Miss Jackie and the girls stop and
stare, and it only makes him laugh harder.

"Woman, you have a screw loose in that head of yours.
God, that was funny." He dries his eyes. "Who adds ice
cream to a curse?"

"I do. I can't believe I forgot how good it is." I move
over to his lounge chair, tucking my feet beneath me. "Are
you still upset with me?"

"No." He cups my face. "I'm upset with myself. I let
him get to me."

"It just means you're human. Welcome to the club."

"Does this mean you forgive your ex?"

"For what he did to me? Yes. But when it comes to
Reese, it's a little harder. I'm working on it though."

He nods. "So what have you been thinking about?"

"I think I want to start my own talent agency for social influencers."

"What? Where is this coming from?"

"From you." His face twists. "Okay, not directly, but you planted a seed. I considered reviving my YouTube channel, but what I want to research is creating brand opportunities for people with smaller, loyal followers."

"I like the sound of that."

"Really?" I sit up taller.

"Yeah, really. What's the next steps?"

"I don't know. I figure I'll help you with relaunching Southern Soul and maybe talk it over with Ebony."

"I can do you one better."

"Not another job offer."

"No, but I know a group of sistas out of Austin that have a company you could consider partnering with to get started."

"Kamal… there you go again."

"It's not mine to give but a hookup. All I can offer is an introduction. You'll have to handle it from there."

I chew on the side of my mouth, not sure.

"Listen, do you think billionaires turn down opportunities to earn more money?"

"No."

"Then take what I'm offering you. It's not an imposition and all you'll owe me is a few more rounds of… What shall we call our little game?" He leans forward and nibbles on my ear. "Kamal Time."

I pull back and look in his eyes. "That sounds so technical."

"It's better than Tasty Ass and Tits."

"Ugh… really, Kamal?"

"Dead ass!"

We laugh and I lean back.

"I'll accept the offer after I make some calls."

"I'm here if you want to run anything by me."

"Thank you."

"No, problem."

Lillian walks over, splashing water everywhere. "Uncle, I'm hungry."

He nods, looking over at Reese. "What about you, princess?"

"Yes, sir."

Miss Jackie helps her out and claims my vacant chair.

"What do you ladies want?" Kamal asks.

"Pizza!"

"Oh no, not more pizza. What about you, love?" He squeezes me. I wonder if he realizes he calls me that aloud.

"I'm fine with pizza. Can we have ice cream for dessert?"

Kamal's head falls back and the girls chant for pizza and ice cream.

"Okay… okay… Momma?" He leans forward.

"Make mine a cheese pizza," Miss Jackie says, and she stares at me with a smile on her face.

Their cheers echo through the room.

Kamal and I strategize about getting the pizza here since we have the place for a few more hours.

"Mommy… mommy… mommy."

"Yes, honey."

"Can I dance?"

"Yes, baby."

Reese starts, and everyone looks on. She twists and turns, using her wet feet to slide around.

"Be careful, baby." I add.

"Yes, ma'am. Dance with me, Mommy."

I shrug and pull Kamal to his feet. He stands with an oversized smile on his face.

"What do I do?" he asks Reese.

"Move to the music in your heart."

All five of us dance. Kamal grabs my hand, spinning me around, and Reese demands, "Do me too."

Our festivities die in a fit of laughter, and I pull out my phone. "Picture time."

We squeeze in, and I snap a picture. Then Reese adds, "Silly face."

"I'll go take care of the pizza." Kamal kisses me and heads to the front desk.

I post the pictures and caption. "Family time is the best time. I have something amazing coming, Gems. Who's ready? Let me see your gems in the comments." I add the kissing lips emoji and toss my phone aside.

CHAPTER 18

I ENTER the dining area and stand in front of the team. This is round two for our Sunday opening. The entire floor is open for customers to eat. This time we removed the open bar and DJ. It's like a regular day, except we changed the hours from noon to eight.

Jayda throws me a discreet thumbs up and motions for me to smile. But the sweat under my collar has me tripping. The front door opens, and I see my family and I'm relieved until I see Kenneth with them. It's been a month, and he still hasn't mentioned our disagreement to Mother.

I dismiss him and focus on the tonight. The kitchen update happened without issue. The dining room took longer than expected, but both sides are ready to go today.

Rashaad has been working with Jayda and Ebony to generate community participation. Demetrius is holding down all the Sunday construction days. The last big step is Miya and Dean are working together to create a new menu.

This is truly a family affair.

"Q, can you give us an update?"

I move aside while he pumps up the team. He's running dual training both here and at his club. The team is moving faster and they're breaking fewer dishes.

I take one last look in the kitchen, so when Q calls me, I'm ready to pray over the meal.

"Heavenly Father…"

I pray over the staff, the food, the families selecting Southern Soul for their Sunday dinner. I pray for the legacy to continue and that future Montgomerys will continue on the path we've paved. We end with a boisterous "Amen."

I have a healthy level of fear about tonight the moment the doors open. Momma gives me a hug before being seated. Catrina and Jayda are splitting the hostess role since Jayda's handling social media.

My boys roll in, and they're seated. I make a mental note to sit with them sometime tonight. I search the room for Jayda, when I see her with Miya.

"Do you see what I see?" Q says.

"What?"

"Check out yo boy." He tips his head towards Dean and Emmitt.

Dean's intense eyes follow Miya and Jayda.

"You better talk to him. I don't trust any of your friends with women."

I almost break my neck looking over at him.

"What?" Q asks.

"You have no room to talk."

"Like hell I can. I can talk because I know. And I'll bust his ass if he messes over my sister."

"And who will bust yours for the way you're slipping numbers in your pockets?"

Q laughs. "Man, mind your business." Then he falls silent.

I glance over and see Ebony. "Don't, Q."

"What?"

"Ebony is off limits. She's like a sister to me."

"She might be your sister, but she's ain't mine."

Q slides off in her direction before I can stop him. I turn to follow him when my eyes are covered.

"Babe, keep playing and I'll demand an intermission…"

"I like the sound of that."

I spin around, peeling away the hands. "Trish, what are you doing here?"

"I came to support you." She reaches out to wrap her arms around me and I pin her hands in place.

"Look, you're welcome to sit and eat. But I'm seeing someone."

"Seeing someone? What about me?"

"What about you?" Jayda pops up from nowhere and I'm sweating bullets.

"Who are you?" Trish asks.

"I'm Jayda and you are…" She extends a hand.

"Trish. Kamal and I are friends."

"Well, any *friend* of Kamal's is a friend of mine."

I pull Jayda to my side and it's not missed on Trish.

The two communicate without words. The longer they stand face to face, the more Trish's fair skin turns red.

"Goodbye, Kamal. Call me when you're ready for an upgrade."

"Don't hold your breath," Jayda offers to her departure. Then she turns on me. "Is there something I should know?"

"No, I didn't invite her. I haven't seen her in months."

"And she just shows up?"

"Yes."

"Right." She walks off.

"Jay."

"Kamal, we need you in the kitchen." I'm torn between my job and my woman. I'll talk with her tonight. "Yeah, man, what's up?"

I burst out the door. Seeing Trish all over Kamal gave me a flashback. I walked over, preparing myself for a repeat of Los Angeles, and I heard him tell her about me.

Kamal isn't Brett.

I look back inside and don't see Kamal or Trish. I sit and take a deep breath. Kamal hasn't given me a reason to distrust him, I remind myself.

Unlike my relationship with Brett, I don't feel jealous about other women. Kamal makes me feel like I'm the only woman in the room. That I'm wanted and desired.

Trish is a nonfactor. I exhale.

"Hey, Jayda! Did we miss the gathering?"

I paste on a smile, "Hey, Gem! No, and we still have room at the table. We're in the far corner. I just need a second."

"Okay, you look amazing!"

"So do you," I call out as the fan goes inside.

I shake off the bad thoughts Trish stirred up. Then I turn on my camera. "Gems! It's not too late. We're hanging at Southern Soul for a few more hours. Come on out. Let's break bread and get glammed up!" I give the address before signing out.

I post on my social media pages and my phone rings. I don't recognize the number. "Jayda Dallas."

"Are you having fun with your little boyfriend?"

This must be fuck with Jayda night. "Brett, what do you want?"

"To check on you and Reese."

"It's almost bedtime, and I told you to call her iPad." I cross my arms, ready for tonight to end. Miss Jackie has Reese, and Kamal and I will finally get a night alone. "Look, I need to go."

"Wait… Jayda wait."

"What, Brett?"

"I miss you."

"We've done this already. Now it's all about Reese."

"Jayda, all couples have issues. Don't you want Reese to have it better than we had. That she deserves to live in her own home with her mother and father under the same roof? Isn't our family worth another shot?"

"I don't have time for this." I shake my head, keeping my eyes on the door.

"Fine. Then I'll let you explain how you quit on our family. Is that something you can live with?"

"Yes. Brett, you're picking a fine time to think about *our* family." I pace back and forth. "I'm supposed to pretend you didn't set up an entire life without us?"

"I fucked up and I'm sorry." His end falls silent and I drop to the bench. "Nobody's perfect. I just want my family back."

The door swings open. "They're ready, Babe."

I press my phone to my chest. "I'll be right there."

Kamal opens the door wider.

"I gotta go. Bye." I disconnect the call.

"Who was that?"

"Brett." I walk over to him. "Who's ready?"

"The partners of Platinum Prestige."

"Oh my god, I'm so nervous." I've worked on my presentation for Gem Talent Agency.

I started with my most recent views and complied with a list of brands that use influencers and I stumbled on my brand specialty, Black-owned beauty brands.

"You got this. I'll be there to cheer you on."

I nod.

"Hey, for the record I didn't invite Trish."

"Okay." I glance inside, trying to spot them, and Kamal turns my face to him.

"Are we good?" he asks.

"Yes, babe, we're perfect."

. . .

I HAVE a hundred-thousand-dollar check signed by Hunter Abbott on behalf of Platinum Prestige. They want to invest in my idea. I sit on the bench outside Southern Soul and it's taking everything not to break out in an ugly cry.

"What are you doing out here?" Catrina sits beside me.

"Trying not to cry. Look."

"Girl, what is this? Wait… Platinum… OMG! You did it! You did it. I've never seen this much money in my life." She runs her nose over the check. "This shit smells rich, *bytch*."

We laugh, jumping up and down.

"We got to dance one time for Reese," I demand and we do my baby justice until the joy overflows.

"What's next?"

"I have to find at least twenty influencers and ten brands willing to take a chance on my agency. But I have the full backing of Platinum and they will set up some brand appointments to help *us* get started."

"Us?"

"Yes, I need you, and they're a twenty-five thousand dollar bonus if you help me build this company."

"You know I got your back. But I don't—" Catrina stops.

"Hey, Jayda and Cat."

"Hey, Rashaad," I respond, but I can't take my eyes off the woman clinging to his arm.

"This is a new agent, Daphne."

"Hello, I'm Jayda and this is Catrina." I bump her with my elbow, but her eyes are glued to Rashaad.

"We have to get inside. I promised Kamal I'd help," Rashaad says.

"Sure, it was nice meeting you." I hold Catrina's shaking hand tight.

"Same to you."

They disappear inside. "Catrina, I know Rashaad has feelings for you."

"Don't, Jay. I've been praying for a sign and that's it. I'm done."

"Catrina…"

"If you say something I'm liable to burst into tears or key his car. Neither one will change how he feels about me. Will you cover for me tonight?"

"Yeah, sure." I gather her in a hug.

"And I'll be all yours after I put in my two-week notice. Have fun with Kamal tonight." She heads to the car.

"Drive safely."

She throws a wave over her shoulder but doesn't look back.

"Why are you still out here? You're supposed to be celebrating." Kamal waves me inside.

"I was… I am."

"What's wrong with you? You seem distracted."

"Catrina left after seeing Rashaad."

"Damn." Kamal shakes his head.

"What's wrong with him? Why are men so blind?"

"Babe, people have to do things in their own time and

their own way. Let's get out of here." He drags me to the parking lot.

"We're going the wrong way."

"No, ma'am. Tonight is a celebration for two. My family will close out the night. Momma is watching Reese and I'm loving on you."

"Why didn't you say so?" I sit in the SUV and bring my lips to his. He kisses me quiet.

"I just did."

THE MOMENT the elevator door closes I'm pinned against the wall, showered with champagne-flavored kisses. Impatient, I yank his pants open. He pulls my skirt over my ass, and I'm lowered to ecstasy.

"Fuck…" Kamal growls, filling me completely.

His cock jumps, stretching me. He feels too big, and just right at the same time.

"Am I hurting you, love?"

I shake and nod my head at the same time. "I want more."

I arch my back using the wall, giving him just enough room to pull out and thrust deeper. I cry out his name and it echoes back, masking our labored breathing.

I grind against him as he settles into a smooth rocking motion. After weeks of pleasure, thanks to his mouth and his fingers, I need this. All of him filling me until I'm climbing the cool metal walls.

He locks the elevator to finish what we started uninterrupted. Then the rhythm increases, he holds on to my hips and the smooth long strokes turn to thrusts, ramming deep and fast and…

"Kamal… Oh… Shit…" I wail from the pit of my soul.

I lose control of my body with my eyes shut tight. But he's not done carrying me inside and slides in from the back.

We both buckle with our hands on the back of his couch. He's claiming every inch of me and it's his to have. The sounds of flesh against flesh, two bodies joined, sealing our fate.

"Jay…" He pulls me hard until his final thrust fades into a growl.

I'm weak, and he's strong, taking me into his arms. We don't stop until we're in the bathroom.

"Anything off limits?"

I shake my head while he slowly removes each article of clothing from my body. He starts the shower and we step inside.

Kamal lathers his hands and slides them across my body. Over my shoulders, while kissing up my neck. Down my back and over the roundness of my backside, while nibbling on my ears. Then he drops to his knees.

I'm pushed up the wall, and he licks up my thighs. He gently spreads my lips, dipping his tongue inside as if checking for my readiness.

"What are you doing, baby?"

"Making you mine," he declares, and he does. I come

for the second time and Kamal isn't done, but I can barely hold myself up. "I got you."

He washes my body again and I'm asleep before my body hits the bed.

LAST WEEK we were tested together, but I didn't expect to make love to her without protection. The weight of it rocks me. Because for the first time, I want a future with someone and I want it with her.

I brush her wet hair over the pillow and tuck the covers around her. The thought of having another Reese with a little Montgomery blood has me rock hard again. I rub my cock over her ass and Jayda rolls her hips against me.

"Kamal… we're taking a big chance…"

"I know." I flip her over and fill her.

We sigh and I make love to my woman, watching the wave of passion cross her face, listening for her desires, giving her what she needs. I kiss over her heart, whispering my love across her moist skin until I hover over her.

"I love you, Jayda."

"Really? I love you too." She cups my face and kisses me until her love is as real as my heartbeat.

We collapse exhausted, and Jayda falls asleep in my arms. But I can't sleep. I don't want the day to end.

CHAPTER 19

I WAKE sore and happy to find a pair of beautiful dark brown eyes.

"Want to hang out today?" he asks, running a finger down the bridge of my nose.

"I need to get my laptop and clothes from Cat's place, then I'm all yours." I lean forward and kiss him. "Will you promise me something?"

"Anything."

"Tell me if this—us—becomes too much. I know you—"

Kamal covers my mouth with a single finger, and I kiss it. "What's going on here?"

"I don't want you loving me out of passion or an amazing sexual encounter."

"Do I strike you as a person who throws words around? That I'd say something I don't mean?"

"No."

"I'm the same man, Jayda. I just never thought I'd meet you."

I nod. "Maybe you should say it again, so I can get used to hearing it."

He blesses me with one of his slow smiles. They're my undoing. Better than a sunset and all the ice cream in the world.

"I love you, Jayda Dallas."

"I love you too, Kamal Montgomery."

I lean up and kiss him, then rest my head over his heart. His "put it in ink" tattoo is colored like graffiti. I run my finger over the letters.

"All right, let's get moving." He slaps my ass with a loud pop and we're off.

WE APPROACH CATRINA'S HOUSE, debating on our plans for the day. It seems I've spoiled her with the spa.

"My vote is for The Galleria. But I'm cool with either," I state for the record.

"Spa it is," Jayda declares.

"I'll call and make the reservation while you grab your stuff."

"Cool."

I turn on the block. There's an unfamiliar car out front. Then someone steps forward, glancing our direction. Her gasp draws my attention.

"What's up?" I look and recognize the man walking this way. "What's he doing here?"

"I don't know."

I stop the SUV and Jayda jumps out. I'm right behind her.

"What are you doing here, Brett?"

"Doing what I should have done four months ago. I miss my family. I'm willing to do whatever it takes to prove it to you."

His words are my worst nightmare. I face Jayda. "Did you know Brett would be here?"

"No." Her inability to hold eye contact gives her away. She knows more than she's saying.

I reframe my question. "Has he been trying to get back with you this entire time?"

"Yes, but—"

I step closer. "Why didn't you tell me?"

"Because I've already made my decision."

"That's not what you said last night." Brett stares at me, and I look at Jayda.

Her mouth drops open, and her recovery is a second too late.

I hear the sound of my heart turning to stone. I broke my rules. This is my fault. But I still don't want to believe she'd deliberately mislead me.

"You need to leave." Jayda points away from the house.

"I'm not giving you up without a fight," Brett declares.

I watch her, watching him leave. She's torn. The

moment the car door shuts, I spin on my heels and get back in my ride.

Jayda runs to my door. "Where are you going?"

"Home. I'm not doing this with you or him."

"Let me get my bag and we'll talk about it."

"Nah, I'm good. I need time to think."

"About what? Brett said that to come between us. He's manipulating the situation." The emotions in her eyes almost break me, and the part of me that loves her more than life prays this is all a misunderstanding.

"Then tell me what you said."

Her mouth snaps shut.

"On one hundred… Isn't that the level of honesty you demanded of me?"

She nods. "He asked for a second chance."

"And your response was…"

"I said 'no,' kind of," she mumbles the last part, but I heard it over the pounding of my heart.

"Your fickle response told him it was okay to fly across the country and sit on your doorstep with the expectation of taking *his* family home."

"That has nothing to do with me. I was done with our relationship the moment he picked her over me."

"People who are done have one answer. No. N-O." I shake my head. "Playing fucking games. Pointing the finger at me like I'm the unreliable person in this relationship while you straddle the fucking fence." I turn over the ignition, slamming the gear into reverse.

"Mr. Kamal."

I look to the porch and over at Jayda. Reese stands, holding her iPad in her hands. I put the vehicle in park and drop my head. "Excuse me."

Jayda steps back. The moment my feet touch the grass, Reese runs, leaping into my arms. "Look at my picture."

I force a smile until I see the drawing. "That's your best one yet."

Reese looks at me. "Are you sad? Mommy, Mr. Kamal is sad. Maybe he needs pizza."

I chuckle. *Pizza can't fix this.*

"I'm just tired." I lower her to the ground and hug her for longer than usual because this might be the last time. Then I kiss the top of her head. "Be a big girl. I gotta go, princess."

"Okay, love you. Bye-bye." She waves, running back in the house.

"Love you too."

I walk beside Kamal, but he won't look at me. "Babe, please listen to me. Please. I should have told you, but I didn't know how."

"You simply say, Kamal, I think I want to work my relationship out with Brett."

"But that's not true."

"But it's not false. Your hesitation is exposing your ass." He climbs behind the wheel, slamming the door.

"Kamal, I love you, please don't do this." I hold on, torn.

"I won't if you answer one question."

I take a deep breath. "Okay."

"Is there a part of you willing to give your relationship with Brett a second chance?"

I drop my head.

"Bye, Jayda."

I DRIVE, refusing to look in the rearview mirror. How can my life change so drastically in twenty-four hours? And somehow I stop at Mother's house.

I drop my head on the steering wheel. I wanted her so bad I ignored the signs. A knock on the window pulls me from my downward spiral and it's Kenneth.

I shake my head. I can't deal with him. I'm too emotional.

"Kamal, please. Jayda called and I've been in your shoes son."

I look up at him but don't move.

"Your mother and I got a divorce because she had an affair."

What is happening? I'm in the Twilight Zone. I hit the locks and Kenneth sits in the passenger seat.

"I never wanted to tell you this way because we both played our part. But I never meant for my heartbreak to affect my kids. I needed time to heal. Every time I talked with her or heard her name, I experienced the pain all over again. It felt easier to block everything out and work. So, that's what I did. But time is a bitch.

"One day turned into two. Two weeks turned into four. Then I looked up and Miya was graduating from culinary school. And it still hurt like the first day."

"*Damn*," is all I can say.

"I'm missing my kids, missing my woman, and I'm making money hand over fist. All I did was work. But I had nothing to show for it because I didn't have y'all." He runs a hand over his face.

"How did you forgive her?"

"My heart wouldn't stop loving her. I've loved no one the way I love Puddin'."

"Damn."

Kenneth laughs. "That about sums it up. My actions and my reasons don't relieve me of my responsibility. I didn't sit by and do nothing for my family. You'll have to talk with your mom about that. My greatest regret is that I didn't try harder sooner."

I think about everything he's said. "Things won't change overnight, but I'm willing to try. I see the way you love my momma and how you look out for her. I just couldn't stand by and let her get hurt again."

"Yeah, I commend you for that. That's why I didn't bust your ass."

"Hold on now, you would have got a surprise messing with me."

Kenneth laughs and I laugh with him. This is the first

time in years we've had a man to man without a misunderstanding.

He opens the door. "Let's get in here and make some
dinner before we mess the moment up."

I holler, getting out and heading inside. I don't know
how I'll handle my relationship with Jayda, but for now I'll
do the job I came here to do.

Q CAME by Momma's and scooped me up for drinks.

"Since when did you let go of Mother?" He tips his nose
in the air.

"You came to console me, not talk shit."

"I talk shit because I'm a shit talker."

I laugh, hating it took losing Jayda for me to have a real
honest talk with Kenneth. I'm thankful for him and the rest
of my family. They're making this day bearable, and it
continues the moment we enter Q's nightclub. Everyone's
here.

"Damn, word travels fast."

Dean, Emmitt, Rashaad, Demetrius, even Baby Miya
hangs with the guys for a few rounds of drinks. Thankfully,
no one mentions Jayda or Reese until I get a tap on my
shoulder.

"Hey, handsome."

I throw back my shot. "What's up, Trish?"

"I thought I'd speak and let you know I'm available
whenever you want to hang out." Trish places a hand on my

knee. I can't believe I'm sitting in this club trying to drown out the love I have for Jayda.

"That's good to know."

The guys snicker and Trish turns around.

"Aren't you a pesky little something."

Jayda.

Trish looks over at me. "You have my numbers. Goodnight."

The others mumble their goodnights, no doubt because they don't want to miss a second of this conversation.

"Can we talk?"

"I'm not ready to talk with you, Jayda."

"If I can't speak with my man, can I please talk with my friend?"

I lower my beer. My heart knows this is my woman, but my pride won't let me hear her out.

"No, because you did the exact thing I asked you not to do. You played me, and I fell for it. We tried. Lesson learned."

"You about to put that shit in ink?" Hurt and longing stare back at me. "People make mistakes, Kamal. You knew my situation was complicated. Now you're acting as if I played you?"

I face the bar, asking for another shot.

"You're exactly who I thought you were, Kamal," she yells over the music.

"Too bad you're not."

CHAPTER 20

EVERYTHING BLEW up in my face. I walked in Q's club and saw Trish with Kamal, and I made my bad situation worse. And my fears of not giving my relationship an honest to God second chance haunted me. I boarded a plane back to Los Angeles in my feelings, and now I'm back where I started.

I turn the lights off in my studio. "Reese, it's time to get ready for bed."

I hear talking and tiptoe down the hall. Brett's back to his same old games, except I'm sleeping in the room with Reese. He said I could return and get the equipment to help launch my company. Then it turned into us staying in our own house instead of living with Catrina. Except he seems to think I come with it, and I don't.

I slow down, following the voices. It must be Brett talking on speaker phone. I stop outside the master bedroom. It's quiet, so I crack the door. Nope, the bed is still made from this morning.

I continue down the hall. Is it coming from Reese's room? I crack the door.

"Let me see what you got, princess."

Kamal.

My heart leaps at the sound of his voice. I miss him so much. Reese holds up the coloring page to her iPad.

"Good job, and everything's inside the lines."

"Let me see yours." She rests her chin on her hand, and he holds up his own coloring page. "That looks like *Finding Nemo.*"

He laughs. "Because it is."

My legs go weak and I lower to the carpet with my head near the door to hear him better. I tried to call the first week I left, then I went to text messages and by the third week I got the picture.

It's been three months and its starting to settle in that Kamal won't give me a second chance. I broke the rules, his trust, and *his heart* so now I have to live with it.

"Are you doing like I asked?" Kamal asks.

I perk up.

"Yes, sir. But Mommy's sad, and pizza doesn't work anymore."

Tears fill my eyes. What am I doing? I tried to make it better, and I only made it worse. I fold my legs to my chest.

"*Maybe*… I think I have an idea," he says.

"Really, can I help?"

"Yes. I need to talk with your Auntie Cat, and I'll tell

you about it tomorrow. But wait, I have a surprise for you."
Then a chorus of voices fill her room. I peek through the
crack and they're all on FaceTime sending her their love.

"All right. It's about time for bed. Sleep tight…"

"Don't let the bedbugs bite." She giggles. "Mr. Kamal?"

"Yes, love."

"Are bedbugs real?"

He laughs, and it brings a smile to my face. "Yes, they
are. Okay. We have a new task for tomorrow. Are you
ready?"

"Yes, sir."

"Ten hugs and ten kisses."

"*Ten* hugs and *ten* kisses." Reese repeats with an
emphasis on ten.

"Let me hear you count them."

Reese counts, and I watch Kamal wiggle his fingers with
each number. I wonder what that's all about? I look back
through the crack.

"Goodnight, Mr. Kamal."

"Goodnight, princess."

I jump up and call Reese from down the hall, louder
this time. "Ready for your bath?"

"Yes, ma'am."

"Then let's do it, honey."

She runs out and gives me a big hug and whispers,
"One."

. . .

Tonight, I tiptoe down the hall earlier than before. Cat must be helping because this is when I record my videos. I'm almost at the point of meeting with Platinum Prestige again, then I think it's about time we make a permanent move.

I sit on the floor waiting to hear his voice. The first week back felt nice. I had my beauty room. Reese had her toys and own space. But now we're missing Houston. This place just isn't our home anymore.

I only hope I can survive living in the same city with Kamal, that's if he plans to stay in Houston. According to Catrina, the official opening on Sundays is tomorrow, and we won't be there.

I close my eyes and pray for him, the staff, his family, and the goodwill they provide to their community. Then I ask God for a special prayer for the child I think I'm carrying.

How will I tell Kamal? What will I do when I see him? I'm already a wreck from the sound of his voice. I shake my head. I went from one man to the other and back again. Only to lose the one I truly love.

"Hey, princess."

"Hey, Mr. Kamal."

I lean closer with my hand on my stomach. They talk for over an hour, coloring like before. This is why kids don't need electronics. What if he was a stranger? I hear Kamal laugh and I peek through the crack, hoping to see his smile.

"How'd the hugs and kisses go?"

"Okay. But…" she twists her body to reposition her crayon, "I think she likes your kisses more."

"What?" He chokes.

Out of the mouths of babes.

"I think you should kiss Mommy and make her happy." She nods her head, approving her own idea.

"I'm sorry, love, I can't do that."

"Why?"

"Because I wasn't a good friend to Mommy. I lost my temper and it might be a while before she'll be my friend again."

"Oh… But Nana Jackie says we're not friends, we're family."

"We are. Always." His head drops and I ache for him, for us. "But I have something better. So, keep an eye out for it."

"Yes, sir."

Nothing is better than you. I really messed this up bad. How can I fix it?

"All right, are you ready for your task?" Kamal says.

"Yes, sir." She hops with too much energy to be an hour out from bedtime.

"Your task tomorrow is fifteen hugs and fifteen kisses."

"*Fifteen* hugs and *fifteen* kisses."

"You are such a big girl. Now let me hear you count it." They count through the numbers and when he runs out of fingers Kamal makes her giggle by lifting his elbows, a pen, a sheet of paper, and a paperclip.

The call winds down and Kamal yawns. It's hard to see

the details of his face from here. I hope he's not working around the clock.

"Mr. Kamal."

"Yes, princess."

"Will you be my daddy?"

The link of resistance chaining me to this place, this house, this city falls. Her question strips me of my pride and my ego. I have to fix us, fix our family.

"What happened?" I hear the edge in his voice.

"I can't play or dance and Mommy's sad and sick."

I fold over, letting my tears flow onto the carpet. Her little eyes miss nothing. It's time for us to go.

"What are you doing?"

Brett stands over me with bloodshot eyes and the stench of sex.

"I thought I felt something sharp in the carpet." I stand, closing Reese's door. "And you?"

I walk to the bathroom to start bath water for Reese. The extra noise will give her privacy to finish her call with Kamal. I need to teach my baby about not sharing our business, but she sees through the lies in this house. Her honesty with Kamal gives me courage.

"Why don't you give Reese her space and move back into our bedroom?" His question brings me back.

"Because, Brett, we are over. You come home smelling like you just rolled out of some woman's cat and expect me to crawl up next to you. What happened to missing your family?"

"He didn't deserve you."

"Who didn't deserve me?"

"Kamal."

"And you do?" My heart drops. I fell for his lines. "How did you know?"

"You post your entire life on social media. I knew everything. About your little spa day, the zoo, the museums, Southern Soul. I'm surprised you haven't posted about your little bastard." He points at my stomach and I feel like I'm about to be sick.

"I don't miss much. You have morning sickness, your breasts are larger, your nose is wider. What I don't get is I had to beg you to have Reese."

"It wasn't about Reese—it was about you. You're selfish, and you only think about yourself. And I knew I'd have to raise our daughter alone.

"Brett, I'm truly sorry I took the comforts of your life knowing you don't love me. You can't. Because to love me you'd have to halfway give a damn, and I… No, *we* deserve more. You're exactly the man I know you to be…"

My knees buckle. I said the same words to Kamal, and I was wrong. *God, I was so wrong.*

We don't belong here.

We're going home.

"I want you back in my bed tonight and keep it down. I had a long day."

I smile, counting the seconds in my head. The moment the bedroom closes, I see Reese peeking through the crack of her door.

This is our exit.

"Get your iPad and your backpack," I say in a hushed whisper with a finger over my mouth. Reese nods. "I'll be right back."

I run to my studio for my phone and my purse. All the qualities I want are in Kamal. He's dependable and loves my baby. I want to spend the rest of my life with him. We'll start over with new clothes, new toys, new makeup. Miss Jackie's words swoop in and I'll do whatever I must to get back to Houston.

Reese and I hold hands, running down the hallway. I keep one eye ahead and the other on the bedroom door. Kamal said if I ever needed, he'd send the plane for us. I fumble with my phone, speed-dialing him as we rush down the stairs.

Taking back my words is impossible but getting my man back is within my power.

"Kamal…"

CHAPTER 21

WILL YOU BE MY DADDY?

I am your daddy not by blood, but in my heart.

I drop my head on the desk. Her voice rings in my head and I have to get to them. I wanted to get through one more day, but Jayda and Reese come first.

Everyone's in town to celebrate the grand reopening with our first official Sunday Family dinner. It took over eight months. This place looks nothing like the original version. Miya and Dean turned in a menu filled with family favorites with the addition of a family-style meal on Sundays.

But my family left, and somehow, I love Jayda more. I miss them so much it hurts.

"What's up? Why is your face long?" Dad asks, sitting in the chair in front of my desk.

"I need to get out of here tonight. I'm not sure when I'll be back."

"Are you going after your woman?"

"Yes." I remove the gifts I have for them from the safe.

"It's about time. I was wondering if you were actually my son."

"It took you twenty years," I remind him and the others laugh. I'm thankful the memory no longer carries the same sting.

"Smartass," Dad bites back. He stands and pulls me into a hug. We hold on and he whispers, "I got you. Go get your lady and bring my grandbaby back. I'm proud of the man you've become, son. Thank you for holding this family together when I couldn't."

I nod, unable to respond. His words are balm to the boy that wanted his father.

"Be careful and keep us posted," Mother says, as I kiss her goodbye.

Montgomerys are strong and I'm grateful for my family. People I can count on and consistently show up in my life.

I returned home to save my family, and my family saved me. Love saved me from myself and the deep resentment I had toward my father. Love is slowly restoring my relationship with my father. And loving Jayda and Reese shows me the beauty in the present and my future.

I head straight to the airport. I'm prepared to do whatever it takes to get another chance to make it right with Jayda and to bring my ladies home.

I'm more like my father than I realized. The type of love he has for Mother is how I feel for Jayda. I can't imagine a world, my world without her love. I only pray we can move forward together.

Thankfully, our jet is scheduled to fly back to Los Angeles for Emmitt. I board okaying takeoff, armed with the address. I place the gifts I have for them beside me and count down the hours until I have them with me.

Hold on… I'm coming.

CHAPTER 22

"Yeah." I answer my phone, half asleep to stop the ringing.

"Kamal…"

"Jay, why are you whispering?" I sit forward, fully awake.

I look at the stewardess and mouth, *What's the ETA?*

She flashes ten with her hands. I nod, focusing on the call.

"I know I messed us up, but I'm more certain than ever that I love you. Everything about you and…"

"Jay, what's going on over there? Where's Reese?"

"She's right here. I have so much to tell you, so much to explain." Her voice shakes with emotions. "Will you send the plane for us?"

I exhale. "Done. Can you hold tight for another hour?"

"Hour. How will you get here in an hour?"

"Because I'm on my way."

"You were coming for us?"

"I told you I would, and I love you too." Her soft sobs fill the line and all I want to do is hold her. "Where are you?"

"At Brett's house."

Her response fills me with pleasure. She no longer sees it as her home. I hope she likes the home I purchased for us. The three of us.

"Are you there alone?"

"No, he's here."

"Do I need to send Emmitt?"

"No, he's in bed. We'll wait here for you."

I put her on speakerphone and send Emmitt a text message. I need him on the ground when I land.

"Catch me up."

WE SIT ON THE COUCH. Reese lays her head in my lap and I talk with my friend, my man. I'm ready to make more memories with Kamal starting with the life growing inside me. I want to tell him, but it's best done in person.

I toss a blanket over Reese and update Kamal on Gem Talent Agency. "I have two proposals left to submit. You're right about those women. They are some bad asses."

"I told you. How's it going with finding the influencers?"

"I have more than enough. Originally I planned to stick with Black beauty brands, and after researching it I've shifted to include other minority-owned brands."

"That's a smart move. How's it feel to be a business owner?"

"I don't know." I play with the end of the blanket.

"On one hundred?"

"Okay, on one hundred, I love the challenge of being creative and the potential to help others. But I'm overwhelmed with all I need to learn."

"It will come. Be patient with yourself."

"Thank you." I exhale. "I sort of thought all men were the same. All the men I've known have been takers around for one reason. So, in my mind, I had to get what I could while the getting was good. But you've changed that."

"Jay…"

"No, I have to say it. I appreciate your friendship as much, if not more, than your love. You are the epitome of who a strong man should be. You've protected us, cared for us, and spoiled us, expecting nothing. Fear almost had me blind to it all. So thank you."

"It's because of you, Jay. You make me want to be better. My relationships with my family are better because of you."

"What about Kenneth?"

"Kenneth is officially Dad again."

"I'm so happy for you. How'd that happen?"

"It's a long story. But I realized we're family, and somebody helped me see the value in a second chance."

"I'm proud of you. So, are you going to get that tattoo covered?"

"Nah. I still have some growing to do." We laugh. "Tonight, he told me to bring his grandbaby back."

"Oh Lord, they will have my child rotten."

"And Miya and Dean are dating. They think I don't know."

"I totally saw that coming."

"What? When?" He chuckles. "I told him if he breaks my sister's heart, I'm busting his ass."

I burst out laughing. "Stop trying to run that woman's life. I can't believe y'all missed it. Dean could melt the clothes off her back with a look."

"I'm not having this conversation."

"Hot, hot, hot."

"We're talking about my sister."

"And Baby Miya is a woman deserving love."

"What about you?" His voice drops to a caress.

"What about me?"

"Are you going to let me love you?" The heat in his voice ignites my longing.

"Yes."

"Forever."

I exhale. "What… what are you saying?"

"You and Reese are my world, and I want to spend the rest of my life showing you how much I love you."

I cover my mouth, unable to control the tears. Tears no longer associated with pain as I feel his love flowing through my body.

"Yes… Can we stay in Houston?"

"Yes, and I have a surprise for you?"

"I have one for you too." I place a hand over my soft stomach. The hairs on the back of my neck stand.

I feel his eyes before I see him. My eyes scan the darkness around us and land on Brett watching me over the banister. I gasp, placing a hand over my racing heart.

"What is it?"

"Brett."

"I'm outside. Put me on speaker."

"We'll be right out."

"Fuck!"

"What?" Emmitt asks, speeding up to the house.

"She hung up."

"Man, what are you about to do?"

"Get my family back and if he's smart we'll be in and out."

"And if he's stupid?"

"Take Jayda and Reese back to Houston."

"Bet." He slams the car to a stop outside the house.

I run over to the door, prepared to break it down, when I hear the garage door.

"Jay?" I run over and see her carrying Reese. "I got her. Let's go."

"She's not going anywhere. You're on private property." Brett exits the house.

I look over at Jayda. "Get in the car."

"Take Reese. I'll be right there," Jayda says with her eyes on Brett.

"I'm not leaving you alone with him," I tell her.

"You will leave, or I'll call the cops. Jayda, you're not going anywhere."

Jayda faces him, and the darkness in her eyes takes me back for a second. She scans the area and I know what she's going for. The baseball bat.

"Emmitt, come get Reese." I pass her off and when I turn around, Jayda has the bat in her hands, standing near a clean black Bugatti.

"Jay's about to fuck his shit up," Emmitt whispers. I swear there's a hint of pride in his voice.

"Baby… listen to me. Just get in the car," I plead with her.

Jayda's eyes focus on Brett and his focus is on the car. "Look at me." Jayda demands.

Brett obeys.

"This is over. All you have to do is be a father to Reese. But my life and who I'm with are none of your concern."

He throws up his hands and I think it's over until he opens his mouth. "Bitch, you'll be back."

"Bitch…" Jayda swings the bat, and it connects with the window. Emmitt's howl blends with the sound of shattering glass. "Call me a bitch again."

Brett looks like he's about to puke.

"Call me a bitch again." She huffs. "All I want is for you to let me go. Just let me go." She demands and I wrap my arms around her, covering my hands over hers.

"Baby, love… let me handle it from here. Okay?"

She heaves, not taking her eyes off Brett.

"I got you. On everything I got you. Trust me and give me the bat."

Her arms go weak and she turns, smothering her face in my chest. I hold her tight with my eyes on Brett.

I kiss the side of her neck and then whisper in her ear. "I love you, but remind me to remove the bats from the house."

Her body shakes with laughter. We will be just fine after I take care of this rodent.

"Go to the car with Emmitt and I'll be there in a second."

Jayda nods. "Thank you for coming."

"Always." I caress the side of her face, happy to have her back. "And don't forget the booster seat."

THE GARAGE DOOR SLIDES CLOSED, and I stare, holding my breath. "Come on, baby."

I look over at Emmitt. He leans back in the seat with his eyes on the door.

"Why didn't you stop him?"

"Stop who? Kamal?" Emmitt chuckles. "You were the one taking a bat to a Bugatti. I bet he won't *eva eva eva eva* mess with you again."

I smile. "He called me a bitch."

Emmitt's laughter fills the car. "My man goes from being single to kicking it with Jackie Robinson. I see why he likes you."

"Are you going to check on him?"

"Kamal is an excellent negotiator."

I shake my head, reaching for the handle to go check for myself, when the garage door opens.

"*What the…*"

Glass is everywhere. Brett looks like he's seen a ghost and the Bugatti looks more like a Hyundai.

Kamal sits in the passenger seat. "Let's get out of here."

"I have to stop rolling with you two. Who vandalizes a Bugatti?"

"Stop for a second," Kamal demands.

"Why? We need to get out of here before you have us on the evening news," Emmitt says.

"He's stupid but he ain't crazy. Just pull over for a second."

Kamal jumps out and opens my door. His mouth covers mine. Slowly, deliberately claiming me as his own. I wrap my hands around his neck, kissing him back and all the angst in my soul dissipates.

KAMAL DROPS TO ONE KNEE, slipping a rock the size of Texas on my finger. My mouth drops open.

"Will you marry me?"

I shake my head, kissing my 'yes' all over his face.

"Thug 1 and Thug 2, we need to bounce," Emmitt yells.

"All right, man."

We jump back in the car. Kamal and Emmitt pound,

then bump fists. "That's the way you handle that shit. Now let's get out of here."

The car zooms out down the street, and I feel free.

"Mr. Kamal."

"Yes, princess."

"Do I get a ring too?"

"No, love, princesses get tiaras." He rounds the seat with a diamond tiara in his hand. "For Princess Reese."

I sit forward, shaking my head. "She's riding with a tiara in a booster seat. The spoiling starts already?"

"That's right. Daughters learn love from their fathers. Any man stepping to her will have big shoes to fill. Right, princess?"

"Yes, sir."

"Reesie, can I dance?" Kamal asks.

She sits up straighter, holding on to her tiara. "In the car?"

"Yes, baby, you can dance anywhere," Kamal answers mid-groove.

I melt hearing the love in his voice toward my baby.

"Yay." Reese claps.

And we dance. Rocking Emmitt's car from side to side.

"Who are you people?" Emmitt asks.

"Shut up and dance," Kamal demands, and my baby laughs until we reach the airport.

CHAPTER 23

"Welcome to Southern Soul Houston." Kamal escorts me inside with his killer smile on deck.

The redesign is breathtaking. Dark wood walls adorned with colorful Black art. A mix of fresh woods of the light and dark variety fills the room, giving the space a homey feel.

This is where we belong. These people are my family, and I've never had that before I met Kamal.

He pulls me to his chest. "What do you think?"

"I love it. It looks and feels larger."

"I agree. Dean did his thing."

"You two work well together. I bet Miss Jackie is elated."

"I am, dear." I turn around and hug her. "Are you back for good?"

"Yes, ma'am."

"Good. I missed you." She hugs me again. "How about you come by the house after you get settled in?"

"I'd love to."

"Now, where's my grandbaby?"

"Back there with Q."

Miss Jackie leaves to find Reese.

I turn around in Kamal's arms. "This is probably not the best time to tell you, but I'm pregnant."

"That's amazing, baby." He hugs me tight, and we kiss.

"Why are you not surprised?"

"Brett told me."

"What? When?"

"Last night."

Panic floods my body.

"It's not worth getting upset over. I'm ready."

"It's yours, Kamal," I feel a need to state. Last night we discussed the status of my relationship with Brett. It had been almost a year since I had sex when Kamal and I made love. But there's no telling what Brett said while they were alone in the garage.

"I know."

I search his eyes for any sign of doubt. "On one hundred?"

"On one hundred. I think it will all hit me later. Two kids and a wife in one year."

"When you go in, you go in. You always said you play to win."

"And I've hit the jackpot." He cups my ass, and he

nibbles on my neck. "Think we can get a little Kamal Time before the dinner starts?"

I look around and back at him. "Now?"

"Now."

He leads me to his office. The contents on his desk hit the floor along with our clothes. I'm on my back with my man deep inside me. Where he belongs. Where I belong with no doubts and no hesitations.

Life doesn't always give you want you want, but I'm so thankful it gave me what I need.

Real love.

Kamal's rhythm increases, and I'm fighting to keep quiet with all our family and friends around. Then he latches on to my tender breast, and I lose it. Screaming my release to the heavens.

"I love you, Jay, but no more Kamal Time for you. Not here."

"I told you. Then you…" I grab my breasts, and he kisses the overflow.

"I couldn't help it. They're so full."

I laugh, searching for my clothes, when there's a knock at the door.

"Y'all do know we can hear you?"

"Bye, Q," Kamal yells.

"Come on, it's time to start," Miya says.

"Wait… who's all out there?" Kamal asks, cracking the door. Then he slams it shut.

A roar of laughter sounds from the other side.

"It was everybody, wasn't it?" I ask, petrified.

"Pretty much. Welcome to the Montgomerys."

I drop my head in my hands, embarrassed. Kamal kisses the top of my head, "Find your panties because we don't play about our food."

I smack his chest and do as he says, ready for our family meal.

THE TABLES ARE PUSHED TOGETHER for the first Southern Soul Sunday Dinner. Months of work and now my entire family and my best friends sit around the table to eat. This is what family is all about.

Fried chicken, fried catfish, baked macaroni and cheese, black-eyed peas, greens, cabbage, hot-water cornbread, and love.

"Are you praying today or tomorrow because I'm hoping to eat while the food is warm?" Q laughs at his own joke.

"You'd think you could keep the food warm with all that hot air," Ebony shoots back.

"I got more than hot air for you." He winks.

"Cute." She rolls her eyes.

All eyes around the table watch them. I look over at Emmitt and decide I'm staying out of it.

"Bow your heads."

"Dear Heavenly Father, thank you for family by birth and by heart. Bless this food for the nourishment of our bodies, the edification of our bond, and the provision of this family. May we live courageously, love wholeheartedly, and trust you implicitly. *Amen.*"

I sit beside Jayda and rub her stomach beneath the table. Southern Soul Houston is profitable again. Infusing new life and updating the environment helped, and I don't have to worry about Mother's bank account.

Jayda has her own business, and I'm not letting her leave my side. Reese is Reese, a happy, loveable, energetic kid, and spoiled princess. Who knows about the little one in the oven? That we plan to keep to ourselves until she finishes the first trimester. I pray for a healthy child and maybe a few more in the future.

"So, what's next?" Jayda asks.

"I'm thinking after a year or so we should renovate Southern Soul Raleigh. That will give us time to have the baby, get married, settle into our new lives. How's that sound to you, Dad?"

Kenneth smiles. "I'm with it. Puddin'?"

"It's about time we align both spaces together. I'm in agreement as long as we do it like this, as a family."

That sounds good to me.

I sit back and scan the table with my boys, my family, and my future. We have a hell of a family, and a hell of a team—the Montgomery compound.

Then I look over at Jayda—pregnant with my child— and across to Reese in her tiara. I'm a blessed man, a very blessed man.

I lean over and nibble on her. "Love you, Jay."

She kisses me softly on the lips and when she pulls back, I see forever in her eyes. "I love you too, *Big Boy*."

I throw my head back, laughing. "Q, you talk too much."

"What—Jay is family now? Family is privy to all the juicy secrets."

"I wonder what secrets they have to tell about you." Ebony doesn't miss a beat. Yeah, she'll fit right in.

We laugh until we cry. Q freezes for a second, and a look of determination settles over his face.

"Oh, boy," Jayda whispers. "Ebony might be next."

"Nah, I say Rashaad and Cat."

"What are you willing to bet?" The smoky texture in her tone matches the passion in her eyes.

I lower my mouth to her ear. "Kamal Time. Same rules on the balcony."

"At forty-five seconds?" Her hand brushes over my cock beneath the table.

"Love, you're playing with fire."

"That's what I'm banking on."

"Bet." I push back. "Momma, you got Reesie Piecie tonight?"

"Yes. Where are you going?"

"To handle some grown folks' business." I pull Jayda up to her feet.

"My son," Dad says with a chuckle.

"Kamal…" Jayda says, shocked. "Now? But it's not time."

"Hell yeah, we need a practice round." I stand up, tossing my napkin on the table. "We'll holler at y'all later."

My boys and brothers cheer. Miya, Ebony, and Catrina roll their eyes. My parents are cuddled up in their own world.

I scoop my baby up and kiss her on the forehead. "See you in the morning, princess."

"Okay. Daddy…" My heart melts into putty in her little hands.

A collective *aaahhhh* rings through the room. On the flight home, Reese asked if she could call me daddy, and I left it to Jayda. Jayda then let Reese decide. Hearing the words makes me want to be the best man I can for them.

"Yes, love."

"Can we dance?"

"Yeah, princess, show Daddy what you got."

The Montgomery compound turns up.

Laughter. Food. Family. I've never felt this much love and hope and drive in my life, all because we played the game of love, and *won*.

Welcome to Southern Gentlemen Series!

You've met the Montgomery Compound! Please take a few minutes and **leave a review**. I'd love you for life. :)

The next book, *All Yours* with Dean and Miya is almost

done. But I'm torn between the next couple. Who do you want to read about next? Q and Ebony or Rashaad and Catrina? Email me at info@janesedixon.com! I'd love to hear from you.

Here's what you can expect from Dean and Miya…

Miya Montgomery is the head chef and one-fifth of Southern Soul, a family-owned soul food restaurant. On the heels of a nasty breakup, Miya welcomes the shift in ownership and preparation for expansion. That's before her brother, Kamal, calls home, his best friend, Dean.

Dean Wellington arrives in Houston, ready to consult the Montgomery family through its management transition, not expecting Little Miya to be the curvy bombshell who steals his heart on sight.

Ignoring their chemistry is impossible. Dean's sweet smile and steamy eyes scorch through Miya's clothes and her objections. However, her tattered heart is counting his casualties, refusing to be Dean's next victim.

Kamal has a strict rule concerning his baby sister: Hands off. But since when has Dean met a rule he didn't want to break. And Miya's finding it harder to ignore his independence and Southern charm.

Dean's hell-bent on making their own rules, and Miya's worried that when he's had his fill, he'll leave her with an irreparable heart. But their late nights have her willing to play with fire, praying...she doesn't get burned.

Get Your Copy!

Be the FIRST to know!

Join My Newsletter
http://www.janesedixon.com/subscribe

Be the first to know about releases and specials. You can unsubscribe anytime.

Rules are meant to be broken, especially when it comes to this curvy chef and infamous playboy.

Rules are meant to be broken, especially when it comes to this curvy chef and infamous playboy.

Miya Montgomery is the head chef and one-fifth of Southern Soul, a family-owned soul food restaurant. On the heels of a nasty breakup, Miya welcomes the shift in ownership and preparation for expansion. That's before her brother, Kamal, calls home, his best friend, Dean.

Dean Wellington arrives in Houston, ready to consult the Montgomery family through its management transition, not expecting Little Miya to be the curvy bombshell who steals his heart on sight.

Ignoring their chemistry is impossible. Dean's sweet smile and steamy eyes scorch through Miya's clothes and her objections. However, her tattered heart is counting his casualties, refusing to be Dean's next victim.

Kamal has a strict rule concerning his baby sister: Hands off. But since when has Dean met a rule he didn't want to break. And Miya's finding it harder to ignore his independence and southern charm.

Dean's hell-bent on making their own rules, and Miya's worried that when he's had his fill, he'll leave her with an irreparable heart. But their late nights have her willing to play with fire, praying...she doesn't get burned.

**Get Your Copy on Amazon
or Read in Kindle Unlimited!**

"HELLO, I'm Miya Montgomery, Executive Chef of Southern Soul Houston. It's a pleasure meeting you." My heart gallops even though I rehearse my new title a million times a day. I extend my hand, pretending for the millionth and one time just to hear it again.

I swirl around in a circle like Julie Andrews in the *Sound of Music*. This is my kitchen.

I'm about to burst. I fold over, holding on to the edge of the table, and run in place, squealing until all the air is out of my lungs. To say I'm happy is an understatement. I'm fucking fantastic. And the f-bomb is required because I earned it. My brothers voted and offered a trial run. But I'll change it to permanent in no time.

Accepting this position could seem evident since it's my family's restaurant. Still, my brothers—Kamal, Rashaad, Demetrius, and Quan—put me through the pacers to prove I'm capable of running this kitchen like our mother. And I can. They'll see when we start testing with a Sunday brunch series next month.

I'm alone in the kitchen, inspecting every drawer and cabinet. We're closed on Sundays, but Kamal—my oldest brother and head Montgomery on this project—asked me to meet him this morning. I didn't expect a totally new kitchen with stainless steel appliances—the prep station, stoves, refrigerators—all new everything.

A fresh bubble of excitement boils over, and I can't control myself. I'm dancing to the music in my head, squealing again. Ass jiggling, boobies swinging until a soft gasp cuts through the air, and I freeze in place.

"What are you doing?"

I spin around, facing the voice. "Minding my business. Who are you, and how did you get in here?"

An unfamiliar man with familiar dark brown eyes stands in the doorway, well, fills it is more like it. I need to adjust my bra and smooth out my clothes. I can only imagine how I look because everybody can't handle these curves. Still, I'm more interested in getting some answers.

He steps closer, and I slide a chef's knife from the block, pointing it in his direction. A smolder descends over his eyes, and the temperature in the room heats up a notch.

"Don't make me turn you into two wings, two legs, and a breast." I flick my wrist with each cut to show him I'm not playing.

"Baby Miya is all grown up." His teasing gaze sends a shudder down my spine.

"Baby Miya? Only my brothers call me that. Who are

you?" I ask while simultaneously trying to place his face—the strong jaw, dark brown hair, and tanned skin—but there's no way I'd ever forget those eyes. They're too distinctive. Too dark. Too knowing. And like a self-defense expert, he claims the knife, pinning my back against the refrigerator.

"You should be careful—you could cut someone."

"I think that was the point, handsome," I bite back, and he smiles, and it's as tasty as cream cheese icing on warm carrot cake.

"How'd you get in?" I ask, moving to free myself, and his grip tightens, not meant to harm. The contour of his biceps through his expensive suit jacket tells me that he's cut, and if he wanted, he could lock me down. But the hold of his strong hands feels more like a caress.

"I'm here with Kamal."

Our chests rise and fall. Inhale, exhale.

Every cell in my body stands at attention. Heart pounding. Lungs demanding. Eyes shifting, openly assessing one another.

His lips, one thin, the other plump, both tempting, hover inches from mine. The scent of spearmint rushes between us every time he exhales.

Caught between cold steel and a rock-hard body, I'm suddenly tongue-tied, which is unlike me. But what's a girl to do with a man like this?

I lick my drying lips, and a deep groan vibrates through his chest and mine, as if in agony. A wave of emotion crosses his face. I'd call it pleasure if I knew him better—or maybe determination as he steps back, freeing me. He replaces the knife in the stand, angling his body towards the door.

"I'm on my way. I need to settle a few things at the restaurant." Kamal talks on his cellphone in his own world.

My eyes jerk to the door. I didn't even hear him. Thank God he didn't walk in and see us. My eyes find *his* again. Kamal sweeps the room, continuing his conversation, opening and closing each of the refrigerator doors.

"Jayda, just make sure you're packed. And babe, you don't need a million bags. We're only going for a couple of days."

I shake my head and laugh. There's no way Jayda's packing light—it's not in her. She's a beauty vlogger and all the way around a glam kind of woman. Three days means at least three outfits per day, accessories, shoes, and makeup. I chuckle. Kamal better drive the SUV.

The stranger's penetrating eyes drag me back.

"So, what's your name?" I ask.

"Dean."

"Dean." I repeat his name a few times, resting a hip against the prep station.

"Hey, Baby Miya, sorry about that." Kamal gathers me to his chest and kisses my temple. "Do you remember Dean? He used to come home with me sometimes for holiday breaks."

"Not really." With four popular brothers, all of their friends are a big blur to me. "Miya Montgomery, Executive Chef of Southern Soul. It's a pleasure meeting you." I extend my hand, reciting my rehearsed introduction, and it feels so damn good.

"Dean Wellington. The pleasure is all mine." The smoky tone in his voice matches the flames in his eyes as he steps forward. He takes my hand in his, and a zap of awareness overtakes me. But instead of lingering, I firmly shake his hand and step back, rejoining my brother. "Nice grip."

"Thanks."

"What do you think of the new kitchen?" Kamal asks.

I blink out of Dean's trance, glancing up at my brother. "It's perfect. How'd you manage to make this happen overnight?"

"I didn't. Dean did." Kamal smiles and returns to examine the new equipment. He opens and closes drawers and then runs his fingers across the handles of the new pots and pans. "I've been working with Dean for months to get this place up to par."

"I busted a move or two when I came in here and saw this place sparkling like new money." I glance over at Dean, curious, and find his waiting eyes. A trail of something sweet ripples through me. But the last thing I need is another man in my life. The ones I have are driving me mad, including Kamal, as we struggle through this transition. "So, what's next? The dining room could use an update too."

"That's on my list. After this, I'm thinking about taking a trip to North Carolina to inspect Southern Soul Raleigh."

"Raleigh?" I gather him in a quick hug. A trip to visit the other location is a major development for Kamal. When our parents divorced, Dad took over Southern Soul Raleigh, and Mom resumed her work at Southern Soul Houston. But we've never been active participants in the operation of the other location. "I'm so proud of you. Dad must be thrilled."

"Don't get gushy. I'd visit it because it's a sound business decision. We can't honestly take on this job without seeing the state of it firsthand. The numbers look good, but..." Kamal shrugs a shoulder, as if not convinced, leaning back against the sink. "Which brings me to today. I called you here because I want you to spend some time with Dean."

Heat flows through my body, remembering the feel of being pinned against the refrigerator beneath Dean. The two of us alone together isn't happening. Not at all.

"And why would I do that?" I ask.

"I want to exploit this feeling of newness. New management. New equipment. New staff. I want the two of you to craft a *new* menu for Southern Soul. We'll test it—"

"*Pause*. You think I need him to create a new menu?" My thumb flicks towards Dean, now resting with his back against the wall, observing us. A slight smile replaces his neutral expression. "No offense."

"You're good." A hint of humor dances in Dean's eyes, and it takes everything in me to look away.

"Kamal, I don't need a babysitter."

"No one said anything about a babysitter, Miya. I hired Dean—"

I halt the words with my hand in the air. The imaginary

party balloons in my head pop like they're taken down by a firing squad.

"You don't have to say he's a babysitter for it to be true." I should have known there was a catch. Kamal towers over me by at least six inches. But it doesn't stop me from walking closer with a hand placed firmly on my hip. "You do realize that's what a head chef does?"

"Miya." He grips my wrist and removes it from my hip. "There's no need for you to huff and puff."

"I'm not huffing and puffing… but I'm about to." I swallow around my disappointment.

Kamal has always encouraged me to pursue my career. He helped me get internships and called in several favors when it was time to secure my first real job. But here he is acting like my old bosses and my ex—like I'm delicate China prone to breaking—and this shit hurts.

"Miya, love, get out of your head. He's here as a tool, a guide, that's it." Kamal throws up his hands as if he's harmless. But he's a wolf covered in faux sheep's wool.

"Don't give me that damn smile. I'm not buying it." My voice cracks, and I'm embarrassed. This is precisely why I didn't join the family business. They don't see me as a professional chef, but Baby Miya, and I'm tired of it. I march to the door, pissed. "I'm out of here."

"Miya, please don't leave." Kamal catches up, placing his hand firmly on my shoulders. "You're the best damn chef we could have hired. Hiring Dean isn't a reflection on you or your position. It's a standard process. When a business makes a transition, they hire outside consultants to make the process as smooth as possible for all parties involved."

I shake my head. "A major chain, maybe. But this is a mom-and-pop business. Southern Soul is family-owned and operated. *We* don't hire consultants to handle *family* business." I yank from his grip.

"And that's the problem," Dean says from behind Kamal. "To take Southern Soul to the next level, you can't continue to operate like a *family* business. No disrespect."

I glance back. "None taken."

"Miya, your work is respected in the industry. You've worked from a commis chef to a sous chef, to your recent Head Chef offer from Torsion. No one doubts your expertise or ability to manage a kitchen."

How did he know? I turn around and face Dean. I didn't tell my brothers or parents about the offer I received from Torsion in Austin. I never wanted to work in other restaurants. I wanted to work in this kitchen—my family's kitchen—my whole life.

"You had an offer from Torsion?" Kamal asks, blocking my view of Dean. "Why didn't you tell us?"

"It didn't matter."

"It *does* matter." Kamal cups my face, and he searches my eyes. He knows how I've fought in other kitchens to be respected as a woman, and a curvy Black woman at that. I did it all to work here. "I'm sorry, Baby Miya."

I nod. It takes everything in me not to shed a tear. I got the nickname Baby Miya because I'm the youngest and the only girl in a family of five children.

A single tear motivates my brothers to move heaven and earth to seek a remedy. I love my brothers, but right now, what I need more than anything is for them to see me as an adult.

Not Baby Miya.

That I can handle myself professionally as a chef and not my abilities to huff and puff and blow all this shit down like a damn baby. Which means if I want this position permanently, they have to trust me, without a consultant standing over my shoulders.

I'll show them. No tears allowed, I remind myself, stepping back.

"I'm listening."

Kamal tips his head to the side. "Look, I was working with Dean before we asked you to take over the kitchen."

"I'm a team player. I think hiring him is a waste of money, but that's why I cook, and you make the decisions."

"Miya…"

I turn my back to Kamal and face Dean head-on. That jab is intentional. We called Kamal back to help us take over the family restaurant and do it the right way. This is my family's business and our legacy. I don't need this handsome consultant to tell me how to cook my Mamma's food. Dean knows my resumé, but he'll see soon enough, he's not needed here. But I'll play along, for now.

"What do you have in mind?"

THE SEXY SMILE on Miya's face comes with the ringing of bells in my head. Kamal gives me a pleading look, and I brush the tip of my nose.

It's our universal sign for *I got you.*

"I need to make a quick call. I'll be right back." Kamal leaves me to convince the very pissed Miya to work with us, not against us.

"What will it take to send you packing?" she asks when Kamal clears the door.

"Trying to get rid of me already?"

"You and I know the head chef handles the menu. I don't need an assistant to do it." The smug look on her face sends a challenge my way, and challenges are my specialty.

"I guess that's why it pays to listen to the extent of my contract for this project because I wouldn't assist you. It's the other way around."

Her head snaps back, and a flutter of laughter spills out.

"You're cute and delusional. Answer the question. What will it take?" She crosses her arms, and her plump breasts perk up higher, serving as a temporary distraction.

I took this job to help my best friend. Little did I know Kamal's kid sister—he affectionately calls "Baby Miya"—isn't a baby. Baby Miya is a curvy woman with a brown-sugar complexion, a round face framed by curls, and hypnotizing almond-shaped eyes.

"Dean?" I blink and Kamal's back.

"Give us a few more minutes."

He heads back out, leaving us alone in the kitchen. I flew into town this morning to walk through the first phase of our renovation before approving the next stage in the dining room and to meet with Miya.

To prepare, I did what I do, researched her history in the industry. Her reputation is impeccable. Her lasting impressions with past chefs boil down to her loyalty to the brand, her kitchen skills, and the energy she infused into the work environment. Not one chef reflected negatively on her employment, and all would gladly hire her again.

That's rare. Cooking is such a personal experience. And to multiply it by thousands and recreate that magic repeatedly takes dedication, and what few realize is it takes heart.

Chefs have to love people in the kitchen and in the dining room. Chefs have to sacrifice days and nights and relationships. And chefs do it all in hopes of one day running a kitchen or their own restaurant.

So, when Kamal called me and told me about the family business's shift, I told him I'd walk him through every step.

He's not a chef on paper, but quiet as it's kept, the man can cook his ass off. And if the man decides to bless a grill, he can convert a vegan to a carnivore. I've seen it with my own eyes. I wonder if Miya has the same ability in the kitchen.

For a man with many talents and the power of persuasion, Kamal is concerned about the petite woman standing in front of me. Miya's revered passion in the kitchen is on full display. And somehow, Kamal's worried about converting his biggest fan, and the core of his heart, Baby Miya.

"I'm here to visit a few local restaurants, to get a feel for the most popular establishments."

"That's easy. The Breakfast Klub, Houston This is Soulfood, Just Oxtails…" She runs down the list. "But nobody serves food like Southern Soul."

"I appreciate your confidence, and I believe you, but that's not the point of my little excursion."

"What's the point?"

"You'll have to join me to find out." I glance away, only for a moment, with a chuckle. "You asked for my plan. That's the beginning. Eventually, we'll have a new menu to present to Kamal before he starts running his test Sundays. The customers will help us filter it down to the final version. Are you in?"

My question hangs in the air, accompanied by the sound of our breathing and Kamal's voice in the distance. He hired me while I'm in-between two large projects, one in New Orleans and the other in New York. But this is important to him, so it's a priority for me.

I'll have to extend my stay, book a hotel, and reschedule a few appointments. No doubt, I'll pay for it, but the opportunity to spend some time with *Baby Miya* is growing more intriguing by the second.

Her neck rolls, causing her bangs to block my view of her beautiful eyes. A slow smile spreads across her face as she runs her tongue along her teeth.

"I'm not on the menu, Mr. Wellington."

The roll of my name off her tongue does something to me. And something tells me she knows it.

"So, is that a yes?" I pull out my phone to review my calendar. Channing and my team will have a fit once I call with the shift in my schedule.

"Did you hear me?"

"Yes, Miya, I hear you loud and clear. I'll remember that." I extend my phone. "I need your address. I can swing by your place and pick you up around six-thirty."

"Wait, this starts tonight?"

"It's one of the reasons for my trip today. I have a reservation at the first place tonight at eight and a tour of the kitchen with the executive chef at seven-thirty. The GPS says it's about an hour from here."

Her forehead wrinkles. "Just the two of us?"

"Yep, you and me."

We exchange phones.

Her screensaver is a family portrait with Mr. and Mrs. Montgomery sitting sideways. Miya is front and center with a toothless smile so full, she's oozing joy. And the boys are behind them with matching grins. They all look so happy.

"How old were you here?"

She turns her head to the ceiling in thought. "Four, maybe five. That was our last family picture. Here." She returns my phone, and I give hers a final look before giving it back. My parents and I never took a family photo.

Kamal re-enters the kitchen as we reclaim our phones. He gathers Miya to his chest, and the desire to hold her fills me. Then I remember I'll have her all to myself tonight.

What's wrong with me?

My eyes sweep from Miya to Kamal, and he squints as if seeing something for the first time. "Dean, this is my sister. None of your player bullshit."

Miya snorts. "Not gonna happen."

"Is that so?" Fireworks explode in my body. I hope she realizes she's playing with the wrong one.

"It is so." Then she tosses a saucy gaze my way. "You're not even my type."

"Are you challenging me, Miya?" I lock my entire focus on her.

"Dean." The warning in Kamal's voice doesn't deter me. We're adults.

Miya leaves her brother's side, walking until I can see the streaks of copper in her eyes. I slide my hands in my pockets to keep from learning firsthand if her skin is as soft as it appears.

"To challenge you would mean I care, and I don't. My priorities are Southern Soul and my family. So, let's get this done."

"Can you handle me?"

"Excuse me?" Miya unfolds her arms and plants them on her full hips. I force myself to watch the lightning crack in her eyes instead of the rise and fall of her chest.

"Can you handle working with me?" I slow down the cadence to get under her skin.

"I can handle anything and *anyone*."

Miya takes another step, and we're almost back where we started. The edible scent of her perfume fills my nose. And the thought of her handling me brings a smile to my face.

"I'll admit, you knowing my resumé surprised me, but you can find that with a basic Google search." She cocks her head to the side, mirroring the one her brother is infamous for. "Do us a favor—leave your suggestive ogling and five-dollar come-ons at your hotel."

Miya straightens my tie, and the heat from her hand penetrates my cotton pinstriped button-up shirt. Then her eyes pop up to mine. The burn in my chest is like I swallowed a tube of wasabi. It overwhelms me, numbing my senses to anything, and everything, except her.

"Are you done, baby girl?" I love nothing more than a woman who knows how to handle her tongue.

Miya rolls her eyes, stepping back. I follow her as if we're dancing.

"I can assure you, what I have in mind will exceed your five-dollar threshold. And for the record, I *love* challenging women."

"That's where you're wrong. I'm not here to challenge you, but to send your ass home." She wags her finger. "Four brothers and a headstrong father means I know every trick in the book. You gotta come better than that. And for the record, I'm not other women."

"Yes, ma'am."

Miya's whipping a red cape in front of a bull, and for the first time in months, I feel alive.

Flying coast to coast, handling my clients' needs, overshadows any resemblance of a personal life. I know the hospitality industry. I eat, sleep, and breathe everything needed to make a restaurant thrive. But right now, I don't give a damn about Southern Soul Houston or my other clients.

All I see is Miya Montgomery, and for that reason alone, she's not like other women. She has blood rushing through my veins and my nose wide open. Something tells me this curvy bombshell's about to wreck my life.

"I'll leave you guys to your business." She speaks to us, but her eyes are on me. "You don't have to pick me up. I'll meet you there." She turns to walk away again but stops short and spins back. "You're officially in my way, and what Miya wants, Miya gets. So, don't unpack your luggage." She winks and double taps my chest. "I'll see you at six-thirty."

The view of this woman from the back stops me dead in my tracks. Her little warning is cute. I can't recall the last time a woman put up a challenge *and* laughed in my face. That shit doesn't bother me one bit. It's a fucking turn on and will only make my victory sweeter.

I watch until she clears the door, and sirens are blaring

in my head. Yet, I hear a soft whisper, a warning: Miya is Kamal Montgomery's sister.

His baby sister.

His only sister.

"Hands off." Kamal's eyes are on me, no doubt reading my mind. "You hurt her, and you'll draw your last breath."

I acknowledge his warning with a nod. That's a bridge I'll have to cross at another time. Plus, we both know I'm not looking for a relationship.

Kamal's a magnet, drawing life to him, including myself and Emmitt Booker. We met in junior high school, and our friendship continued through college and into playing professional football. But it was sometime in college when the three of us made a pact to remain single for life.

We each have our reasons. Kamal's issues with divorce. Emmitt's upbringing in the foster care system. As for me, it wasn't my parent's divorce, but their dysfunctional relationships afterward. The examples I've seen in "committed" relationships" haven't been the best, and I don't want to add to the staggering statistics.

Living single agrees with my work schedule and lifestyle —I'm a modern-day nomad. The three of us, self-proclaimed, life-long bachelors, have traveled the world. And I can work without restrictions. But lately, I feel off, like a part of me is missing, and I don't know what it is or where to find it.

I've vacationed.

I've partied.

I've worked.

The weight of not knowing feels suffocating until I walked in and saw Miya dancing around in the kitchen, without music, without a care in the world. I try to recall the last time I was happy enough to dance without reservation, without music, and with my damn self. That shit must be dope.

I stop before opening one of the ovens and ask Kamal, "When's the last time you've looked forward to something?"

"Today." He beams, sitting on the table. "Jayda has this thing she started with Reese since they moved to Houston. She calls it 'making memories.' And it's all about them having fun in a new city, familiarizing themselves with the local attractions. But to me, I see my city through their eyes. The zoo, museums, restaurants. Last weekend we went to the spa."

"You at the spa?" I laugh. Seeing Kamal in a relationship makes me wonder if he plans to actually settle down. It's mind-blowing.

"Yep, me and my little ladies. I took Lillian, Reese, and Jayda for the works, and…" His eyes glaze over. The light of the memory covers his face, and for a moment, I let myself wonder what it must be like to have people in my life that I can count on other than Emmitt and Kamal.

My mother has a new family. My father travels the world cooking and bedding every woman he can. I have no siblings, a few close cousins in New York, and have my trusted staff. But I spend the majority of my time alone or with my boys—Emmitt and Kamal.

Kamal is the most sensible and responsible of us. He has his parents, siblings, and now, Jayda, his girlfriend, and her daughter Reese.

"You're a lucky man."

"I'm a *blessed* man," Kamal corrects.

"Sounds like you're about to break the pact."

"I would in a heartbeat if I thought Jayda was ready."

I'm surprised by his admission. I wait for him to explain, but my friend seems to be far away in thought.

I'd never intentionally cross him. I'd never intentionally jeopardize our friendship. But electricity hangs in the air, and the heat of her touch lingers on my skin, long after Miya's departure.

Is it selfish to want more?

Blazin' Love (Contemporary Romance)

Complete Series

Platinum Love (Book 1)

Privileged Love (Book 2)

Exclusive Love (Book 3)

Chosen Love (Book 4)

Special Love (Book 5)

Absolute Love (Book 6)

Pretend for Me (A Short Story)

Devoted Love (Book 7)

Select Love (Book 8)

Lavish Love (Book 9)

Total Love (Book 10)

Forbidden Chords Series (Contemporary Romance)

Complete Series

Hidden Desire (Prequel)

Rockstar Seduction (Prequel)

Rockstar Secrets (Book 1)

Rockstar Sinners (Book 2)

Rockstar Savages (Book 3)

Waiting for You (A Short Story)

This Song's for You (A Short Story)

Rockstar Scandals (Book 4)

Precious Stones Series (Romantic Suspense)

Before Black Diamond (Prequel)

Black Diamond (Book 1)

African Emerald (Book 2)

Fire Opal (Book 3)

Southern Gentlemen (Slow Burn Steamy Romance)

Play to Win (Book 1)

All Yours (Book 2)

Honest & True (Book 3)

Smith Pact Duo (Contemporary Romance)

Complete Series

Yuki's Luck (Book 1)

Tempting Asher (Book 2)

Smith Surprise (Book 3)

When It Comes to Love Boxed Set (Books 1 - 3)

Weekend Reads

Resort to Love

You Owe Me

Grown and Sexy for Christmas

Standalone Novels

Her Last Man

See all of my books on my website:

http://www.janesedixon.com/books.

USA Today Bestseller, Ja'Nese Dixon writes tales of romance laced with strong women, stronger men, and family values that based on more than blood. Her happily ever afters are written to inspire. So, if you're looking for a page turner that will leave you blushing, with your heart racing, and lying to yourself about reading "just one more chapter" then grab one of the author's thirty-something books.

Ja'Nese is an avid reader and coffee drinker living in Houston, TX with her husband, three adult children, and her spoiled diva dog. Want to learn more? Join her newsletter and get exclusive reads, all the inside details, and a first look at what's to come at www.janesedixon.com.

Stay in Touch:
www.janesedixon.com
info@janesedixon.com

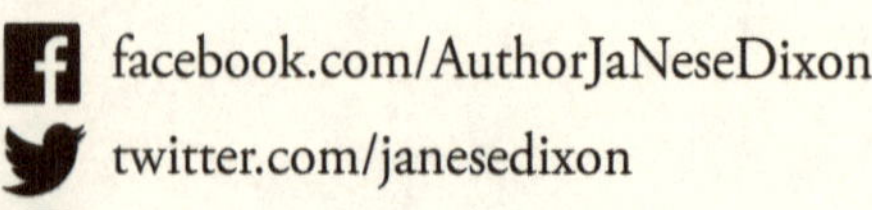

facebook.com/AuthorJaNeseDixon

twitter.com/janesedixon

instagram.com/authorjanesedixon

amazon.com/author/janesedixon

bookbub.com/authors/ja-nese-dixon

ABOUT THE PUBLISHER

Purpose Prevails Publishing
2231B Center St. STE 144
Deer Park, TX 77536
www.purposeprevailspublishing.com

Get Waiting for You for FREE!

Do you love second chance romances? Then here's another sweet, steamy romance for your device.

https://geni.us/waitingforyougift

www.ingramcontent.com/pod-product-compliance
Lightning Source LLC
Chambersburg PA
CBHW061218190726

48288CB00001B/234